Books by Phyllis A. Whitney

Woman
Without
a Past

PHYLLIS A. WHITNEY

Woman
Without
a Past

DOUBLEDAY

NEW YORK   LONDON   TORONTO   SYDNEY   AUCKLAND

PUBLISHED BY DOUBLEDAY
a division of Bantam Doubleday Dell Publishing Group, Inc.
666 Fifth Avenue, New York, New York 10103

DOUBLEDAY and the portrayal of an anchor with a dolphin
are trademarks of Doubleday, a division of
Bantam Doubleday Dell Publishing Group, Inc.

Designed by Anne Ling

Library of Congress Cataloging-in-Publication Data

Whitney, Phyllis A., 1903–
Woman without a past / Phyllis A. Whitney. — 1st ed.
p.   cm.
I. Title.
PS3545.H8363W6   1991
813'.54—dc20   90-3860
                                                                       CIP

ISBN 0-385-41784-5
ISBN 0-385-41988-0 (large print)
Copyright © 1991 by Phyllis A. Whitney
All Rights Reserved
Printed in the United States of America
June 1991
10   9   8   7   6   5   4   3   2   1
FIRST EDITION

For Sally Arteseros,
my editor and good friend
for so many years—

With Affection and Gratitude

Foreword

I visited Charleston, South Carolina, in May of 1989. A few months later Hugo swept in with devastating force to change portions of the landscape forever. The Charleston I have written about here is the city I saw before the hurricane; a city that has recovered from a good many disastrous blows over the years, yet with its spirit always intact.

Friends tell me that the Historic District, which is the main setting for my novel, came through with minor damage to those sturdy old buildings. The plantation houses up the peninsula stand as they did before the storm. Perhaps the major, irreparable loss to the entire area was the hundreds of beautiful trees—some of them a century old and more. As I wrote, nothing had touched them, and I could see them in my mind as they were.

The plantation house I've called Mountfort Hall is a composite of the houses I visited, though with an emphasis on Drayton Hall.

The people of Charleston are resilient and have always carried on their lives with grace and courage. Several residents of the Historic District opened their homes to me while I was there, inviting me back of the scenes.

Anne Wall's lovely South Battery house crept into my narrative, with a few changes that bow to the needs of plot. I fell in love with a child's rocking horse I saw in an upper room, and it became a "character" in my story.

My thanks to Helen and Harold Tinley for showing me their charming home in one of Charleston's "single houses." Helen was my "scout" on an occasion when I needed the exact details for one of my scenes. She also sent me a vivid account of what it was like to live through Hugo.

Catherine Boykin introduced me to Patricia Dwight, whose street-level house was filled with treasures from the Far East. Fortunately, these were removed to an upper floor before the storm brought in two feet of mud. I thank both these women for their help with my project.

With each new setting that I write about, I turn first to the local public library for help. I am especially grateful to Jan Buvinger, director of the Charleston County Library, who arranged for members of her staff to assist me.

Michael Leonard, Public Service Manager for the library at the time, gave me some of my best scenes. Thanks to him, I learned about the Footlight Players, and was able to wander backstage in the old warehouse that houses their theater. Michael also showed me the inspiring view of St. Philip's lighted steeple from the alley that runs past the stage door. Sparks for my imagination!

While in Charleston, I stayed at the Ansonborough Inn, which also occupies an old cotton warehouse, and gave me some eerie scenes for my book. I've changed its name to the Gadsden

Inn, and have taken only a few liberties with the setting. My thanks to the staff for being endlessly helpful.

Visitors are thronging back to Charleston, as they always have —and a city that is like no other is welcoming its guests.

Woman
Without
a Past

One

I felt *almost* wonderful.

If it hadn't been for the other occupant of my publisher's waiting room, there'd have been no "almost." A recently completed manuscript rested safely in the briefcase on my knees, while the hardcover of my newly published suspense novel, *Crystal Fire,* stood prominently displayed on a shelf across the room.

All of this gave me a good feeling——something I needed more than ever these days. It was satisfying to have published four successful mystery-suspense titles by the time I was thirty, with the fifth one ready to submit. I'd had my early years of rejection and discouragement until Douglas Hillyard had "discovered" me. Hillyard Publishers was family-owned—a small oasis in the midst of huge conglomerates that wanted to swallow it.

More than anything else, my glow of happiness indicated that I'd finally begun to heal. It had been two years since Doug's death in a multiple automobile accident. Sudden death could be more devastating than a slow, expected death, which was the way my mother had gone. Writing had always been my lifeline—an escape into that imaginary world where hurts were fictional and endings happy. Now, on this bright spring day in New York, I could sense new stirrings of life in me. I was ready for something good to happen.

My new novel was open on a nearby shelf to show both the front and back of the jacket. The gray-blue painting on the front had a woman's face floating mysteriously in mist, and my name, MOLLY HUNT, in large, clear lettering just below the title. I wasn't famous enough yet to have it placed above.

The photograph on the back of the jacket was a variation of the "signature" photo Doug had invented for me. He had wanted something more glamorous and intriguing than the usual author's picture, and he'd suggested a clever disguise. I enjoyed hiding behind the dark glasses, pulling the black fedora down over my forehead, and concealing the lower part of my face with the upturned collar of a trench coat. It was a takeoff, of course, and we'd changed the pose for every new title. Norman Hillyard, my present editor, and Doug's younger brother, wanted something different for my next book, but I was still happy with the current Lady-in-Fedora. She seemed to hold more possibilities for adventure than I'd ever experienced in real life. I was sure she was much more like one of my intrepid heroines.

In a moment Norman's receptionist would summon me to his office, and I would brace myself against the familiar pain. The car accident that had killed Doug had been a tragedy for Norman as well, but it had also promoted him to senior editor, and given him Doug's office. Doug and I were to have been married the following month, and I couldn't step into the room where we'd held so many conferences without the sense of loss striking me all over again.

My attention focused again on the man who sat across from me in the waiting room pretending to read a magazine. He had been stealing glances at me ever since he came in, glances that came close to open stares. When I caught him looking at me, he turned his eyes quickly away, but his attention came back to me repeatedly.

The moment he'd entered the room, I'd been aware of his startled expression. With my writer's habit of quick observation, I'd registered his appearance. He was tall and strikingly good-looking, with thick, fair hair, and eyes that were a tawny brown. He wore a well-cut, conservative business suit, gray and light-weight, the material intended for summer. But this was early May and the weather in New York was cool.

Any minute now I expected him to try the old ploy: Haven't we met somewhere before? Deliberately I shut him out of my mind, and felt relieved when Norman came to the door. Before I could gather up my briefcase and rise to join him, however, he stopped me.

"Hello, Molly. Will you forgive me if I see Mr. Landry first? He's here from out of town, and we'll talk for just a moment."

Norman took my agreement for granted, and with a last, oddly doubtful look in my direction, the man "from out of town" disappeared through the door to Norman's office.

I settled back to wait, glad that I was rid of him, for the

moment. With a new manuscript ready to deliver, I was already turning to ideas for the next book. That's what I would think about now. No matter where I was, I could go off "into space," as my father called it, and lose myself in my imagination.

With a notebook open on my briefcase desk, I jotted down a few ideas I didn't want to lose, and thus preoccupied, I hardly noticed that it was more than a "moment" before the two men returned to the waiting room. To my dismay, Norman brought Mr. Landry over to introduce him.

"We're doing a book about Mountfort Hall Plantation outside of Charleston, South Carolina," Norman explained. "Charles Landry represents the present owner of Mountfort Hall."

Landry took my hand in his and held it for a moment, looking deeply into my eyes. "Astonishing," he said. "Absolutely astonishing!"

I took my hand back quickly and walked into Norman's office, hoping this would be the last I'd see of Charles Landry. His intensity made me uncomfortable. I was always writing about "intense" men, but my heroines knew how to deal with them. I didn't.

Norman spoiled my hope at once. "Landry is going to ask you to have lunch with him, Molly, and it might be interesting to accept."

This was even more disturbing. "But I'm having lunch with you—remember?"

Sometimes Norman's resemblance to Doug made me feel stricken, as it did now, though he was doing something Doug would never have done.

"I'm sorry, Molly, but something has come up that I can't help, so I'll have to offer a rain check."

I didn't believe him. For some unexplainable reason he had given up our luncheon date to this stranger. I didn't want to be left alone with Charles Landry. His very look made me uncomfortable.

Even as I was shaking my head, Norman went on abruptly. "You were adopted when you were a baby, weren't you, Molly?"

"What has that got to do with anything?" I asked, my instinctive alarm increasing.

"Do you care about where you might have come from? About your real parents?"

I answered defensively. "I still don't know what this has to do with anything. Has this man seen what he thinks is a family resemblance? My *real* parents are Richard and Florence Hunt, who adopted me and loved me all my life. My parents were never able to learn much about my birth parents. They've told me that. People who didn't want me gave me up, and I don't care who they were."

I was being much too emphatic. Something about this situation and that man frightened me. Perhaps it was my own dreaming that made me afraid. Ever since I was a little girl, I'd created a make-believe family for myself. A family with none of the shortcomings of my own. I knew that reality would be disappointing and never match my imagination, so it was better not to risk anything.

Norman frowned at me. "It's up to you, of course, Molly, but I think you ought to hear what Landry has to say. Things like this are too important to dismiss. But let's forget him for now. You've brought me your new book?"

Glad to drop the subject, I handed him the big folder with my typed pages. I'd talked the novel over with him early in the writing, but Norman had seen none of it until now. When Douglas was my editor, I had always kept him as a fresh eye for the first complete reading, and I followed the same course with Norman.

"You'll find some scribbling on the back of page twenty-three. I thought of a good touch, and had to write it in."

"Fine. I'll spend the weekend enjoying this. Then we'll have that lunch and talk when I've read it."

I felt thoroughly let down. Norman was the nearest I could come to Doug these days, and I enjoyed being with him. Now there was nothing more to talk about until he'd read the manuscript. I no longer felt even a little wonderful.

Norman came with me to the door, started to say something more, then broke off. Probably the set of my chin warned him that I wanted to hear no more about Charles Landry, so he simply said, "I'll phone you," and went back to his desk. Though I noticed he left the door open, as though curious to see what I would do.

The moment I appeared, Landry rose, looking not at all apologetic.

I stopped him before he could speak. "Look—I don't want to seem rude, but Mr. Hillyard was wrong in supposing—"

He interrupted me with the assurance of a man who usually got what he wanted. "Don't say no until you've heard something I have to tell you that can't help but interest you."

I caught the soft southern cadence in his speech, and the writer in me compared him again with the hero in one of my novels, even as I continued to resist his attractive smile.

"If this has something to do with my adoption—I was adopted, yes. But I'm not looking for answers from the past. Even if you think you see a family resemblance, I really don't want to follow it up."

"You don't? Really?" Startling me, he reached for my right hand and turned my wrist over. For a moment he stared at my birthmark—a flat red strawberry stain on the under part of my wrist. "I've seen the duplicate of that mark."

I froze as he went on quietly. "I have very strong reasons to believe that I am engaged to marry your twin sister in Charleston. Your identical twin sister."

That was a blow to the body—something I could neither deal with nor absorb. Suddenly I felt out of breath and totally vulnerable.

"Please have lunch with me," he said. "Let me talk with you for a little while. There's a pretty big mystery here, and I can't go home until I've at least tried to clear it up."

My resistance was gone and I allowed him to guide me to the elevator, and out to the sidewalk at the lower level.

"There's a place across the street," he told me as we waited for a stoplight to turn green. "It's still early and we'll get a table at the back, where we'll have privacy."

We crossed the busy street with the flow of the late-morning crowd. The shadows of the high buildings all around us formed that eternal man-made twilight of Manhattan.

A revolving door led into a hotel lobby, and the restaurant we entered at its far end seemed quietly expensive.

"The food's not bad, and I'm staying in the hotel, so it's convenient," he said.

Food didn't interest me and I felt unable to deal with a menu. Landry ordered for us—a clear soup, cold salmon, and a salad.

When the waiter had gone, he spoke to me quietly, gently. Back in the office I had been ready to think him rude and arrogant, but now he seemed concerned, and even a bit helpless himself to deal with what was happening.

"You were a shock when I walked into the Hillyard waiting room. I couldn't take my eyes off you. Let me show you Amelia's picture." He took a small color photo from his wallet and handed it across the table.

Reluctantly, I looked at a beautiful, smiling face framed by a

7

sweep of long, straight brown hair. I was looking into a mirror—except that this woman was much more beautiful than Molly Hunt, and I wore my own hair in a short cut that curled in just above my shoulders. Astonishingly, the woman in the picture wore a blue bandeau over the top of her head—and so did I. In some way the headband was even more confounding than our obvious resemblance.

My hand shook. "What does this mean? If she's my twin sister, why did her family give me up—if that's what happened?"

"It's not what happened. You were born in Charleston and your father and mother loved you a great deal. You were the firstborn twin—a few minutes ahead of your sister. When you were a year old, you were stolen. Kidnapped. Though there was never any demand for ransom—that would have been paid. *Any-thing* would have been done to get you back. Believe me, your parents spent a great deal of time and money trying to find you. I was only eight years old, but I vividly remember all the excitement. For years private detectives, hired by the family, attempted to track you down. There wasn't a clue. It was suspected that an underworld ring that sold babies to couples who were willing to pay large sums and ask no questions was at work in Charleston. Of course, they wouldn't have stayed around long, and probably skipped to some other part of the country after a successful snatch. What do you know about your adoption, Molly?"

I still found it hard to breathe. "Very little. My mother used to tell me that the moment she set eyes on me she knew I belonged to her. But neither my mother nor my father ever wanted to talk about the details. I can't believe they would have accepted a stolen child."

"They probably wouldn't have known. They'd have been told some story. Longing for a child can make a couple victims and ready to be gulled. Would your adoptive parents have had that sort of money?"

I wasn't sure. "My mother inherited some family money, but we weren't rich. I still live in their house in Bellport, halfway out on Long Island, where I grew up. My mother died a year ago, and my father is retired as a professor. None of my grandparents are living."

What I was saying didn't seem to matter very much. Important questions that needed to be asked were crowding through my mind, bewildering me with their ramifications.

"If I am this woman's twin, what was my name?"

"Your mother named you Amelia and Cecelia, and Simon Mountfort, your father, always gave Valerie everything she wanted. Though I think he'd have liked simpler names. You are Cecelia."

I'd never liked Cecelia as a name, and I rejected it now. "I could never get used to that name. I'll always be Molly Hunt."

"Of course," he agreed. "For now, that's what you're comfortable with."

Sometimes he still stared at me intently, as though he wanted to see past my surface resemblance to the woman in Charleston, and those words, "for now," frightened me. I felt as though a tide I couldn't resist were sweeping me toward a shore that might be strange and inhospitable. Did I want the make-believe family that I'd created in my dreams to be replaced by a real family that wouldn't serve my secret longings any better than my adoptive parents had?

"Haven't you ever tried to imagine what your real family was like?" Charles Landry asked.

"Of course I have! I was just thinking that. When my parents did something I resented, or when they punished me, I'd go off in my mind and visit the family I'd made up. Sometimes that family became more real to me than the one I lived with. I even made up a sister for myself—and named her Polly."

"A twin sister?"

"I didn't call her that, but of course she was my age." I didn't tell him that Polly had sometimes been a guiding factor in my life. She could make up her mind more quickly than I could, and she always knew what I ought to do. When I grew up and began to publish my stories, I turned Polly into a model for my strong, clever heroines. Then Douglas Hillyard came into my life and became my wise counselor and guide—at first for my fiction, and then for me. Romantic love was another dream that I'd never really experienced, but I could use it in my writing.

"Am I at all like her?" I asked, looking again at the picture. "If she is my twin."

"Yes—and no. I can't help watching you and trying to figure out the difference."

"From this picture, she must be very beautiful. I would look like her only superficially."

"Dressed alike, with your hair long, or hers short, I don't think anyone could tell you apart. Not until you moved or spoke. You're more animated than Amelia, and quicker in your gestures. She has a lovely serenity, an acceptance of herself and her place in society. Of course, there have always been men at her feet—it's an old southern custom when you're born a belle like Amelia Mountfort."

"I'd never fit into that sort of life."

Perhaps I'd sounded a bit scornful, for he raised his eyebrows, though he didn't comment. "Mr. Hillyard says you're a writer."

"Yes—of mystery novels." I always explained this quickly, lest anyone expect me to be "literary."

"My favorite kind of reading, though I lean toward the Elmore Leonard type of mystery. I gather you are more—that is, more—"

"Romantic? Yes. You needn't be afraid of the word, though sometimes it's used as a put-down. I have to be careful not to wear a chip on my shoulder. The way I like to think of the word is in its older definition, meaning something strange and exotic and mysteriously beautiful. Mystery without detectives. I suppose I go my own way in what I write, as every author must."

I wondered why I was explaining this to Charles Landry. Somehow he had begun to disarm me, even to win me over a little.

"I'm sure you don't need to carry a chip about your writing, Molly. One of your many cousins, Daphne Phelps, runs a bookstore in Charleston. When I get home I'll go straight to her store and buy your books—for me as well as for Amelia."

I could see why women would like Charles Landry. He knew how to reach past my defenses. However, his next words shocked me all over again.

"Molly, come to Charleston with me. Just for a few days. You can make up your own mind after you meet your family. Shouldn't you know who you really are?"

I rejected this at once, backing away fearfully. "I'm not ready for that. I didn't grow up with these people you're talking about, and I have a life I enjoy."

"You needn't be so prickly." He was teasing now, and I hated that. I felt cross and confused.

"Mr. Hillyard told me you usually visit some new place for the setting of each book. So why not Charleston? There'd be a rich background there for you to write about."

"I like to choose places I feel sympathetic toward. I'm a Northerner—I wouldn't fit in."

"What if every drop of your blood is southern?"

11

I'd heard enough, and I couldn't finish my salmon. I set down my fork. "May I have coffee, please? Then I'd like to go."

"Of course. Landry signaled the waiter and asked for two coffees.

I found myself watching him now, as he had watched me. His movements were graceful, and his classic good looks matched my notion of a typical southern gentleman. He would have come from old family, old wealth. I could easily imagine him in the dress of the 1800s. Perhaps in uniform—Confederate gray, of course.

"You came to see Norman Hillyard about a book—what is your connection with Mountfort Hall Plantation?" I asked directly.

He answered without embarrassment, collapsing my fantasy of his position and wealth.

"Your family owns Mountfort Hall and my mother was—still is—housekeeper there. Her name is Evaline Landry and she's quite a woman. She and your mother were good friends when they were young girls. I know the family has hushed up an escapade or two indulged in by Valerie and Evaline. It's going to be nice for my mother to step out of her role as housekeeper when Amelia and I marry. It will be her home then too, although she will go right on supervising everything, since Amelia won't want to take over and no one else can manage the Hall better. I don't know if she'll want to live in the main house."

"Why not?"

"She still lives in the little cottage I grew up in. It was originally a slave cabin on what they used to call Slave Row. The other cabins are gone now. My father enlarged this one into something comfortable and attractive."

"Tell me about your father." I was revising my conclusion about Charles—in part, at least.

"Jim Landry was a bricklayer. An artisan who could make his own beautiful bricks from clay on the land and match what was used on the plantation originally. When Porter Phelps, your mother's cousin, renovated the wing at Mountfort Hall that was shelled by Sherman's army during the War, it was my father he hired to do the work. Of course, I grew up with the Mountfort and Phelps families, and after we marry I'll be living at the Hall with Amelia."

For some reason I sensed a hint of uncertainty, and wondered why they hadn't married when they were younger. Yet, I liked the open way he spoke of his mother and father, with no suggestion that he was anything but proud of them.

I could imagine that young boy he'd been, growing up with the Mountforts, yet never quite part of the family. It was interesting, too, the way he spoke of the "War." For the South, there was still only one War that would receive the capital letter which I heard in his voice when he used the word.

It was at this moment when I really began to relent toward him, that a devastating realization hit me. Perhaps I wasn't the person I'd always believed myself to be. Charleston, the South— all that plantation world I'd read about, and that whole dim war the North sometimes forgot, could be my history too. Though I would always be an outsider, something I hardly recognized stirred in anticipation. I'd never thought I'd have real blood ties, since my own blood was a mystery. What if my mystery were solved and I became—what? Who would I be? Did I really want to know?

Worst of all, though I had friends, there was no one close enough to whom I could turn to for counseling about any of this. Doug was gone—Norman was only my editor. My father, under the circumstances, would be worse than useless. My mother would have known immediately what to do; I had lost her recently and I missed her. I suspected Charles would welcome my leaning on him, but that was out of the question.

I plunged into safer waters. "Tell me about this book Norman Hillyard is interested in."

Our waiter poured more coffee and I sipped it black, listening to Landry's answer.

"It's Porter Phelps's project—your second cousin. He and your mother are both Mountforts on their mothers' side. Your father, Simon, carried the Mountfort name, as does Amelia. And you. Your mother is very much alive, but Simon Mountfort died about ten years after you were kidnapped."

He had made up his mind about me fully. But I hadn't made up mine. So why, when I wasn't sure of anything, did I feel a pang of loss for a father whom I would never meet? And why feel something that was almost a longing for the mother who had lost me?

I made myself pay attention to what Charles Landry was saying.

"Since your mother has never lifted a finger out at the plantation, everything has been left to Porter to manage since your father died. Porter has always been fascinated by the history of the house and the family. He's a proud, tradition-bound old South Carolinian. But he's no writer himself, so the book will be ghostwritten."

"Are you doing that?"

"Hardly. My work is restoring houses. As my father's son, I suppose that's what I had to do. I was too young to help restore Mountfort Hall, but there's still plenty to be done, both at the plantation and in the Historic District of Charleston, where we have a strong preservation society. The man who's working on the book is, oddly enough, from the North. He had a job with a Charleston paper—the *Courier News*—when Porter got to know him. Garrett Burke has become nearly as obsessed with Mountfort Hall as Porter is, even though he moved south only two years ago. I wouldn't have given him the assignment, but Porter didn't ask for my opinion."

"Why wouldn't you have chosen Garrett Burke?"

Charles Landry looked uncomfortable. "I'm not sure I can explain. Perhaps I don't trust him, though I must say he's thrown himself into this work as if he'd grown up in our Low Country. That can happen, you know. Strangers visit us, fall in love with Charleston and the whole peninsula, and become its greatest champions. Perhaps this will happen to you, Molly, if you give it a chance. After all, you have roots you never dreamed of."

He used my first name easily, though I still couldn't call him Charles.

"Your mother needs you," he went on. "She's never stopped grieving over the child she lost. And I know that your sister will be beside herself with joy at the prospect of knowing you. Besides, both Simon and Porter always believed in cultivating dependency when it came to women. You, I suspect, are a whole other breed —and that may come as a shock. Perhaps you'll be good for all of them."

I must have been better at bluffing than I'd thought! If I wasn't as dependent as Amelia, it was only because there was no one around to lean on.

"You're going much too fast," I objected, needing to step back from this tide that seemed to be sweeping me along. My ties were here. I loved the picturesque little village of Bellport, with parts of it dating well into the past. This was my history. It meant more to me than that of the South ever could, and I said so emphatically.

"I'll always be a Yankee."

His eyes crinkled at the corners. "Famous last words." He

15

took a card from his wallet and handed it to me. "Here's where you can reach me—whether I'm in Charleston or at Mountfort Hall. I'm not going to say anything to your sister or anyone else until you've had time to adjust. Then I think you'll come—if only for a short visit. You'll need to know. When I'm sure that you're coming, I'll break it to the family. It won't be easy for them either, you know."

I didn't argue with him. I would take his card, but I would never use it. I wanted no borrowed trouble in my life.

When we left the restaurant, Charles Landry put me into a cab to Penn Station. I wouldn't let him come with me to the train. It was a relief to be on the way to Patchogue, where I'd left my car. All I wanted was to reach Bellport and home. I knew very well where my real home was.

Historically, Bellport had always held a charm for writers and artists. Now theatrical and movie people were discovering its quiet seclusion, though perhaps their presence might eventually threaten the very qualities they sought. My father constantly complained that there was too much traffic these days on South Country Road.

My drive home from the Patchogue station took less than twenty minutes, and I turned off South Country down the blind side-road that ended at the house I'd lived in since I was a baby. A stolen baby?

Our home wasn't one of Bellport's historic houses, but it was old enough to look down on the upstarts that were springing up everywhere. I loved the big frame structure with its wide porch and generous, welcoming rooms. When I was little it had been painted yellow, but I preferred its present shining white.

As I climbed the front steps I realized how utterly weary I felt, yet I knew I couldn't rest until I'd talked to my father and put a pressure on him that I'd never exerted before. I couldn't let go of the things Charles Landry had told me, after all.

Several years ago Dad had retired from teaching English Lit at a local college. Mostly these days he puttered in the garden, took long walks to the village, and visited the Sou'wester bookshop, where he bought more books than he would ever read. He also wrote a little, mostly reviews or articles for scholarly magazines. I suspected that it pained him that his daughter dabbled— he never quite considered me a writer—in such a commercial field as mystery fiction.

I loved him dearly, though I'd never given up the make-believe dream father who would be really mine. Of course, that father would read my books with pleasure and be proud of what I did. Now, thanks to the man from Charleston, not even he existed.

Dad was in his small study at the back of the house—a room he had long ago partitioned off from what had been a rear parlor. He still used an old, manual typewriter, and the very thought of an electric machine, or a word processor, distressed him. He preferred a good fountain pen. Perhaps some of his prejudice had rubbed off on me. Although I wrote on an electric typewriter, I enjoyed the feeling of a pencil in my fingers when I was thinking and jotting down notes for when I came to revision.

I tapped on the door and he looked up as I came into the room, his smile warm and loving as always, and as always a little absent.

"Did it go well in New York?" he asked. He and Douglas had been good friends, and he knew how I felt about visiting New York.

I dropped into a big shabby armchair—one of two in front of a fireplace that he never used anymore. He hadn't recovered from my mother's death, and I hated what was happening to him; his loss of interest in life. Sometimes his memory failed these days, and I couldn't bear it if that happened now. Today I had to get him to remember and talk to me, as he'd never been willing to do before.

There was no way to soften what I had to tell him, so I plunged in abruptly. "Someone seemed to recognize me in New York today, Dad. A man who believes that I am the natural daughter of a family in Charleston, South Carolina. Please—it's time for me to know the truth."

He put down his pen and looked at me sadly, though without surprise. Perhaps he'd always known that someday I'd ask questions in a more searching way than I had in the past.

"I wish I knew more. When you were adopted it seemed best not to ask too many questions. All the adoption agencies knew we were looking for a baby, and once we had made up our minds, we didn't want to wait. We'd never had children of our own, and we were afraid we'd soon be too old to think about raising even an adopted child. You were already more than a year old, but as we've told you, from the moment the agency woman brought you here, Florence knew that you were our daughter."

"What agency, Dad?"

He looked uncomfortable. "I—I'm sorry, Molly. I can't remember now. There are papers somewhere. I do know that when we tried to get in touch with them later—just to fill in your medical background a little more—we couldn't find them. They had told us a few things about you. That you were born in Chicago and your mother died at the time of your birth. Your father had a daytime job and couldn't keep you. There were no relatives to help."

Dad had never told me this much before, and I wondered if he hadn't always been a little suspicious of the story they'd been given.

"You came from a good middle-class family—we were assured of that."

"Assured?"

"I don't know how it is today, but back then laws could be very strict, Molly, when it came to revealing details about an adopted child's birth parents. It wasn't unusual to know very little."

"How much money did you pay for me?"

I hated the sound of those words, and hated myself for the tears that came into his eyes, but I had to go through with this.

He answered softly. "It took most of our savings at the time, and all of your mother's inheritance. A pretty large sum, but we never thought about the cost. We weren't *buying* you—we were sacrificing."

I wanted to put my arms around him and ease his pain, but I couldn't stop now.

"Didn't the amount you had to pay tell you anything?"

Agitation drove him to push his chair back from his desk and get shakily to his feet. "Babies weren't available quickly, Molly, darling. And Florence wanted you more than she'd ever wanted anything in her life."

I remembered how strong my mother's desires could be, though I knew they would surely pale in comparison with Valerie Mountfort's devastation over the loss of one twin daughter.

"Did you ever suspect that I might have been stolen?"

"No—of course not!" He answered so vehemently that I guessed the thought had certainly occurred to him, and that he hadn't dared to spoil my mother's happiness by voicing it.

I put my arms around him, aware of the frailty of his body, sensing his trembling. "I'm sorry, Dad. Please don't be upset—it doesn't matter. You and Mother gave me a wonderful, loving home, and you will always be my parents. I feel reluctant to go to

19

Charleston, but perhaps I need to clear the record. There's probably nothing to any of this, but I ought to find out."

Somehow I had made up my mind without being aware of it. I helped my father into his armchair, and took his weight as I lowered him into it. He walked with a cane these days, and I put the ivory knob close to his hand.

"You must do whatever you need to do, Molly," he told me bleakly. "I understand. Go along now. I'd like to be alone."

Alone with thoughts of my mother, with whom he would talk about what had happened. Once more I sensed that in spite of his tears, he didn't care about much of anything since her death. My adoption belonged to a dim past, and his interest in recalling it was gone. I didn't think he would remain upset for long about my going to Charleston.

It would not be a matter of leaving him alone. After Mother died, my father's youngest sister, Dora McIntyre, had bought the house next door. She looked after my father, and she also supervised a cleaning woman who took care of both houses and did a little cooking. He would be in good hands while I was gone. And I wasn't planning to stay for more than a week, if that long.

I kept telling myself that I must do nothing too sudden or impulsive. I had responsibilities here. There might be revision needed on my new book, and Norman Hillyard must be consulted. There were a few friends I needed to talk to about my plans, though I wanted to give no details. I was on my own now. That was a worrying feeling, yet one that brought a certain sense of freedom.

I decided to get in touch with Charles Landry while he was still in New York. My private phone was in my bedroom and I dialed the number of the hotel where we'd had lunch and where he was staying. He answered at once, and somehow his voice, with its soft southern accent, reassured me. It also excited me a little. I could no longer think calmly about a twin sister and a mother who had never stopped grieving for me.

"I can't come with you now," I told him, "but I'll arrange to fly to Charleston in a week or two. Can you suggest a place where I can stay?"

He didn't sound surprised, and I had a feeling that he had expected my call—perhaps waited for it. "There's an interesting inn not far from Porter's house. Let me know the date you'll arrive and I'll make a reservation for you."

I was pleased that he had suggested an inn. I had no desire to move in with strangers who might, or might not, be my family.

"I'll take care of everything," he went on, "including your plane tickets. Of course, I'll meet you at the airport."

He sounded as assured as I remembered, but something of the same excitement I felt had caught him up as well. I could hear its quickening in his voice.

I thanked him, feeling relieved, now that everything was out of my hands.

"I'm glad you've made up your mind, Molly," he went on. "Look at this as the sort of adventure you may write about some-day. Just let your imagination go. Incidentally, I was able to pick up your new book at the store near the hotel, and I've started reading it. You *are* a good storyteller."

He couldn't have said anything that would have pleased me more, and when we hung up I began to relax for the first time in a good many hours.

I lay on my bed and held up my left hand so I could stare at the mark on my wrist. But it was the blue bandeaux that both Amelia Mountfort and I wore that convinced me most of all. Of course, they matched the blue of our eyes, but even then . . . Tomorrow I would go to the library and learn all about twins, and about Charleston, South Carolina.

Two

There was an unexpected hitch about my leaving for Charleston. In a day or two, when he reached home, Charles Landry phoned, sounding apologetic.

"Your mother hasn't been told yet, Molly. We're afraid she might become excited and build her expectations too high. So your cousin Porter has advised against it. However, your sister knows, and she's anticipating your coming. She cried when I told her. I think she's happy, but a bit fearful."

The way he used these relationships—mother, cousin, sister —made me fearful too. I wouldn't blame them for not wanting to accept me. I could hardly accept all this myself.

Charles Landry went on. "One unexpected problem about your coming is Honoria Phelps, Porter's wife. I don't know exactly how to tell you about Honoria. You'll understand better when you meet her. Her connection with the family is only by marriage, but her ties with Mountfort Hall are strong. Honoria believes in portents, and sometimes we listen. She's been reading her tarot cards, and she doesn't like what she sees."

He waited for some response from me—which I didn't know how to make. I knew nothing about tarot and felt dismayed by this turn of events.

When I was silent, he went on reassuringly. "Don't let this upset you, Molly. Even Honoria is quick to say that what she sees is vague and unspecific. I probably shouldn't have told you."

"Has Mr. Phelps decided that I shouldn't come because of this?"

"He hasn't gone that far. Daphne is eager to meet you, and she may be strong enough to prevail."

"I'm lost! Who is Daphne?"

"She's Porter's daughter by his first marriage—another cousin. He married Honoria after his wife died. Daphne is the one who owns the bookstore in Charleston. She already has your new book and she's pleased about your coming. Daphne doesn't pay much attention to her stepmother's psychic spells, though she's tolerant and quite fond of Honoria."

"So what do I do now? Would you prefer that I not come?"

He sounded more uncertain than when we'd talked in New York. "No, I think you must come. I've talked it over with my mother. She's practical in her approach and feels that you should come. She wants to meet you. So if you're willing I'll go ahead with plans for you to come next week. This is a good time, since you'll be here before the worst hot weather, though you'll miss the azaleas. They were early this year."

I might as well go now and put the experience behind me, so I could get on with my life.

"Tell me when and I'll come," I said.

"Fine! I'll let you know as soon as I've made the arrangements. I can't wait to see you and Amelia together."

It was left at that.

For now, I stayed away from my typewriter, glad that I was between books. I needed a quiet mind in order to lose myself in an imaginary world, and my thoughts were churning over the events that lay ahead of me.

During this interval I dipped into a pile of books I'd brought home from the library. A surprising amount of material had been published about twins. I narrowed my reading to the subject of identical twins who had been raised apart.

Apparently three different contributing elements had to be considered. Heredity and environment seemed obvious, but the third element, coincidence, was given a good deal of consideration. Some of the astonishing likenesses discovered among twins who met each other after they were adults had been studied in great detail. I remembered the story of Minneapolis twins—boys —who had fascinated researchers with their amazing similarities. However, it was pointed out that coincidences happen all the time to everyone. Perhaps Molly Hunt and Amelia Mountfort wore blue bandeaux because we had fine straight hair that needed to be held back, and the color blue matched our eyes.

Physical resemblance was easily explained in identical twins, of course—so the birthmark on our wrists simply confirmed this. Now a new science called chronogenetics was being explored— dealing with the role genes play in making twins alike, not only in terms of physical characteristics, but in terms of similar traits and tastes, even though the twins were far apart. Yet even here upbringing played a strong role, and in the end anything seemed to go when it came to twins. There were a good many twins who were more different than alike, and ultimately my reading left me confused and uncertain.

Probably none of this mattered anyway. I suspected that when Amelia and I met we would know, one way or another, and theories, or even the opinions of others in Amelia's family, wouldn't matter.

Charles Landry sent my plane tickets promptly and let me know that I'd be staying at the Gadsden Inn on Hasell Street—which was pronounced Hazel. I was not to worry about anything, he assured me, and said nothing more about any opposition from the family in Charleston. Valerie Mountfort had still not been told of my coming. Porter wanted to meet me before anything was said to his cousin. Wise, perhaps, but troubling.

When the time came, the trip seemed anticlimactic. My father let me go easily enough, and that left me feeling oddly alone. Norman Hillyard said our conference about the new book could wait—he wanted to read it again anyway. I couldn't worry about that now. Planes and airports were pretty much alike these days, and even the first-class travel Charles Landry provided was nothing special.

When he met me in Charleston he seemed reserved, in spite of the effort he made to welcome me and make me feel comfortable. After we'd picked up my bags and were in his car, an uneasy silence settled between us. I wondered what sort of family crisis might have arisen that he wasn't telling me about.

By this time I had studied maps and was acquainted with the

configuration of land on which Charleston had been built. I even knew a bit of its history. In 1670 the first colonists arrived from England and discovered a fine harbor at the foot of this peninsula of land. They sailed up what would be named the Ashley River to the spot that was now Charles Towne Landing. The new settlement was, of course, called Charles Towne in honor of King Charles II, whose merry, hedonistic ways would be imprinted upon his namesake city.

The land itself was limited by the arms of two rivers, the Ashley and the Cooper, which met at the tip of the peninsula to "form the Atlantic Ocean," as Charleston had long boasted. Fort Sumter—where the first shots between North and South had been fired—was only a dot out in the harbor. Parts of the older Fort Moultrie, which also guarded the harbor, dated back to the Revolutionary War, and was now a museum.

We traveled south through North Charleston and down toward the Historic District, where the family lived. This was Old Charleston. Hasell Street ran east and west for a few blocks, and as we turned onto it, Charles came out of his silence to explain about the Gadsden Inn.

It occupied what had been an old cotton warehouse and was named after Christopher Gadsden. Brilliant and wealthy, Gadsden had been an early agitator against the British. The Sons of Liberty had drawn in young lawyers, mechanics, and planters— all angry with the injustices of British rule—and Gadsden had played his own patriotic role.

The big redbrick inn, foresquare and sturdy in its construction, edged the sidewalk. Its windows had been trimmed with red-and-green-striped awnings, and there were plantings of tropical shrubbery and palmetto palms where a narrow strip of earth permitted.

Several entrance steps led up to the lobby, and a porter came to help with my bags. While Charles stopped at the desk, I stood looking around with the interest of a writer who knew a mystery setting when she saw one.

The lobby was punctuated by massive brown beams that were part of the original warehouse and formed columns that reached several stories up, leaving a vast open space in the center. Huge beams rimmed the opening, and supports reached clear to the distant roof, where skylights threw down muted daylight. I could glimpse doorways beyond the great beams that formed the railings above, and all this stirred my imagination. I could almost see one of my characters leaning on a beam to look down upon tiny figures on the lobby floor far below. A dizzying height from which to fall!

The lobby floor was of dark red tile, with a handsome oriental rug covering a small portion. Striking paintings decorated the walls, and my eye was caught by a scene of jungle animals that hung above a grouping of chairs, sofa, and lamps—all with the signature of Africa in their pattern. But the lobby was not African in its overall effect, for on another wall hung a huge painting of a golden Japanese carp created on fabric and dominating its own space. This was certainly no ordinary hotel lobby.

Charles returned and the porter came with us to enter an open-sided elevator, from which we could look down through glass as we rose to the third floor. Here we followed a narrow gallery behind a beamed railing, and I could look over it down to the reception desk.

Walls up here had been painted a light buff, and a door at the end opened into the suite Charles had reserved for me. The living area was furnished in bright tropical prints, and a strip of galley kitchen opened off it. A hallway led back to bedroom and bath. Restoration had left bits of the old warehouse visible in portions of brick wall and a strip of wooden post.

27

"Thank you," I said to Charles when the porter had gone. "I love this place."

We sat down on a sofa bright with azaleas, and he smiled at me.

"We want you to be comfortable while you're here, Molly. Tonight Porter Phelps and I would like to take you out for dinner. There will be just the three of us, since he feels it will be best to meet your sister after you've settled a bit."

There was no mention of Valerie Mountfort. "You haven't told me much," I said. "Has anything happened that I ought to know about?"

"Not really." His good looks seemed shadowed by something somber that I hadn't seen when I'd met him in New York. When I waited, he went on hesitantly. "You've stepped into a family of individuals who are apt to go their own ways. I don't know what will happen when they meet you. Not even with your sister. You might as well brace yourself for the unexpected, and be a little on guard."

"Against what?"

"I'm not exactly sure. We'll see what develops." He promised to call for me at six-thirty.

"I'll be in the lobby," I said, and gave him my hand.

He took it with the warmth I'd sensed in him at our first meeting.

"The problem isn't you, Molly. You'll do fine. It's just that some of the family refuse to believe that you really are Cecelia Mountfort. They're curious, of course, but don't expect open arms. You'll need to relax and let the tide carry you. What will happen, will happen."

"That sounds pretty fatalistic. They're right to be cautious, of course. I still wonder whether I can possibly be Amelia's lost

28

twin. I do know that I'm Molly Hunt, and that's who I'll be, no matter what happens. Nothing will change for me."

Even as I spoke, I wondered if that were true. Perhaps just coming here had changed me a little.

Charles held my hand for a moment and I felt again the charm he could exert when he chose, and I hoped it was genuine, and that he wasn't holding something back.

When he'd gone I washed away travel grime and changed into slacks and a light blouse, so I could be comfortable until the dinner hour. I stepped outside my door to look down upon the great open space of beams and wooden crosspieces made from the trunks of full-grown trees, the whole structure probably well over a hundred years old.

The inn's guest rooms were set against the outer walls of the building, while the interior formed this dark, cathedral-like space that dropped to the lobby—a dusky emptiness with galleries all around and dozens of closed doors. The central space rose another floor above me, narrower at one end than the other. I had no geometric name for this irregular enclosure.

The beam under my arms had been planed so that it felt smooth, and as I leaned upon it, I had the sense that someone was watching me. When I looked up to the opposite rail on the floor above, I discovered that a child seemed to be peering down over a beam she could hardly reach. I couldn't tell whether the head belonged to a boy or a girl, since only a shock of pale curly hair was visible in the dim light across that cavernous void. A pair of eyes studied me with an unwavering stare beneath a patch of white forehead.

I called out to the watching child. "Hello there!"

She put one foot on a slat and raised herself so that her entire delicately formed head was visible—and definitely feminine.

This alarmed me and I called out again. "Be careful! Don't climb any higher!"

She answered with an assurance that belonged to no child. "Stay right there, Molly Hunt. I want to talk to you."

The voice startled me—adult and not particularly young. I could hear her small feet along the corridor as she moved to a stairway at the far end. In a moment a tiny woman emerged on my own level and ran lightly toward me.

She wore a pleated white skirt and embroidered tunic blouse —clearly made to her small measurements. She was definitely not a child, but a perfect person who was smaller than average. Her movements were airy, as though she floated along the hallway where I stood. Now I could see that her eyes were a silvery gray, and her hair had the same light silvery cast. Her features were perfectly formed, from small, pert nose to a chin that squared a little. She carried herself with a dignity that would protect her from the giants in her life. She was probably in her late fifties, though it was difficult to guess for sure. As a young girl she must have been very beautiful. Exquisite, perhaps.

"I had to see you for myself," she announced without preliminaries. "Though I didn't want Charles or Porter to know I was coming. I am Honoria Phelps." The accent was there. I would come to realize that the Charleston accent was special and had its own musical sound.

"I've heard about you." I held out my hand. "Charles Landry says you didn't want me to come to Charleston."

Honoria stared at my offered hand as though she might be reluctant to touch it. Then she put out her own small hand, and I found that taking it was like holding the fingers of a child, and I was surprised at the responsive strength of her handclasp. For a moment she seemed to cling to me, as though she didn't want to let me go.

30

"I was afraid to touch you," she confessed. "I didn't know what I might feel, but it all seems positive. It's true—what Charles said—you *are* Cecelia Mountfort."

"I'm Molly Hunt," I said quietly, "and I expect I always will be." I might grow tired of asserting this, since I had the feeling that no one would pay much attention to my claim to be *me*.

"Where is your room?" Honoria asked. "Let's go where we can talk."

Charles had said that he didn't know how to explain Honoria Phelps, and I was beginning to see what he meant. Feeling more bemused than alarmed, I led the way to my room.

"My pantry isn't stocked, Mrs. Phelps," I told her. "So I can't offer coffee, but please sit down. You are Porter Phelps's wife?"

"I am indeed." Honoria seated herself in a corner of the sofa, taking up very little space. Her sandaled feet didn't reach the floor, but she sat erect, her short legs dangling, her hands clasped in her lap—and she said nothing at all. I was the one who had a tendency to fidget. Her silence was almost like a reverie, and it made me self-conscious.

I managed a few unnecessary words. "I'm having dinner tonight with Charles Landry and your husband. Will you be joining us?" I already knew she wouldn't, but it seemed something to say in this weird silence.

She returned from whatever distant space she'd gone to. "Call me Honoria, please. After all, you are family. No, I won't be there. Porter thinks it's best for me to stay away. Of course, he doesn't dream that I'd come here to meet you ahead of time. He will have a fit when he finds out." Her laughter sounded mischievous and included me, as though we shared some secret amusement.

"Porter is terribly proper, you know," she went on. "You'll have time to find out—if you stay. He couldn't trust me not to

31

have one of what he calls my spells at dinner. Though everyone is used to me, and no one really minds. They expect me to be a little off. But Porter thought it might be a shock for you if this happened too soon, so it seemed safer to leave me at home."

She still smiled with bright mischief, and I couldn't help smiling back, though I hadn't the faintest idea what this small, vital person was talking about.

Honoria recognized my bewilderment and explained. "I am able to channel, and sometimes that upsets people. Or do you know what channeling is? I find it surprising that even today so many people don't understand."

"I'm afraid I'm a bit vague on the subject."

"It can happen to me anytime, whether I invite it or not. And it takes different forms. Sometimes words appear on paper that I don't expect to write. Or I hear a voice coming from my mouth that isn't my voice, and which brings in the entity who speaks through me. His name is Nathanial." She spoke the name affectionately. "Or sometimes only strong thoughts may form in my mind—so strong that I must respond to them in some way. Nathanial told me to come here to see you today. And I'm glad he did."

I was beginning to feel a bit spooked, and I could see why Porter Phelps might be uneasy about having me meet his wife before I had been prepared.

"I'm fascinated," I told her. "Do go on."

"I thought you would be. Of course you'll use me in one of your stories."

It was my turn to laugh. "I never use real people. They'd get in my way and not do what I want them to do." I'd often found it difficult to explain this to a layman who didn't write and couldn't imagine making up a new person out of bits and pieces that might be present in a writer's consciousness. All I needed was a springboard.

Honoria understood, however. "I can see how that would be. You'd have a lot of trouble with me. Now then—show me the mark on your wrist. Charles says it's there."

Compelled, I held out my hand, and Honoria slipped down from the sofa to stand before me, her eyes on a level with mine. One tiny finger touched the flat strawberry mark and rested there for a moment as she closed her eyes. A slight tingling sensation centered where her finger touched my wrist. When she had apparently gathered whatever information she wanted, she went back to her erect perch on the sofa, not bothering with any propping cushions behind her.

"That was the final corroboration," she said. "You are the stolen baby—grown up. So what will you do, now that you're here?"

"I haven't any idea. I suppose I'll meet the family and then go back home where I belong."

Honoria shook her head vigorously and her pewter curls trembled with their own life. "I don't think you'll be able to do that. In a little while it will all begin to sink in and take hold of you. All that heritage you know nothing about. If you want to go home, this is the time to go. Tomorrow—at once. Before the connection begins to take hold and the curiosity you'll feel becomes irresistible. Then you won't be able to escape."

"I can't turn and run," I said. "Not until I've met these people who are supposed to be my family."

"Never mind. Once you've had time to understand why you're here, you'll know what you must do. Whether it's to go or stay."

There was no need to deny or argue. I remembered Charles's words: "What will happen, will happen."

"Of course, there's another way," she added. "If you can let yourself drift with the tide and take no action, you may be safe."

This was too much. "Safe from what?"

Honoria's eyes opened wide—almost staring, though not at me—and she uttered a single word. Her voice was suddenly hoarse, very different from her own light tones. The word, however, was clear: *Murder.*

Immediately she was herself again. "There—you see! I didn't say that. It's a fair warning, though I don't know what it means. Is he indicating that there's been a murder? Or that there will be one? And what are we supposed to do? He's often vague and not very helpful. Though I never ignore what comes through."

How much of this might be an act, and how much Honoria really believed, I couldn't tell. She seemed direct enough, though, and convinced in her own mind. Before I could ask any questions, she took a sudden new road.

"I have something for you at home. It's a letter. Nathanial told me to wait before giving it to you. You should have it soon, but this is enough for you to think about now."

That startled me. Who could possibly have written a letter to me here in Charleston that would have come into Honoria's hands? But before I could protest, she floated to the door and left without another word. I stared after her, not understanding much of anything. Perhaps not even wanting to. I seemed to stand at the edge of dangerous ground, hesitant to take a step forward.

For a few moments I sat waiting for the air around me to quiet. Honoria Phelps seemed to move in a certain radiation of her own—if that was the word. Something around her reached out to touch others, probably shaking them up as it had shaken me. When I saw Charles I would have even more questions to ask —particularly about Honoria Phelps.

I showered and even napped a little until it was time to dress for the evening. I'd brought a creamy silk blouse, scattered with tiny blue gentians—because Amelia had worn blue in the picture Charles had shown me. And—even more deliberately—I fastened on the blue velvet bandeau to hold back my shoulder-length hair. I might as well astonish Porter Phelps, who was still doubtful about me. Though no more doubtful than I was.

Charles picked me up in the lobby and we went out into an early evening that was still light. He'd come alone, and he explained as we got into his car.

"Porter's tied up with something unexpected. He'll meet us at the restaurant. I'm rather glad, because this will give me a chance to show you some of the Historic District before we have dinner."

Pride came into his voice as he talked, and I found myself watching with a writer's eye as I listened.

"More preservation has been accomplished here than in Williamsburg. Of course, this isn't an exhibit to show what the past was like. This is where people still live and work. Some Charleston families go back to the Revolution. But there are a great many newcomers from other parts of the country who have stayed because they fell in love with what they found here."

He drove slowly so that I could savor the charm of this old part of the city. As he talked I could tell how close to his heart the scenes around us were. If Charles was in love with Amelia Mountfort, he was also in love with this city at the tip of the peninsula.

Except for the through streets of King and Meeting, most of these streets were narrow, the houses close to the sidewalks and curiously narrow themselves. Often there were side gardens, with the thin houses stretching back beside them. Lovely verandas often edged the private gardens. We slowed still more to allow a horse-drawn carriage filled with sightseers to pull out of our way.

Charles explained about the houses. "We call them single

houses, or sometimes double houses when they are wider. The single houses are one room and a hallway wide, and usually two stories in height. The piazzas—we never call them porches or verandas here—are built at the side to offer privacy from the street. They usually face south or west to catch whatever breezes there are in summer. Sometimes the front door opens directly onto a piazza. Or sometimes you enter from the sidewalk through a decorative iron gate leading into a side garden."

I noticed as we drove along that larger houses were also in evidence—mansions that revealed the beauty and dignity of another era. Here gardens might be placed at the front and were more generous in size, more luxurious with tropical growth. Many of the single houses were pale pastels—blue, pink, green, yellow. Or sometimes gray or buff. Occasionally a wrought-iron balcony overhung the sidewalk, reminding me of New Orleans's French Quarter. Of course, wealthy planters had fled here from slave revolts in Barbados and other parts of the West Indies, and they had brought touches of their own tropical architecture to the area. Various periods and cultures mingled in more than three hundred years of history.

Of necessity, traffic moved at a decorous pace, and no one tried to hurry. Coming so recently from the North, I was aware of the difference. Here I might find time to draw deep breaths and stop the blind running I'd been doing ever since Douglas died.

"This is a good time to be here," Charles said. "Before heat and humidity drive us indoors, or away from the Low Country altogether. We're lucky to have kept so much of Old Charleston intact, in spite of hurricanes, fires, and earthquakes. Charleston will always recover and go on." He spoke with deep affection, and I knew how much he valued all of this.

"I've been reading whatever I could find to orient myself," I told him. "But really seeing it is wonderful."

He pointed to a building we were passing. "Do you see those iron patches on some of the houses? They hide earthquake bolts, where rods go through from wall to wall to hold a house together." His tone grew almost dreamy, as though he relished his city's history. "The clocks stopped at nine fifty-one on the evening of the great 1886 earthquake—the largest ever to hit the East Coast, and Charleston took the brunt. Nearly every building in the city was damaged, yet Charleston survived. In a way, we can thank the poverty that existed after the War for all that has lasted here."

I began to notice the iron rosettes covering ugly bolts. "What do you mean?"

"Any other place might have torn itself down after a disaster and rebuilt in some faddy new design. But after the War, Charlestonians had no money for rebuilding, so they painted and repaired and saved all these beautiful structures. Now when a new building goes up it must be in keeping with the old. Though, unfortunately, we've lost a few of our most distinctive older buildings—among them the first orphanage asylum in the country. Torn down because of people who didn't appreciate what they had."

Charles had played his own role in this preservation, and I was glad he could care so deeply.

"It's your city too, Molly," he told me.

"Not yet!" I spoke quickly. "Give me time, Charles. Everything has happened too quickly. I'm only a very new visitor."

"A special visitor. Whether you're ready to accept it or not, your origins are here. Now that you've seen all this, you'll have to write about us."

I probably would, since I was never happy unless a book was stirring at the back of my mind. But in order to write, I would need to stay longer than I might want to. I would need to learn a

37

great deal about Charleston—though research could always come later, once I'd experienced a new setting with my own feelings and responses. Of course, I would never presume to write from the viewpoint of a longtime resident. A stranger's viewpoint was my own. In this case, however, that viewpoint might be flavored and affected by more than I was as yet ready to accept.

"Here's a parking space," Charles said. "Let's stop for a moment. Daphne's bookshop hasn't closed yet, so we can look in and give her a surprise."

He'd pulled the car over to the curb, and there was no way for me to back out—though this was happening a little too suddenly. A spark of impudent fun seemed to touch Charles, and I knew he was playing his own little game and using me to surprise Daphne Phelps.

When we went up the few steps into the Book Loft, only a last-minute customer was being waited on by a clerk. Charles spoke to Daphne and she came toward us at once—a tall woman, perhaps in her mid-thirties, and distinctive-looking rather than pretty. Green eyes widened when she saw me, and she ran a startled hand through brightly tinted red hair that had been cut short in a straight twenties bob.

"My God!" she said. "For a moment I thought you were Amelia. You're as much like her as Charles claimed you were." She paused, appraising me disconcertingly. "Yet you're different in subtle ways. And it's more than the cut of your hair."

She held out her hand in a strong, direct clasp, and I sensed a woman of assurance and strength. Perhaps an assurance that had even placed a few hard lines in her face.

"You mustn't be engulfed and overwhelmed by the Mountforts," she warned.

"This is Molly Hunt, Daphne," Charles said quickly, coming

in on cue. "She doesn't want to be called Cecelia. This is your cousin Daphne Phelps, Molly."

Daphne grinned—not exactly a smile—and waved a hand in the direction of a table piled with my new book. "You can see we've been expecting you."

The misty blue jacket of *Crystal Fire* looked fine on display, and I felt pleased to see it, as I always did when I found my books in a shop. A mother proudly recognizing her newest baby!

"My amnesia story," I said. "I hope your customers will like it."

"They will. I read it before I knew I was to meet you. That photo on the back is a good disguise. It must seem strange to come into an entire family you never dreamed existed."

"Right now," I told her uneasily, "I'm not sure who I am."

She patted my arm. "I don't envy your meeting the Mountforts all at once. Never mind—will you sign some books for me, Molly Hunt?"

Charles intervened. "I'll bring Molly in another day to sign copies. We're meeting your father for dinner at Jilich's, so we'd better go along."

"That should be interesting," Daphne said. "Don't let him blow you down, Molly. I wish I could be there to see what happens. I don't suppose . . . ?" She looked at Charles hopefully.

"Not a chance," Charles said. "Porter wants to meet her alone and make up his mind what to do."

"That's my father! Captain of the ship, and aye, aye, sir! Cousin Valerie still doesn't know?"

"I've tried to persuade Porter to tell her before someone else lets it slip."

"Does he have Honoria's spirits muzzled?"

They laughed at a private joke—one that I was in on more than they knew.

Daphne put out her hand to me. "I'll look forward to seeing you soon, cousin. Perhaps you'll visit me? I'm in the phone book. I can be an antidote to too many Mountforts, if you need me."

I returned her warm clasp, liking Daphne Phelps, and never dreaming that by the time I visited her in her apartment several happenings would have changed and frightened me.

Just as Charles and I reached the door, a man came in with a comfortable informality that told me he knew everyone, and was at home in Daphne's shop. His easy smile vanished, however, when he saw me and he stared openly. I knew that look by now and I stared back defensively. He was a rugged young man, perhaps a little older than I was. His unruly dark hair had been cut a bit long, and his too penetrating look reminded me of a few villains I'd written about. I wondered if he were typecast in this drama I seemed to be living.

He didn't wait for an introduction. "Hello, Cecelia. I'm glad to meet the mystery woman everyone's been talking about." His accent was as northern as mine, and he lacked the easy charm I'd seen in Charles.

Charles corrected him, sighing. "Garrett, this is Molly Hunt. Molly, this is Garrett Burke, who's ghostwriting Porter's book about the Mountforts."

"Let's say I'm collaborating." He held out his hand to me after a slight hesitation, as though the gesture were an afterthought. When I gave him mine, he disconcerted me further by turning my wrist over to reveal the strawberry mark. I snatched my hand away at once, but his direct, searching look never left my face. He seemed to be questioning my existence, no matter what the resemblance.

"Be careful what you say to Garrett," Daphne warned. "He's a journalist and you'd make good copy."

Garrett paid no attention, but turned to Charles as though he could dismiss me as being of no importance. "Are you coming to the rehearsal tomorrow night, Charles? We need to go through that phony duel a few more times. You nearly poked my eye out in the last go-round."

"We'll get to it soon," Charles promised. "In the meantime you need to work on your other scenes." He turned to me to explain. "We have an acting company here—semipro. We call ourselves Stage Center and we're rehearsing a play about the War Between the States. Garrett makes a good Union officer for me to kill off—even if he can't act." His tone was joking, but I caught an edge to his voice that surprised me.

The look in Garrett's eyes told me that he might give as good as he got. So hooray for the North, I thought scornfully, all my sympathies with Charles.

"Incidentally," Charles continued, "your sister Amelia wrote *The Shadow Soldier*. It's turning into a family production by this time. Even Honoria is helping out as director—at which she's pretty good. Help from her spirits, I'm sure."

His words about Amelia struck home. Amelia Mountfort and I were both writers!

Charles caught my look of astonishment. "Oh, Amelia's not as serious as you are. She just likes to dabble."

"It's a damn good play," Daphne said. "She's hit all the clichés about North and South and written past them. So you needn't apologize for Amelia. And Honoria is a whiz of a director. Wait till you meet her, Molly. The experience will blow you away!"

"I've already met her," I said quietly.

Charles and Daphne both stared at me. Garrett had moved to

the stack of my books and picked up a copy of *Crystal Fire*. I could feel his attention on me rather than on the book in his hands.

I hurried to explain. "Mrs. Phelps came to see me at the inn. I suppose she was curious, like everyone else."

Daphne shook her head, marveling. "Honoria does what her guides tell her to do, and that can lead to unexpected action."

I caught her up. "What do you mean—guides?"

"I suppose you could call them spirit guides, if you believe in all that stuff."

Since my meeting with Honoria, I no longer knew what I believed. "I liked her," I admitted. "Though I didn't know what she was talking about half the time. She thinks I should go back home as soon as possible. Her portents aren't very good for my staying around in Charleston."

Charles seemed to have forgotten that we were about to leave. He and Daphne were silent, while Garrett Burke pretended to study the book he held. I felt a concentration about him that was disturbing, and I went on, unsure of my ground.

"Mrs. Phelps talked about channeling. I'm not sure I know what she meant."

Daphne and Charles exchanged looks that held some meaning which was beyond me.

"Did Honoria give you an example?" Daphne asked.

"I suppose that's what it was. Without any warning she used a different voice. Someone she called Nathanial apparently speaks through her."

Charles smiled. "Our Mountfort Hall ghost! You might as well accept him, Molly, since he comes with the territory these days. Thanks to Honoria and her cat."

"What did Nathanial say?" Daphne persisted.

I hated to repeat the word aloud—it sounded too melodramatic. "She used a rather deep, spooky voice and she said just one word: *Murder.*"

No one spoke for a moment, and the silence chilled me. Garrett seemed to be reading the flap copy of my book, but he must have read it over several times by now.

"We must leave, Molly," Charles said abruptly. "The restaurant's nearby, so we'll walk. 'Bye, Daphne. I'll see you at rehearsal, Garrett."

As Charles swept me toward the door, I looked back and met Garrett's dark gaze for a moment.

Outside, the evening air felt sea-fresh. A scent of magnolia blossoms came to me from over an iron fence. In the next block, lighted shop windows offered an endless variety of treasures that would have fascinated me at another time. What had happened— silently—in Daphne's shop was all that concerned me now, as though swampy ground had opened at my feet and I didn't know where to step.

Jilich's was a distraction and a relief. Again I found myself in a huge space that had once been a warehouse. The headwaiter knew Charles and showed us promptly to our table, where I looked about in appreciation. Walls—except for the exposure of brick at one end—had been painted a pale peach, with matching tablecloths and napkins. Faraway ceiling fans set among old wooden beams stirred air-conditioned currents gently.

"These old warehouses have been put to good use," Charles said. "Rice, indigo, cotton—those were the staples before the War. Slaves brought their own knowledge of raising all three, back where they came from. Of course, the economy collapsed during the War. When the soldiers came home, the devastation was numbing."

I didn't want to think about that confusing war and all the

southern slave owners who might have been related to me, so I was relieved when Charles picked up his menu.

"Porter said not to wait, so let's go ahead and order."

I studied the big card with interest and decided on Sea Island crab cakes and a salad of spinach, artichoke, and hearts of palm. Charles ordered a Jilich's specialty—coconut deep-fried shrimp with a sweet chutney.

When the waiter had taken our orders, I returned to what had happened in the bookshop, unable to leave it alone.

"*Has* someone been murdered?" I asked Charles.

"Of course! This is bloodstained ground, Molly—has been since the Revolution. Which murder do you want to talk about?" His tone was light, teasing, his words completely evasive.

"Honoria's—voice—seemed to have made a choice."

"He would. Isn't a ghost supposed to haunt the place where he died? Especially if he left his human existence unwillingly."

"You mean Nathanial was a real person—not some entity out of—wherever? Was *he* murdered?"

"He was real enough, but he wasn't murdered. It's a long story. Do we have to talk about this now?"

"Perhaps we do," I said, unsure of why I felt this urgent need to know. "Please tell me about Nathanial. He tried to speak to me through Honoria, which was more than a little unsettling, as I'm sure you can imagine."

Charles fiddled with his silverware, and I knew how little he wanted to talk about this.

"Go on," I persisted. "Tell me."

Three

"I'm sorry if Honoria upset you," Charles said. He was still evasive.

"She didn't. I found her fascinating. Though she never told me that Nathanial was a Mountfort ghost. Does he date back to the early history of the house?"

"No, no. Mountfort Hall was built by Edward Mountfort early in the eighteenth century. Nathanial Amory was much more recent. In fact, I knew him very well when I was a young boy. He was the tutor at Mountfort when I was a child. Daphne was a bit older, but he tutored her too. Honoria knew him because she was a young docent taking visitors through the plantation house. It's still open at certain hours for public tours. These days it costs too much to keep up an old mansion, and those tourist dollars help. There's a shed on the grounds where pottery making and weaving are demonstrated. The family has private quarters above the first floor, so visitors are not allowed upstairs."

"How did Nathanial become a ghost?"

"He drowned in the Ashley River not far from Mountfort landing. A boating accident. It happened a short time after you were kidnapped. Rumor has it that he and Honoria were a pretty hot item in those days. Of course, this was while Porter's first wife was still alive. After both she and Nathanial died, Porter married Honoria, but Daphne thinks Honoria was rebounding from a broken heart."

"So now Honoria has created a loving ghost for herself?" I asked.

"I don't know about *loving*. He's a bit of a pest, really, since Honoria uses him happily for her eccentric purposes."

"Have you ever seen him?"

"Never. Only Honoria and her cat are in touch with him. You'll meet Miss Kitty eventually."

"A psychic cat?"

"Aren't most cats? Never mind—here comes Porter, so let's not talk about Nathanial. Ghosts aren't Porter's favorite subject."

The man being led to our table by the headwaiter was in his late sixties, more than six feet tall, and he needed his height to balance a figure grown portly. I knew he had retired from management of a Charleston bank, and was wealthy in his own right. He looked like my idea of an old-fashioned southern gentleman straight out of Central Casting—immaculate white suit, a black string tie, white shoes. The fact that he was bald except for a circle of white hair that ran from his ears around the back of his head seemed to add to his air of dignity and command. It was hard to imagine this big, overpowering man married to Honoria. What a contrast they must make together.

Unlike other family members, Porter Phelps showed no surprise over my resemblance to his cousin Valerie's daughter. When Charles rose, his manner respectful, I had no doubt about who was head of the clan these days.

Charles's introduction was formal, and Porter bowed over my hand, though his fingers seemed to release mine quickly. The look he gave me from pale blue eyes carried no warmth. Porter had clearly decided that I must be an impostor and that he wanted me gone.

"You told us not to wait," Charles said as Porter joined us.

"Yes, of course," Porter said. "I had a late tea at the house with Valerie and I'm afraid I'm not very hungry."

"You've told her?" Charles asked.

"Told her? I'm not sure there's anything to tell," Porter said, and asked the waiter for a salad and the wine he preferred. Then he settled back in his chair and looked around the big dining room as though he were sitting alone.

Charles attempted conversation. "I was telling Molly that she really must see the plantation while she's here, Porter. If you have no objection."

Porter raised one thick white eyebrow. "Of course not. I will be glad to offer Miss Hunt our hospitality."

For all his respect for Porter Phelps, I suspected that Charles was growing restive over the way I was being treated. "Show him your wrist, Molly," he ordered suddenly.

I kept my hands in my lap and spoke directly to Porter.

"Please let me explain how I feel, Mr. Phelps. I've never had any sense that I was a twin. I'm fascinated by Charleston, but I'm still a Yankee, and I find it hard to believe that I was taken from your family when I was a baby. However, after meeting Charles, it seemed necessary to come here and find out the truth—if that's possible."

"There are blood tests. Pretty sophisticated ones these days," Charles added.

Porter waved this aside. "Inconclusive." But he had begun to relax a little, as though my words had reassured him to some extent.

"I admit there's a real likeness between you and Amelia— enough to satisfy Charles's eye. Though perhaps there are many more differences."

"Cut Amelia's hair and dress them alike—and they'd be identical," Charles insisted.

"Perhaps. I don't blame you for getting carried away, Charles." Porter turned to me. "At least, you must visit my cousin Valerie's house tomorrow. Not to meet her. I don't think that would be wise. We mustn't disturb her when she isn't well. But you and Amelia could see each other. She would never forgive Charles and me if we allowed you to leave without meeting."

This discussion was beginning to upset me. Of course Amelia and I must meet. These two men couldn't decide for us. I changed the subject deliberately.

"Do you all live in the same house in Charleston?"

"Certainly not," Porter said. "The Mountfort house is on South Battery and was built in 1790. Houses on East Battery were built after the War, when the waterfront was made safe by sea-walls. So they're a more recent vintage. Our home, Phelps Place, is on Church Street and dates back to 1735. When we are in Charleston, Honoria and I live there. My daughter, Daphne, has taken her own apartment—though we have plenty of room for her."

His resentment of Daphne's independence came through, and I could only sympathize with his daughter. Obviously, there had been a rift here.

Smoothly, Charles distracted Porter from this irritating subject. "Have you seen Honoria since she visited Molly this afternoon?"

His effort was fully successful. "She visited you, Miss Hunt? I might have known!" However, he sounded more fond than annoyed. "I purposely didn't invite her to join us because she sometimes takes matters into her own hands. Tell me what happened, Miss Hunt."

"Your wife believes that I'm Cecelia," I said quietly.

"Did she say why?" He seemed only mildly curious, his own conviction unshaken.

"She touched the mark on my wrist—here, you might as well see it, though it's begun to embarrass me." I held out my hand across the table. Porter flicked his eyes in the direction of my wrist and looked away.

"I don't think it's the same," he said. "Probably coincidence anyway. Go on about my wife."

"She touched my wrist and seemed to get some sort of information that convinced her. But as I've said, I am not convinced. Not yet."

"That's wise of you. Perhaps we'd better not wait until tomorrow. Why can't we get this over with now? When you've finished dinner, we'll go directly to South Battery and you can meet Amelia. I'll phone ahead to let her know, and to make sure that my cousin will be upstairs in her own room. I hope it won't be necessary to have Valerie see you at all before you leave."

"What if Molly *is* her daughter—would Valerie ever forgive you?"

"My cousin is very emotional and not at all well; she listens to me," Porter said stiffly.

"I'm still confused by the family ties," I told him. "Are you a Mountfort by blood?"

"Simon, Valerie's husband and Amelia's father, was another second cousin, though he carried the name and I didn't. Old families here can be confusingly interrelated," he explained coolly. "If Simon had lived, I would not be in full charge at Mountfort Hall."

"It's a good thing you are," Charles put in, turning to me. "Next to my mother, Porter cares about the plantation more than anyone else, and he's done a lot toward its preservation. By the way, Porter, how is Garrett Burke working out? Is the book nearly completed? When I was in New York I couldn't give Hillyard all the details."

"Garrett works at his own pace," Porter said, "but I like what I've seen, and I'd rather read the whole thing fresh when it's done. Then we can talk about any changes or additions. I tell you, it was a real break for us when he came to Charleston to find out more about the southern branch of his own family. Of course, Honoria says there are no accidents, and that he was drawn here because he is the right man to work on this book."

"We saw Garrett just now in Daphne's shop," Charles said. "I'm afraid he puts me off. Maybe I'm not happy about having to duel with him in Amelia's play. He seems so eager to show me up; at least I've taken more fencing lessons than he has. But, in all honesty, we both need a lot of practice. Sometimes I wish Amelia had put dueling pistols into our hands instead of swords."

Porter's interest in such theatricals was clearly slight, and he shrugged Charles's words aside.

We had been served our entrées, and wine was poured in tall glasses. For the moment my butterflies were calm and I found I was hungry.

"Tell me about the theater where you'll put on the play," I said to Charles.

"It was originally another of our old Charleston warehouses, but it's perfect for our purpose. There's plenty of room for stage and audience, and an enormous area backstage for dressing rooms and for scenery and prop storage. Since the warehouse was owned by the Mountforts until the 1890s, and they've contributed to converting it into a theater, it carries the Mountfort name. I suspect the family has a bit of influence when it comes to taking an occasional part in activities. It would have been hard for the theater management to turn down Amelia's play, so it's a good thing she's done a fine job of writing it. Charleston will love it. This is a city that enjoys laughing at itself."

"I've never thought of Amelia as especially humorous," Porter said.

"She surprised me too. Have you read the play?"

Porter shook his head. Watching the two men, I was aware of a strange dynamic between them. In spite of his obvious respect for Porter Phelps, and all Porter had apparently done for him, Charles seemed a bit edgy with him. Under-the-surface conflicts were my business as a writer, and this hint of antagonism interested me. I wondered again why Charles and Amelia had waited so long to be married. Perhaps, growing up together, they'd taken each other for granted, and only fallen in love when they were older.

While we finished our coffee, Porter went off to telephone Amelia and let her know that we were coming.

"You don't really like Porter very much, do you?" I asked Charles when we were alone.

51

He looked surprised. "Of course I do. He's done a great deal for my mother and me, and for my father when he was alive. Perhaps it's human nature to resent our benefactors when they take us over. Perhaps when I'm married to Amelia I'll feel less in Porter's debt."

Something about the way Charles said this made me uneasy. I hoped he was truly in love with Amelia and not marrying the Mountfort name and wealth.

"How do you feel?" he asked abruptly. "I mean, now that this meeting between you and Amelia is about to happen? Are you all right?"

"I'm not sure. I still haven't any intuitive feeling that I have a twin sister, yet at the same time I feel keyed up and anxious. Why doesn't Mr. Phelps want me to be the lost twin?"

Charles shrugged. "Who knows? He always likes to be top dog. Simon died when Amelia was ten and she has looked up to Cousin Porter ever since. Perhaps you might furnish some unwelcome competition."

"What does Valerie think?"

"She thinks today is Tuesday and tomorrow is Wednesday— or whatever. She's a bit difficult, Molly. That's probably why Porter is keeping you away from her. She could be excited and pleased—or she could fall apart. Valerie is the most unreliable person I've ever met. Don't count on anything there."

"I'm not counting on anything anywhere," I told him, and his smile was sympathetic. He reached out and gave my hand an encouraging pat.

Porter returned, looking brisk and purposeful. "Amelia's waiting for us, so we'll go straight to the house."

Clearly he wanted to put all this nonsense behind him.

"How did Amelia react?" Charles asked as we left the restaurant.

"She's nervous. I've warned her not to expect too much."

"And Valerie is out of the way?"

"She's gone to bed early with one of her headaches. She'll be safely up on the third floor in her room."

We drove to South Battery in separate cars, and turned along the park, where live oaks kept the area green the year round. The seawall along the Cooper River offered a view of the harbor, and Charles said I must come see it one day at sunset.

All along the street that fronted the park stood great white mansions built closely side by side to use every inch of waterfront ground. The Mountfort house was fronted by balconies with white balustrades, since there was not room for a generous piazza.

Charles parked his car behind Porter's and we got out to climb wide steps that ended beneath an arched doorway.

"Amelia's waiting for us upstairs," Porter said, unlocking the door with his own key.

Inside, we passed a formal drawing room on the first floor, and I glimpsed a beautiful old Persian rug and graceful antique furniture and bric-a-brac. As we climbed carpeted stairs, it was not this impressive house that held my first attention. The moment of my meeting with the woman who might be my twin sister was here, and my knees felt weak.

Doors opened off a space at the top of the stairs, and Porter led the way into a generous, informal sitting room. At the front windows a woman stood with her back to us, looking out across the park toward the water.

Porter spoke to her gently and I sensed his fondness for his cousin. "Amelia, I'd like you to meet Molly Hunt, who is visiting us from Long Island." A safe introduction.

The woman didn't turn at once, and I knew exactly how she felt. My own heart was thumping, my emotions ready to fly frighteningly out of control. Charles touched my elbow, under-

standing, steadying me. When Amelia turned, I could only stare
—as she stared at me. Here was no mirror image; nothing was in
reverse. When other people looked at me, this was what they saw.
True, Amelia's dark hair hung long down her back, and in some
subtle way—as I'd already recognized—she was more beautiful
than the reflection I knew as Molly Hunt. Perhaps there seemed a
serenity about her that I lacked, and a poise that came from good
breeding and an old family.

We both wore blue—her dress blue-flowered, simply cut, and
wide-belted in black leather. Blue bandeaux held back our fine,
straight hair, and I began to feel my own identity slipping away.

It was Amelia who saved me from some foolish, jittery collapse into tears and trembling. For a moment longer she stood
staring across the room at me, almost as if she feared what she
might see. Then she ran toward me with a little cry of joy and put
both arms around my stiff, resistant body.

I knew why I resisted. If my life in the North was to continue
happily, I would need to save myself from Amelia Mountfort.
Instead, I began to relax in her embrace. The outpouring of
emotion between us was totally unexpected for me. This was the
unreasoning, accepting love of twin for identical twin, and I
knew neither of us could ever be free of the other again.

"I've always known I'd find you," she whispered, her wet
cheek against mine. "I've been afraid ever since Charles told me
—afraid it was all a mistake. But the minute I saw you I *knew.*"

She dropped her arms and led me to a sofa covered in a
pattern of pale yellow primroses. We sat side by side, my hand in
Amelia's, and she spoke to Charles and Porter with the assurance
of a woman who knew her request would be obeyed.

"Please go somewhere else—both of you. My sister and I
need to be alone for a little while."

Porter might have objected—clearly he didn't approve of this

54

quick recognition between Amelia and me—but Charles nudged him toward the door and they went through to another part of the house.

Strangely, now that we were alone, there seemed to be nothing to say. Amelia's hand didn't release my own, and perhaps something of her own happy emotion began to convey itself to me. When her fingers tightened, I could return the pressure in a sort of wonderment.

"Where shall we begin?" she asked softly. "The last time we were together was in this very room, but we were babies, and now I don't know how to get to know you."

I made an effort to put my confusion into words. "You've always known you had a twin, but I grew up as an only child in another part of the country—with people I called my parents, who knew nothing about where I came from."

"We needn't hurry," Amelia said gently. "We can do this a little at a time, Cecelia. I need you—I need you terribly!"

She was reaching out too far, too quickly, and I had to step back a little.

"There can't be a bridge between us if you call me Cecelia. That's not my name."

"Of course it isn't. I won't use it again—though it's the way I've always thought of you."

How strange to have existed in her mind, in whatever her fantasies were of a real sister, when I had created a make-believe sister in my friend Polly. I envied Amelia her simple, straightforward acceptance.

She went on almost shyly. "I've read your books, Molly. Daphne Phelps gave them to me even before I knew who you were. I love them—and you'll never know how often I studied that photo on the back jacket and wondered what the author was really like. Perhaps something in me was guessing, even then. You're what I've always wanted to be—a successful writer."

This, at least, was safer territory. "Charles says you've written a fine play that's in rehearsal now."

"Oh, that. It was only written for fun. And maybe mischief. I enjoyed setting Charles and Garrett in opposition to each other. Of course, I'm the heroine in the play and they're both in love with me! Which is giving them fits. Because Charles is jealous, and Garrett isn't even interested. Isn't it strange that we both like to write? Oh, there's so much to catch up on!"

I could easily be beguiled by this newly found sister, yet I was still not sure whether I should give that much of myself away.

"I can't stay in Charleston very long—" I began, only to have the sudden alarm in her eyes stop me.

"You mustn't say that! We've only just found each other. Sometimes things go too fast for me and there's no one to talk to. It would be so wonderful to have a sister who would listen. You must feel the same way too." I nodded cautiously and she continued. "Later, perhaps we'll have time. Right now we must think of Mama and how this may affect her. She's never really recovered from losing you."

I touched Amelia's arm to stop this flood of words. "You need to understand that I have had a mother whom I loved. And still do. She died only last year."

Amelia seemed not to hear. "We lost our father when we were ten, Molly. I'm sorry that you can never get to know him. I was very close to him, and I've never stopped missing him. In a way, he belonged to me, while Mama belonged to you."

I couldn't listen to all this. I left my place beside her, where her very proximity troubled me, and went to stand in the middle of the room. At once she was quiet, watching me.

For the first time since I'd entered the room, I allowed myself to sense it—experience it. A room I would have grown up knowing, if it hadn't been for the kidnapping. The soft primrose of walls and carpet seemed warm, friendly, soothing. Paintings on the walls were mostly watercolors of Charleston scenes. And of course the long bookcase with its bright jackets invited me to browse.

When I was last in this room I must have been a little over a year old. Babies have no memories—do they? So why did I have this almost comforting sense of familiarity, as though the room knew *me?* Its very colors must have changed many times over the years—yet there was this strange sense of recognition that was inner and emotional.

Amelia waited, watching me, and a darker feeling seemed to touch me, bringing with it an eerie chill. At once Amelia sensed the change.

"What is it, Molly? What are you feeling?"

I couldn't explain. I just wanted to escape. I went into the small hallway, where the stairs came up on one side from the front hall below, with a narrower flight rising opposite, curving out of sight to an upper floor. From a skylight over this second flight, evening radiance from the city beamed down upon the steps.

When Amelia came to stand beside me, I spoke quickly. "I can't move into this house. Perhaps I'll come back sometime for a visit, and I hope you'll visit me up north. I have another life to return to. I met Honoria Phelps earlier today, and she thinks I mustn't stay. Now that I've come here I'm sure she's right."

"We'll talk again," Amelia said softly, and I knew she hadn't given up.

The hall space opened into a dining room, with a small balcony beyond. Through French doors I could see Charles and Porter sitting outside near the rail.

The moment he was aware of us, Charles jumped to his feet and came inside. "You're all right, Amelia?"

His concern for her was as clear as Amelia's joy in seeing him. With sudden clarity I knew that what Amelia felt for Charles was something very different from my quieter love for Douglas Hillyard, and in that instant I envied her. The differences between us were very great.

When we joined Porter on the balcony, his impatience showed as he spoke directly to my sister. "Well? What do you think?"

She answered with simple conviction. "Molly is my twin sister, Cousin Porter. There isn't any doubt. Not for either of us—is there, Molly?"

I could only nod my agreement.

"I want Molly to move into this house right away," she told him. "Please help me to persuade her."

I suspected that Porter would do nothing of the kind, and I spoke quickly to avoid anything he might say. "That isn't possible, Amelia. Not right now."

"Why not, Molly?" Charles asked. "It seems like a sensible idea. If you're going to write a book about Charleston, this would be a way to begin." His face lighted as something occurred to him. "Amelia, let's take her out to Mountfort Hall tomorrow. That's a first important step, don't you think?"

Before I could manage a further protest, he hurried on, and somehow the arrangements were out of my hands.

"You must meet my mother, Molly," he said. "And of course you must see some of that wonderful history that is yours too."

"I come from Long Island, New York," I told them quietly— and realized for the first time that I knew nothing about my history. I'd always accepted this, but now I felt a strange longing to know all that had never touched me before.

58

Amelia waved my words aside. "That's a wonderful idea, Charles! I must go to a meeting at our Historical Society tomorrow morning, but you two can drive out to the Hall early, and I'll get away to join you there for lunch. Will you let Evaline know we're coming? Evaline Landry is Charles's mother, Molly, and I know she'll be happy to give us lunch."

Porter looked displeased, and I suspected that he wasn't accustomed to having his wishes ignored. For once, Amelia and Charles seemed to be out of hand, and he didn't like this at all.

By now I knew that there would be no use in my saying that I'd prefer to go home tomorrow. The curious sensation I'd experienced in the primrose room still unsettled me. It was as though some time warp that had lasted only seconds had shaken up my entire sense of reality.

At least, now that everything had been decided, I could relax and give in to the tide that was sweeping me along. That the shore ahead might be rocky was not something I could cope with now.

From my balcony chair I looked out over the dusky garden that spread below us behind the house. This space of shrubbery and flowering trees ran through to the next street and was gently illumined by lights at the far end. The sea-scented breeze and the fragrance of gardens were Charleston as it must have been for centuries, and it could make one forget the cars driving by just beyond the garden walls.

This was no high-rise city. Rooftops were only two or three stories high, with a few cupolas and church steeples overlooking the rest.

Charles pointed out St. Michael's and St. Philip's—both Charleston landmarks, their spires illuminated.

As I sat there in the dim light close to Amelia, I could feel myself begin to surrender my individual and independent self. We

59

were more like one—as identical twins must surely be. But if I accepted this, then I must begin to ask questions. How had I been stolen? And what about the mother I still hadn't met, and whom everyone seemed to be protecting? What would Valerie Mountfort and I feel toward each other? And why did Porter Phelps seem determined to keep us apart?

"When is our mother to be told?" I asked abruptly.

None of them answered, but I sensed the underlying uneasiness.

Before I could insist on a response, something happened that startled us all. At a sound from the room behind, we turned, and Amelia gasped in dismay. I saw that a beautiful woman in a long robe the color of marigolds stood in the opening of French doors. A scent of roses clung to her and wafted toward us more eloquently than the garden scents. When she saw me she raised a shocked hand to one cheek and her blue eyes widened. There was no question as to who she was, and a sense of something like terror rose in me. If Valerie Mountfort rejected me, then who was I? I could only stare at her in that moment of silence.

I could see her clearly in the light from the dining room, and there seemed few lines on her smooth skin. She was still slender, and unlike Amelia and me, she was very fair. Her long pale hair hung in a braid down her back, and a lacy frill of white nightgown showed at her throat.

"I—I heard voices," she faltered, staring at me uncertainly.

"Mama!" Amelia cried, and I heard desperation in her voice.

Charles said, "Val, dear, this is your other daughter. She has come back to you."

As she faltered in the doorway, Porter moved swiftly and caught her as she crumpled. He picked her up, his anger directed at the rest of us. He carried her into the sitting room, where he lowered her gently to the long sofa with its pale yellow blooms that matched her fair hair.

Amelia ran to kneel beside her mother and then looked up at Charles and me. "Do something!" she cried.

Valerie's color had turned ashen. Long fair lashes touched her cheeks, and from her parted lips came the sound of faint breathing.

"Let me." A voice spoke from the doorway, and I looked around at Honoria Phelps—a tiny figurine, whose only use, surely, would be to decorate a shelf. But she came quickly across the room, already in charge. She pushed Amelia aside and sat on the edge of the sofa beside Valerie. When she had rubbed her palms together briskly until they almost crackled with electricity, she placed them near Valerie's temples and closed her eyes.

No one in the room spoke or moved. In a few moments Valerie looked up into her face and sighed deeply. Honoria whispered reassuringly, though we couldn't hear her words.

"Honoria knew," Porter marveled. "She always knows when she's needed."

It was Valerie Mountfort, however, returning from an experience that had shocked her into unconsciousness, who held my full attention. The scent of roses seemed heavy in the room, and I remembered that the fragrance of roses had always made me feel sad. Perhaps now I knew why.

I looked deeply into the eyes of this woman who was my mother, and she looked as deeply into mine. I couldn't speak or move. When her rejection came, I felt a little sick.

"No!" Valerie Mountfort said, her voice perfectly strong now. "This isn't my darling lost Cecelia."

Four

Honoria looked around at us and stood up. "Which one of you is going to explain?"

"I will." Amelia hurried to take Honoria's place beside her mother, and held Valerie's hands in hers. Watching her, I was aware of a deep love on Amelia's part.

For myself, I felt only numb. What had happened didn't really matter—or so I tried to tell myself as I listened to Amelia explaining how Charles had found me in New York, and brought me here.

When she finished, Valerie's eyes filled with tears. "I'm sorry," she told me. "It was such a shock." She held out her hand in apology. "Of course you must be Amelia's twin."

She didn't claim me as her daughter, however, and I took her hand reluctantly. Her first rejection of me had seemed more real than these easy tears.

She must have sensed my hesitation, for she drew her hand back quickly, and for an instant flashed me a look that I couldn't interpret. A look that seemed more than rejection—even something as strong as hostility. Then she looked away and I could hardly believe what I'd glimpsed.

Once more, it was Honoria who saved the moment. "Look, Val, honey, you've just had a shock. And I'm sure that Molly has had nothing but shocks since she's come here. So let's turn off all the emotion until tomorrow. You belong in bed, Valerie, and so does Molly."

Valerie allowed herself to be drawn to her feet by Honoria's small, strong hands, while Amelia hovered anxiously. Before she went into the hall, however, leaning on Honoria's shoulder, Valerie looked back at me again.

There seemed no rejection now, no hostility, but only a questioning.

"It shouldn't have happened like this," Charles said when they had gone upstairs. "Never mind—it can't be helped now. Let me take you back to the inn, Molly. Honoria is right. You need to rest."

All of Porter's attention seemed to be focused on listening intently for any sound from the floor above. He hardly noticed as I took my leave, and I was thankful to put myself in Charles's hands.

PHYLLIS A. WHITNEY

We went out to his car and drove through dark streets that were quiet and nearly empty. Rows of closely packed houses crowded the sidewalk, or gave way in a block or two to single and double houses, their side piazzas overlooking gardens. I felt as though I moved in a dream and none of this were real. Only that look Valerie Mountfort had first given me was real, and could not be erased by her later apology and tears.

Charles drove slowly, pointing out houses of special interest, allowing me to rest—to simply be. When we reached the inn, he didn't move at once to get out of the car.

"Are you all right, Molly? I had a feeling back at the house that things were going badly for you. You mustn't mind Valerie— she isn't well."

"I don't know," I said. "Perhaps I shouldn't stay. There are things I'd like to know, but . . . I can't be a real daughter to Valerie, and if I stay she'll only be hurt."

He said strangely, "I don't think I can let you go now," and then went on quickly, as though he'd said something he hadn't meant to. "I'll call for you around nine in the morning, if that's all right. They serve breakfast in the lobby of the inn, if you get up early, and then we can drive out to Mountfort Hall. You can't possibly leave before you see your family's most prestigious ancestral home."

I supposed he was right, and gave in. He came around to open my door, took my hand as I got out and held it for a moment. "Thank you for coming, Molly. I know it hasn't been easy. Valerie is emotionally fragile—even more so than Amelia— and you must be gentle with her. She wasn't always like this. I can remember her when I was a young boy—a happy, spirited lady. The loss of you, coupled with your father's death, has made it hard for her."

Unexpected emotion that had nothing to do with Valerie

64

Mountfort choked me. "I was stolen as a baby! I was taken away from my family—a horrible crime. Kidnapped! I want to know how it happened. I must know how it happened. I *must* know! Before I leave I have to know!"

I must have startled him, but he spoke quietly. "I was only a boy at the time, Molly, but I remember a little from hearing people talk."

"Where was I when I was taken?"

"You were in the upstairs sitting room of the house we were just in."

"That's what Amelia meant when she said the last time we were together was in that room. Somehow I had a sense—a feeling—about the room that I can't name. What else do you know?"

"You and Amelia were playing together on a blanket spread on the floor of the sitting room. Your nurse was there. Later, of course, they relieved her of her duties for not taking good care of you. Someone came into the house, wrapped you up in that very blanket, and carried you away, leaving Amelia behind. I don't know why they didn't take both babies. Valerie was upstairs. She heard Amelia screaming and came down to find that one of her daughters was gone, and the nurse, who had been put out with ether, tied up in another room. It must have been a nightmare. Simon rushed home from his office, and the police were summoned—with no results whatsoever. No one had a clue as to your whereabouts until I walked into Hillyard's waiting room and saw you there. Thank God I did!"

"I'm not sure I can thank anyone. Perhaps I've only brought more trouble and grief."

Even as I spoke the words, I wondered what I meant. I couldn't explain them, even to myself. Amelia hadn't reacted as Valerie had. I told Charles good night and went quickly up the steps into the entry hall of the inn. When I reached the lobby, I stood for a moment looking up into that eerie, cavernous space. Irregular beams rimmed the open area, all shadowy in spite of lights set in the faraway ceiling. At least no one peered down at me tonight from some high railing.

In the elevator I pushed the button for the third floor. A narrow length of hall led to my room, and I hurried to close myself away from those empty spaces above the lobby. When I reached the bedroom, I turned on several lamps and then stood at a window to look out over the rooftops of Charleston. Yet all I could see in my mind's eye was the room with the primrose carpet and pale walls.

What was it in that room that had so moved me? Something had seemed to reach into the past—to have been a part of the terror of being snatched up in rough hands and spirited away. Did anyone really know what sensory memories might impress themselves upon us when we were babies, and leave a residue that could surface years later?

The ringing of a telephone startled me, and I lifted the receiver to hear Honoria's voice. "I must see you soon, Molly. I'll drive out to the plantation tomorrow, since I understand you'll be there. We'll find a way to talk—*alone*. Terrible things have happened in the past. At first I only wanted you to leave, but now I've been told that you must stay. Tonight I sensed very strongly that you are the instrument I've waited for all these years. Besides, I have a letter for you, and you must see it soon.

"You must stay, you know. You haven't any choice. The road has opened and you must take it. In the meantime I want you to sleep well tonight—with no disturbing dreams. I left some comfrey tea for you, with a touch of my own herbs in the packet. Make yourself a tisane and be peaceful, Molly. You are very tired and you will sleep."

The very quality of Honoria's voice quieted me, and when I hung up I made myself a cup of the tea she'd left me. Sleep came quickly, with no dreams that I remembered when I awoke refreshed in the morning.

Today I would begin my search for the "truth," whatever it might be. Honoria had been "told" that I must stay, and for the moment I would accept that. There would be a way—an opening through which I could step—and I must watch for it. Perhaps something of Honoria's hypnotic influence had lasted through the night, and whatever guidance she offered me, I would use.

The early-morning sunlight streamed through my windows, and last night's alarms and fears seemed almost silly now. I could look forward to my visit to the plantation and to being with Charles again. My sister valued him, and I must too. Most of all, a sense of this sister to whom I was already drawn strengthened me and lifted my spirits. I didn't need the imaginary "Polly" of my childhood anymore. Later today I would meet my real sister again, and how could I not be happy? I put aside the thought of Valerie and her disturbing behavior.

For a few moments longer I lay in bed, looking about with more interest than I'd felt last night. One side of the bedroom had been stripped to original bare brick, and the walls were thick, as evidenced by the deep recesses of the windows. In one corner a tall strip of wooden post had been left exposed, and these touches gave one a sense of the past and the very old.

When I'd showered and dressed in fawn slacks and a pale yellow blouse with an embroidered yoke, I stood before the full-length bathroom mirror, looking for some identifiable change in myself. Except for my shorter hair, curling in just above my shoulders, I was looking at Amelia Mountfort, and that fact made me somehow uncertain. I didn't really know this woman who had my face, my body. Today I didn't bother to put on a matching bandeau.

Only a few guests were in the lobby when I went down to breakfast. I helped myself to toast and coffee and a slice of melon, and as I ate I refrained from looking up into the dusky reaches overhead. I wanted nothing to blight my spirits this morning.

Charles was prompt and arrived just as I finished eating. He approved of my appearance—"You even like the same colors that Amelia likes," he marveled. "She wears that same shade of yellow. But there's a difference. I'd never confuse the two of you."

That reassured me a little—I felt a desperate need to hold on to my own identity.

We walked down to Charles's car, parked at the curb, and as I got in I wondered if I should tell him about Honoria's call last night. Quickly intuiting that it might be a disturbing element to introduce, I decided against it. I wanted to enjoy everything about this trip to Mountfort Hall.

"We're going south first," Charles told me as we moved into traffic. "It's only a little out of our way. You haven't seen the lower tip of the peninsula yet."

We followed East Bay Street to the Battery, where we got out of the car and climbed up on the wall. A breeze blew in from the water, still fresh in the warming morning.

Charles pointed. "There it is out there—Fort Sumter. It's only a sandy rise above the water. That's where all the trouble started—because of Lincoln's perfidious strategy. Charleston is where the curtain rose, but the stage directions were coming from Montgomery, the capital of the Confederacy, and most of all, from Washington. It's pretty clear that Lincoln forced the South to fire the first shot. He wanted to enter the War with the Union seemingly blameless."

I had a different view of Lincoln, but I said nothing and Charles went on.

"When the battle began, the people of Charleston climbed to their rooftops to watch—until the shells came too close for comfort. It was only then that they realized that a real war had started."

Old passions, the history of an entire people, were close to the surface in his voice, and I listened in amazement. In the South the effects of a terrible war that should never have been fought were still too recent to be forgotten. Charleston walls still bore the marks of shelling. Plantation houses had been looted and burned. An entire people had been impoverished. The stories were still handed down from grandmother to granddaughter, from father to son. I could only feel that war itself was to blame —strange means of settling arguments that men still seemed to accept as natural.

"Where do I belong?" I asked ruefully. "I've grown up away from all this. It has nothing to do with me."

"Blood matters," Charles told me. "You are a member of this family." Something in his voice quickened. "I wish I could have lived in Charleston before the War. It was a lively, exciting city, and there's still nothing we like better than a good party. They say wonderful parties and balls were held out at the old plantations—before everything fell apart."

I stared out across the busy harbor at the tiny rise of the fort above the water. Charles's fervor was something I might use in a story, but I would not be otherwise beguiled by it. I *knew* who I was.

"General Beauregard was part of all that," Charles went on. "He came from Louisiana, but he was the Confederate hero at Fort Sumter. Charleston ladies adored him and made him their ideal of a soldier."

I felt as though I had somehow stepped into the pages of *Gone with the Wind,* yet all this had really happened. This was bloody ground where history had been lived by men and women, some of whom might have been my ancestors.

"Sumter belongs to one war," Charles said more quietly. "But Fort Moultrie is our Revolutionary fort. They both guard our harbor. I just wanted you to have a sense of the city's past, Molly, before I take you out to find your own."

We drove up through North Charleston to where great bridge spans crossed strips of water in what seemed a confusing maze— one over the Ashley River, one over the Cooper, with more bridges reaching out to the Sea Islands, sometimes in the path of hurricanes.

"Since our rivers were the highways to Charleston in the early days, the great plantations were built near the water," Charles told me. "Only Drayton Hall and Mountfort Hall remain on the Ashley today."

By car, the trip to the plantation took no more than a half hour, and the highway ran unnotably through this Low Country. Charles turned down a side road leading toward the river.

"My mother's family was made destitute by the War, as the Mountforts were for a time. The two families were friends and she was invited to their home often as a young girl. That's how she met my father, since he worked for the plantation. Of course, people thought it was an unsuitable marriage—a young woman of a good family and a bricklayer—but my mother did as she liked, just as her friend Valerie Mountfort did. So when a head housekeeper was needed, my mother insisted she was right for the job, and she's worked there happily since I was a little boy."

Again we turned off the main road, this time onto a wide driveway with moss-hung live oaks reaching their branches across to meet overhead. A picture I'd seen in a dozen movies.

Charles was still speaking of his mother, and he laughed softly. "Valerie and Evaline ran off together on some escapade one time, when they'd had too much Mountfort discipline. Of course, they were brought back chastened and never broke away again. I wish I could have known them in those days."

I hardly listened, my attention riveted to the long avenue of beautiful, arching trees. An excitement of recognition—of the spirit?—filled me.

"The slave cabins were over on the left," Charles said. "My father restored the only one left and turned it into a comfortable cottage, where we lived. And where my mother still lives. In the old days slaves were kept away from the main house at night, and plantation owners took care that the people who worked for one household did not grow chummy with those of another. In spite of the luxury and wealth that slaves afforded them, families were uneasy at times. Revolts like those in the West Indies might break out here, so it wasn't always a comfortable life."

Charles's home was a small, charming cottage. A rose garden had been planted under the white frames of windows set into the original brick—bricks that had faded to a soft, dusty pink that glowed softly in sunlight.

"We have quite a few visitors at certain times of the year. You can see one of the demonstration sheds over there." Charles pointed. "Local craftspeople make pottery, candles, do weaving and basketmaking. You can visit it whenever you like. But first we meet my mother. She's probably waiting at the house for us. Look —there ahead!"

The driveway curved, and now I could see Mountfort Hall looming at the far end. Set squarely across the end of the drive-way, it had been built before the Greek Revival movement—a great structure of rosy brick, with a high basement and noble Palladian portico two stories high. A doorway, Charles said, that

71

was one of the earliest of its kind in the country. Wide steps climbed on either side, meeting at a landing behind which were the slim white columns of a recessed porch. Duplicate columns on the level above supported the small peak of a frontal roof, separated from the larger roof rising behind.

"This is really the back of the house," Charles said. "The front has twin flights of steps and faces on the river, where guests once approached by boat. The rise of the ground here protects the house from flooding. That corner of the structure was shelled during the War, though the rest escaped damage. I think I may have told you that when Porter had it restored, my father matched the old bricks that had been made here on the plantation, using the same clay."

I liked the pride in his voice when he spoke of his father. "Did any of your family fight in the War?"

"Several died. One great-grandfather was a foot soldier. He was killed at Gettysburg—a long way from home."

As we left Charles's car and walked toward the house, a woman came through the high doorway above us to stand in the portico. Charles waved to his mother, and she bowed courteously toward me—a hostess welcoming a guest.

Evaline Landry was an impressive figure, standing high above us—tall and straight, her graying hair combed simply back with no part. She resembled her son, though with a stronger, more determined cast of features. Her dress of silky gray cotton had been cut severely, so that it just missed being a uniform, her one decoration a long chain of gold, silver, and gunmetal beads that hung nearly to her waist.

As I came up the right wing of steps, she held out her hand to clasp mine, and her dark eyes examined me gravely. "Yes," she said, deciding quickly, "there's no mistaking the likeness."

Charles kissed his mother's cheek. "Just don't call her Cecelia.

This is Molly Hunt, Mother. Molly, this is my mother, Mrs. Evaline Landry."

Mrs. Landry smiled rather coolly, as though she measured me in some way. "My son didn't mention whether you are to stay with us. There is plenty of space, of course, and a guest room is always ready."

"Thank you," I said, "but I'll be returning to Charleston for the night."

Again she bowed to my decision, but I couldn't tell whether I was good or bad news to Evaline Landry. She obviously belonged as much to Mountfort Hall as any of the family, and even as she admitted my likeness to Amelia, I suspected that she would wait for her lead from Porter Phelps, who undoubtedly made all decisions out here.

She gestured us inside. "May I show you a little of the house, Miss Hunt?"

I sensed Charles relax, as though his mother's acceptance was a relief to him.

We entered a hall carpeted in a neutral color, which led straight through to doors on the river side. I glimpsed the shrubbery on far green banks and could see the water through glass doors at the far end.

Mrs. Landry took us first into a splendid drawing room, where two crystal chandeliers hung from plaster carvings on the ceiling. A huge floor-to-ceiling mirror, the frame heavy with ornate gilt, reflected the room at one end, making it seem even larger. At the opposite end stood a fireplace of veined white marble. It was the portrait above the mantel, however, that held my attention.

The subject was a handsome, commanding man in the British dress of Revolutionary times. Perhaps it had been painted before the colonies had rebelled. Strangely, he had chosen to be seated at the entrance to what might have been a Greek temple.

Mrs. Landry spoke respectfully. "That is Edward Mountfort, who built this house. Your ancestor, Miss Hunt."

I returned the portrait's rather challenging look, and found a certain amusement in the eyes. Did the old boy find humor in my presence here?

"He must have been a colorful fellow," Charles said. "Amelia always talks to him when she comes out. He fought a duel in his late sixties, at an age when he had no business taking on a younger man. They fought out there on the lawn, where we just came in, and old Edward died of his wounds. Amelia has adapted bits and pieces of all that in the play we're doing, though of course she's moved the action up to the War Against Northern Invasion."

I bristled a little, and caught Charles's smile and knew that he was deliberately baiting me—the Yankee visitor.

He went on. "In the play Garrett Burke, whom you met yesterday in Daphne's shop, and I are supposed to fight that duel. Though Garrett is no Edward Mountfort, and neither am I. Mother, is Garrett working here today?"

She nodded, her tone disparaging. "He's in his upstairs office."

"Good. I've brought our swords along in the car—so this is the time for some practice. I'll go look for him. You'll be in good hands with my mother, Molly."

Mrs. Landry stood looking after her son, her eyebrows quizzical, as though she didn't altogether approve of his breezy ways. Then she made an effort to relax, and her smile was warmer, accepting me.

"Let's go on with our tour, Molly. May I call you that?"

"Of course," I said, and followed her into the adjoining dining room.

A Hepplewhite table, with matching shield-back chairs, had been set for six, though it would seat many more. Woven grass mats held elegant Royal Crown Derby china, and the silver looked old and heavy.

Mrs. Landry explained. "The table would have been laid with linen in the days before the War, when there were slaves to take care of all the washing and ironing. The silver was made here on the plantation by slaves who were skilled artisans, and during the War it was successfully hidden from possible looters. Of course, these chandeliers are the original Waterford. The house was never burned to the ground, as so many others were."

She spoke with the authority and knowledge of one who had taken guests through this house a great many times, and she caught my unspoken question.

"I've trained a few docents in my day—Honoria Phelps among them, before she was married to Porter. Sometimes, if no one else is available, I still take a tour through myself."

The library across the hall came next, and then the music room. Mrs. Landry allowed me to look briefly into each in turn. The library was a dark room, paneled in West Indian mahogany, rather than the pine more commonly used in early houses. Its burgundy rug showed patches of wear, as did dark green leather armchairs, networked with thin cracks.

The music room was brighter, with sun coming through long Palladian windows set in deep walls. However, except for the piano, the furniture remained shrouded in sheets, and unused. Mrs. Landry stood in the doorway without entering, and I experienced a strange sense of uneasiness, as though this were a haunted place.

"We don't show this room on our tours anymore." I caught a note of restraint in her voice that made me curious.

"Why not?"

Her glance rested for a moment on the piano and then she looked away. "Mrs. Phelps prefers to keep this room closed."

This was evasion, and I knew she meant to tell me nothing about the music room. Secrets, I wondered, my writer's sense alerted. While I made no written notes as we moved about the house, I was constantly observing, registering, storing away. I had no strong feeling of connection with any of this, but as a writer I found it all wonderful background material.

Again we followed the wide central hallway to where a staircase curved gracefully up along one wall. Mrs. Landry gestured upward.

"These days the family stays on the upper floors when they come out, and we never take visitors up there on the tours. Though, of course, when there's a party, the downstairs rooms are used, as they have always been. Amelia's wedding to my son will be held there."

"When is that to be?" I asked.

"In September," she said as she led the way up the staircase.

Each of the downstairs rooms had displayed handsome oriental rugs on the floors—from China and old Persia. The stairs, however, were uncarpeted, covered in dark varnish, while the walls were a pale, pearly gray.

The upstairs sitting room was less formal than the rooms below, and had been furnished with comfortable modern pieces. There was evidence here of people living their lives. A woven basket held someone's knitting. Books and magazines lay on the coffee table. At one end an arched doorway opened on what must have been the family dining room, smaller than the formal room downstairs. Another Waterford chandelier hung from a plaster rosette in the ceiling, and cornices were elaborately carved with a pattern of dogwood blossoms that ran all the way around the room.

Mrs. Landry caught the direction of my interest and spoke with pride. "It took great skill to create all that plaster ornamentation. The carving had to be done very quickly while the plaster was wet, and then not disturbed until it had time to set."

I felt like a stranger, visiting Mountfort Hall as any tourist might have done. Nothing tugged at me from the past to make me feel that I belonged. I would have no trouble going home when the time came. The events I felt driven to learn about had happened back in Charleston, and out here I was only stirred now and then as anyone might be who read a tragic and romantic tale.

Just once did I sit to jot down a few impressions and some information in my notebook—details I might not remember.

Mrs. Landry watched me with interest. "Do you put real people into your books, as well as real settings?"

I shook my head. "I work out my characters carefully in detail, but they're born in my own imagination."

"Of course, Garrett Burke is already writing about Mountfort Hall," she added. "But I suppose fiction writing is very different."

I assured her that it was, and watched as she stopped before an album bound in leather that lay open on a table in the sitting room.

"I found this for you before you came," she said. "Has anyone shown you a picture of your father?"

My sense of shock was sudden and unexpected. I was no longer uninvolved and untouched. I shook my head.

"Simon Mountfort," Mrs. Landry said, placing a finger on one small snapshot. "Though of course these don't do him justice. You must ask your sister to show you the splendid portrait that hangs in the South Battery house."

No physical sense of recognition came to me as I studied the tiny picture of a tall man who seemed to possess an air of authority about him. What I experienced was more like a sensing— something I couldn't put into words—a feeling of conviction that this was my father. A far stronger feeling than anything I'd felt for Valerie Mountfort's flesh and blood. This was nothing I wanted to share with Charles's mother, however.

"I know so little about him," I said. "What was his profession?"

"I suppose the family will tell you about him gradually. Perhaps I can save them the pain. His profession was the law. Twelve years before he died, he became a judge. Porter Phelps has always believed that you were stolen by someone whom Judge Mountfort sent to prison. Someone who wanted revenge."

"But wouldn't they have found such a person?"

"Of course certain leads were followed through, but no real clues ever surfaced."

I turned away from the album, experiencing for the first time the pain that Simon Mountfort and his wife Valerie must have suffered over the loss of their baby.

"This must be difficult for you," Mrs. Landry said. "And terribly confusing. Would you like to take a little time for yourself —perhaps go outdoors and walk down to the river?"

Before either of us could move to implement this, I heard someone running lightly up the stairs, calling my name as she came.

"Molly? Molly, where are you?"

"That's Honoria Phelps," Mrs. Landry said. "You needn't stay and talk to her, unless you want to." Her tone indicated that she wasn't happy about Honoria's appearance.

I didn't accept the offer of escape, but thanked her and called out a response to Honoria. She came running into the sitting room, to greet me warmly.

Today she wore a long, engulfing garment of dark yellow and indigo batik—somehow entirely right for her small person. Along one arm she carried—wore—a small gray-and-white cat, like a decoration. The little creature stared at me with bright amber eyes, the vertical irises narrowed.

"Hello, Molly," she greeted me. "Hi, Evaline. I suppose you've already given Molly the grand tour? I can take over now, if you like."

As Porter's wife, Honoria was still mistress of Mountfort Hall, and Evaline its housekeeper. Losing none of her dignity in spite of the abrupt dismissal, Mrs. Landry said she would see us when luncheon was served, and went out of the room.

Honoria sighed. "There! I've done it again. I never mean to act as though I own the house—I certainly don't. But Evaline and I disagree on a number of things, and I let that surface more often than she does. This is Miss Kitty, Molly. She lives in Charleston with Valerie and Amelia, but she's *my* special friend, and she loves to come out here whenever I can bring her."

Gray markings on white fur were distinctive, attractive, and Miss Kitty's small face was a perfect triangle, with pink nose and pointed pink ears alert. She seemed to be sniffing the air as though some tantalizing scent had reached her—something she recognized.

"Miss Kitty is psychic," Honoria said. "She probably knows that you are one of the family."

I let that pass, scratched the little cat's ears, and was rewarded with a purr.

The photograph album still lay open on the table, and Honoria's attention was caught. "Evaline's been showing you pictures of your father, I suppose? Poor Simon. If only he could have

79

believed that you would return. I always told him you'd be found. It was such a misfortune that he had to suffer a heart attack. He died in the music room of this house—right at the piano. I've always wondered why."

"What do you mean—why?"

"Nothing, really, it's only a feeling I have. Perhaps you will be the one to bring us answers. That's what I wanted to talk to you about."

She'd hinted at something of this sort before, and I wanted none of it. "I need to find answers—not give them."

"You won't be able to help yourself," she went on. "The moment will come—before long, I think—when you will have to decide."

"If you mean about staying—permanently—I don't belong here. The past that built all this isn't mine. I'm not even in sympathy with it."

Honoria smiled gently. "You need time to get used to us. I shouldn't have startled you the way I did. Sometimes words come out of my mouth that I don't expect. Anyway, when the time is right we will both be *shown.*"

I stroked the cat without answering. Miss Kitty stirred and looked at me with increasingly focused interest, her long tail thumping on Honoria's arm.

Honoria spoke briskly. "I want to show you the room I like best in this house. For me it has a special fascination. Come along, Molly."

I followed her, still intent on my own questions that no one so far had been able to answer. Since I now knew where Simon Mountfort had died, and that Honoria had some sort of doubt about the reason for his heart attack, it occurred to me that answers might exist under the roof of Mountfort Hall, as well as in Charleston.

Before she reached the door, I stopped her. "You told me you had a letter for me. Who is it from?"

"Why—from your father, of course. Didn't I mention that? But I don't have it with me here. I hid it a long time ago in a very safe place. Fortunately, I can remember where. Let's have no more talk about the letter now, Molly. And don't tell anyone else about it."

Five

Honoria flitted ahead of me into the hall, the thin stuff of her batik rippling as she moved. The cat climbed onto her shoulder and looked back at me with intense interest, though I wasn't sure whether to be flattered or dismayed.

Honoria's words about a letter from my father had electrified me. I wanted to ask questions, yet I had the feeling that she would tell me nothing until she was ready. My tingling anticipation—partly excitement and new longing, partly pure anxiety—would have to be contained until we were back in Charleston.

We paused before a closed door. "This is where Garrett Burke works," Honoria indicated. "But the next room is the one I want you to see—and experience."

A strange word, since the room we entered seemed small and unnotable. It was obvious that it had been closed for a time, and she hurried to open windows that looked toward the river. When she put the cat down, it settled on its haunches, still watching me with fixed interest.

The room was a bedroom, simply furnished, with a narrow single bed, two armchairs, a desk with a straight chair set before it, and a small round table with a drop leaf. The fireplace had been screened, no longer in use with the coming of central heating. No ornaments or personal belongings indicated occupancy, so this was not a room also used by Garrett. An unfamiliar scent that might be coming from the river was replacing mustiness in the room. I chose one of the two armchairs and sat down, still brimming with questions I wasn't sure how to ask.

Miss Kitty made up her mind. She came over to me, looking up with a tiny mew that showed her open pink mouth.

"She's not a talker," Honoria said. "But she's asking."

I understood the request: Make a lap. I uncrossed my knees. At once the cat sprang onto them and arranged herself carefully, resting her head in the crook of my arm. I stroked her, feeling ridiculously flattered.

"I think I'm in love," I said.

Honoria smiled. "I do believe she connects you with Amelia. She doesn't usually accept strangers. I suspect she already knows a lot more about you than you dream."

"Aren't you reading a good deal into her intentions?"

Honoria answered me earnestly. "Humans are much too arrogant when it comes to animals. We think that without words there can be no thought. But it's possible to think in images, pictures. Perhaps that's what the more intelligent animals do. You can watch them figuring something out. Though I don't know about chickens."

I stroked Miss Kitty's fine, soft fur—never coarsened by outdoor living. "I think she must be one of T. S. Eliot's 'amiable Jellicle cats.' "

"Maybe. Just don't take her good nature for granted. She has a mind of her own, like most cats."

Somehow, holding the little cat, who was purring contentedly now, had quieted and soothed me. I spoke to her softly. "What a good kitty. What a nice kitty." Silly baby talk, but she opened her eyes and looked up at me, approving. I blinked and she blinked back at me, clearly feeling safe and unchallenged. I hoped that our friendship had been established.

"Miss Kitty is the only one who can see Nathanial," Honoria went on. "He was the children's tutor and lived here at the time when I was a docent. This was his bedroom, so this is where he sometimes appears." She looked about the room dreamily, and then went on, surprising me. "We were very much in love, Molly. Of course, this was long before I married Porter. That's why Nathanial channels through me."

I continued to stroke the cat, not looking at Honoria, trying to find some footing in this nebulous atmosphere she created wherever she went.

Something I'd been told returned to me. "Nathanial drowned in a boating accident, didn't he?"

"Yes. People whispered that he killed himself. A lie! He was murdered. He has told me so himself—the first time he came back to speak through me."

I tried to hold on to what I knew of "reality." "Has he told you who murdered him?"

"He doesn't know, Molly. That's the terrible part. Someone damaged his boat before he took it out, and it sank when he was in the middle of the river—out there way beyond the landing. Everyone knew he couldn't swim, yet he loved to fish."

Honoria went to a door leading onto a small balcony. She opened it and stepped outside. I followed her, carrying Miss Kitty. The river flowed past below the steep rise on which the house was built. A grass-grown road originally intended for carriages wound to the landing, with a brick footpath running down more directly.

"It's not possible for Nathanial to go on to the next plane"— Honoria spoke sadly—"until his murderer has been exposed. He has told me that you will be the instrument to help him, Molly."

I could understand that Honoria, in her long-ago unhappiness, had built up this fantasy in her mind. But she had been married to Porter Phelps for years, and I wondered that a past tragedy should be kept alive in this eerie way. Nor did I want to take part in her make-believe.

"Please," I said, "don't put anything like that on me!"

Miss Kitty began to squirm in my arms, and a squirming cat can never be held. I carried her back inside and let her go. She flew into the center of the room and began leaping and shadow-boxing with her front paws. It was as though she followed some moving presence invisible to us, though I told myself she was simply chasing dust motes in a sunbeam that streaked into the room.

"We've evoked Nathanial," Honoria said softly, fondly. "If only I could see him—as Miss Kitty does. Let's be very quiet, Molly, and try to communicate with him. Perhaps he has something to tell us, now that you are here."

I still wanted no part of this, but before I could walk out of the room, she spoke again in that deeper voice I had heard from her yesterday.

It is time to give her the letter. The words came haltingly, as though human vocal cords were strange to the speaker.

Honoria answered quickly in her own voice. "I know. It will be done today. But tell us now how we can help you, Nathanial."

The uncanny conversation Honoria was having with herself went on in that deeper voice. *She will find the way. Then—I can —go at last.* The voice was growing fainter.

"Wait! Please, Nathanial—"

Whatever had happened in this room was now over. Miss Kitty lost interest in her sunbeam and sat down to lick a forepaw and wash behind an ear. Honoria dropped into a chair and covered her face with her hands. I waited helplessly, not knowing how to deal with any of this. Nothing in my life had prepared me for this spirit world Honoria believed in and took for granted.

When she lowered her hands and opened her eyes, she had clearly come to some decision. "It's settled," she told me. "We'll take care of the letter as soon as we get back to Charleston."

Voices reached us suddenly through the open windows and I heard the clanging sound of metal striking metal. Honoria ran into the hall toward the land side of the house, and the cat and I followed her. When I stood beside her in the porch enclosure a story above the door on the land side, I could look down on the front lawn.

Beyond the driveway two men were engaged in what I hoped was a mock duel—though the fury with which they thrust at each other was hardly reassuring. Charles had the skill to parry Garrett's attacks, though Garrett was using his untrained strength in a not ineffective way. Charles looked both grim and angry, while Garrett appeared to be enjoying himself. I heard his shout of triumph as Charles's sword went flying out of his hand.

Honoria called down to them. "That's terrible! That's not the way Amelia wrote the duel scene in her play—or the way I've directed it! Oh dear, I think Charles is hurt."

Charles appeared to be nursing one hand as he scowled at Garrett, who was still laughing. Honoria ran inside and down the stairs, and again I followed. Miss Kitty, uninterested in all this human passion, stayed behind.

When we came out through the lower door, Honoria sped down the right-hand flight of steps to the ground where Garrett was already apologizing good-naturedly.

"Sorry, Charles, I know that wasn't in the script. I promise to let you kill me the next time!"

Honoria, tiny and furious, scolded both men, while I stood on the steps and watched in astonishment. Charles, in shirtsleeves and fawn trousers, looked as tall and slender and elegant as a southern aristocrat out of an old novel. Garrett, on the other hand, was stocky and plebeian, and obviously belonged to the present—yet there was something strange about him, something unreadable.

"You were showing off, Garrett!" Honoria scolded. "Unless you accept Charles's thrust and carry out the duel as it's been planned, how can you come back from the spirit world in the next act? Stop fooling around and play your part as Amelia has written it!"

This was major miscasting, I thought. Not for a moment could I see Garrett Burke returning as a spirit. The need for a northern accent had done them all in.

Garrett apologized all over again, still sounding lighthearted, and promised to behave himself from now on.

Honoria turned her back on him and went to Charles. "You've hurt your wrist, haven't you?"

Charles flexed his fingers. "It was numb for a few moments.

Garrett nearly broke it when he struck my sword, but I'll be all right in a minute."

"It's probably a sprain," Honoria told him. "Come inside and let me bandage it. Molly, why don't you take a walk down to the river, and I'll join you later."

"I'll show you the way," Garrett offered, and came with me without waiting for me to accept.

We followed the herringbone-patterned brick path down a bank and along the river's edge toward a landing. Was this the dock, I wondered, from which Nathanial Amory had rowed out on that fateful day?

A marble bench under the branches of live oak offered a spot of shade, and we sat down on its cool surface.

"Do you know when Nathanial Amory died?" I asked Garrett.

He looked startled, but answered readily enough. "I believe it was a few months after the kidnapping."

A good many years ago for Honoria to be carrying a torch. How unfaithful could one be with a ghost?

"Why do you want to know?" Garrett asked. He was studying me in the same absorbed way that he'd done in the bookstore, and it made me uncomfortable. I'd have preferred to sit quietly by the river alone.

"I suppose I'm curious about everything that concerns Mountfort Hall," I said carefully. "And Honoria was just telling me about Nathanial."

"And his haunting of the bedroom?"

I didn't want to discuss this. "How did you come to be interested in Mountfort Hall?"

Garrett persisted. "Have you met the spirit that Honoria communes with?"

"I've met Miss Kitty," I said evasively.

He laughed. "All right, I'll answer your question first. When I came down south, I got a job on a Charleston paper and became interested in doing a piece on Mountfort Hall. I did a lot of research and talked to everyone, including Porter Phelps. He liked the article when it was published and asked me to consider working with him on his own history of Mountfort. I jumped at the chance and I've been working out here ever since."

Simple enough, yet I wondered if there was anything he might be leaving out. "Why did you knock that sword out of Charles's hand? You have to admit that was pretty aggressive."

"I suppose because of his arrogance. He was so sure of his skill and my ignorance. What I did was hardly good fencing. That's two questions for you. Tell me now what you think of Honoria and her talents."

"I like her," I admitted. "At first she warned me to leave—it was a bit spooky. But now she seems to feel that my being here is of great importance."

"Somehow that doesn't surprise me," he said enigmatically and changed the subject. "They'll invite you to stay for the wedding, of course. Since you're family. That is, if those two actually make it to the altar."

"Why haven't they married before this?"

"Who knows? Charles's mother seems more enthusiastic than Valerie, but no one's standing in their way. Perhaps Amelia needs you, Molly."

This man had too many sides to keep up with. He sounded kind now and concerned for Amelia. But I still didn't trust him.

"How can she need me?"

"She seems afraid of something. Can't you sense it when you're with her? Perhaps she'll tell you what's troubling her." We stared at each other for a moment and then he changed the subject again. "Molly, are you coming to the rehearsal tonight?"

"It might be fun. Perhaps I can come with Amelia."

He was silent for a few moments, and I made up my mind that I would certainly go to the rehearsal.

"I've just finished reading your new book, Molly Hunt," he said out of nowhere.

I could think of no comment and I waited.

"You're a good writer except when it comes to your hero. I think you could have done better there."

"I'm not writing for men," I said stiffly. "Women readers seem to enjoy my books."

"Sure—Mr. Rochester and good old Heathcliff are always popular. But not exactly up to date."

I hadn't asked for his criticism and I didn't want it. I could feel him watching me for a response, and I stared straight ahead at the flowing river.

"You might consider Harry Lime as a beginning model in your next book," he said mildly. "It's useful to get a new springboard occasionally."

"I don't know what you're talking about."

"You remember the movie *The Third Man,* don't you?"

"Of course. Orson Welles played Harry Lime. A thoroughly despicable villain."

"Right. That was well established before Harry ever showed his face. Orson Welles was on-screen for about six minutes—and we never forget Harry Lime. He was pretty rotten, yes—but he was a mixed bag. There were characters in the movie who loved him, no matter what. If you're not going to use real-life models for your next hero, you could do worse than let Harry Lime spark your imagination. Or maybe you just need to think of Orson Welles."

I felt disconcerted and resentful, and aware that he was still watching me. When I looked at him he was smiling, not unkindly.

"I've just attacked your youngest child, haven't I, Molly? Believe me, as a writer I know the feeling. But we all have to learn how to take criticism with our minds, not our emotions. Think about Harry—without the evil. You might find a whole new road to your next hero."

"But there isn't any Harry Lime without the evil."

"Don't we all have a dark side? Rochester and Heathcliff certainly did—that's part of their appeal. But isn't it time for a different kind of hero?"

Before I could answer, Charles hailed us, waving his bandaged hand.

Garrett stood up. "I'd better get back to work. Don't let them get to you, Molly. The Mountforts tend to swallow people up, and Charles is so close to them he's one of the clan."

It wasn't the Mountforts who had upset me and I was glad to be free of Garrett's company. As he climbed toward the house, he exchanged a few words in passing with Charles. I couldn't hear what they said, but Charles didn't look happy.

However, by the time he reached me he seemed so pleased to see me that my irritation with Garrett subsided.

"Amelia's car is coming up the driveway," he told me. "I'd hoped to have more time to show you around, but this damage to my hand threw me off. Mother says we can come right in to lunch as soon as you and Amelia are ready."

When we reached the far side of the house, Amelia was getting out of her car, and she ran happily into Charles's embrace. When he'd kissed her warmly, she held out both hands to me.

"Hello, Molly. Isn't Mountfort Hall wonderful? Are you beginning to get the feeling that you belong here?"

"It's beautiful and fascinating," I agreed. "I've been learning

91

a little about its history." *Belonging,* however, was a long way off for me.

Evaline Landry had opened the formal dining room for us. As hostess, she sat at the head of the table, with me on her right and Amelia on her left. Garrett didn't join us, so there were only Charles and Honoria to fill out the five places that were set.

Now I could note a few more details about the room. Here the Chinese rug was of lustrous gold, green, and dark blue, and of more recent vintage than the beautifully faded orientals. The mahogany sideboard, with its brass drawer pulls, displayed pieces of heavy silver—a tray and an elaborate coffee service. Draperies at the long windows were of dark green brocade that seemed heavy for weather that was already warming. Upstairs, preparations for hot weather had been made, with lighter curtains and cool slipcovers. In this room, formality would probably prevail the year round, since it was shown to visitors.

A Chinese bowl filled with freshly picked magnolia blossoms made a centerpiece that perfumed the room. Fireplace and mantel were of delicately veined white marble, while the walls carried a silvery tone. All around the moldings an intricate design of scrollwork had been carved in the plaster.

Still looking around, my eye was caught by a corner cabinet where several shelves displayed tiny porcelain figures. Dresden shepherdesses, coquettish little milkmaids, farm maidens—all perfect in every colored detail.

Amelia saw my interest. "That's Cousin Porter's collection. You must really examine it sometime."

I glanced at Honoria and saw that she was watching me with a wry expression. The thought struck me that perhaps Honoria, too, was a miniature that Porter had collected. Not that I would have expected this of him from my slight acquaintance. He was much more in character as the retired bank president. But why shouldn't a bank president collect miniatures?

"Perhaps you'll put Mountfort Hall into your story, Molly," Charles said.

"I don't know yet," I admitted. "I write mystery stories—I'd hate to disturb this beautiful place with evil doings."

Honoria caught up my words. "Do you think a house as old as this one hasn't known terror and crime and death? Nothing you could invent can match what has really happened here. There's always been the same old struggle between good and evil."

I thought of the music room across the hall, where Simon Mountfort had died, and I wondered if I could ever match in fiction the ominous quality that haunted that room. Too many of my questions had gone unasked or had been evaded, and I wondered if a direct challenge might startle someone into giving me some answers.

"I met one of your ghosts this morning," I said, not looking at Honoria.

The sudden silence, the arrested attention, startled me. I had certainly touched a sensitive nerve. For a few seconds the room hushed completely. Then the moment of crisis was saved, or at least postponed, by the appearance of one of the black servants who worked at Mountfort Hall.

She carried a silver tureen of black-bean soup that she set before Evaline Landry. The servingwoman's manner, while self-effacing, was one of quiet, confident belonging, and my interest was immediately caught. I wondered if her ancestors might have been slaves at Mountfort Hall in the days before the War.

She was striking in appearance—tall and rather angular, her dark skin evidence of purity of blood. Graying hair, cut short and full, had been drawn back and held in place with two gold half-moon combs. Tiny gold hoop earrings were fastened in pierced ears. She wore a light gray uniform, and the combs and earrings were her only decorative touches. She moved to serve us with an easy grace and the skill of long experience. I didn't believe her self-effacing manner, however, and suspected that she had been a part of this family for so long that she would miss nothing of interest. There was no doubt that the family knew this as well, since no one commented on my small bombshell as long as the woman was in the room.

At some point she must have become aware of my interest in her, for she raised her eyes and met mine across the table. She knew instantly who I was. I caught the shock of her recognition, and suddenly knew that no one had told her of my coming.

"Thank you, Orva," Evaline Landry said, and picked up her soupspoon. The black woman went quietly from the room, turning once to look at me again.

The moment she was gone, Amelia followed up on my remark about the ghost. "You've actually met Nathanial, Molly? What fun! What did he have to say?"

I sipped a spoonful of soup before answering—and choked over the burning sensation in my mouth and throat.

"Oh dear!" Honoria said. "We should have warned you. Drink some water, Molly."

Mrs. Landry smiled. "I didn't think it worth mentioning. If Miss Hunt is a Mountfort, she must get used to our Low Country dishes. It's only a matter of educating her palate."

I drank several swallows of ice water. "I don't think I'll be here long enough for that. Amelia, I didn't actually meet Nathanial. He communicated through Honoria and seemed full of warnings that I didn't understand. I expect Honoria will need to interpret."

I'd spoken lightly, and Honoria shook her head at me. "None of Nathanial's words were in fun, Molly. I am only the channel through which he speaks, but I know how serious he is. However, he hasn't made it clear to me exactly what he wants of me—or of Molly."

Charles sighed. "Here we go again! What can Molly possibly do about the past?"

"She is a part of the past, even though she was too young to have any memory of this family or her kidnapping," Honoria persisted. "Nathanial evidently thinks she has an important role to play now."

"Let's not go off the deep end," Charles said. "Don't worry about any of this, Molly. It's all ancient history."

But I found myself interested in ancient history. "If Nathanial drowned," I said, "how was his body recovered?"

Again there seemed a stricken pause. Evaline Landry rang a small silver bell at her place, summoning Orva and preventing any answer to my question. They were all in this together, I thought in annoyance. And they didn't want me to have answers —in spite of their apparent acceptance of me as Amelia's twin.

If the black woman sensed a self-conscious silence, she gave no sign as she directed a young woman to take away our plates on a big tray. She herself brought in a platter of chicken, dumplings, and hot corn bread.

Honoria began to chat about the wonderful weather we were having—not too hot yet—so that the inconsequential took over our conversation. For me, the meal seemed much too heavy, and I nibbled at my fresh salad, which was kinder to my tongue than black-bean soup.

Not until Orva had left us alone did Mrs. Landry return to my question, which had been left hanging in the air.

"Your mother found the body, Miss Hunt," she told me quietly.

At once Honoria flew into words. "It was so terrible! We didn't even know that Nathanial was missing! River currents brought his body to the bank and swept it under pilings down at the dock. A storm had come up and Nathanial was caught there, instead of being swept out into the river again. After the sky cleared, Valerie went down to walk out on the dock and look at the sunset. So she was the one who found him. I'm glad I was away from the house at the time and missed the whole terrible discovery."

Anguish sounded under her excitement, and Amelia put out a hand to quiet her. "Don't, Cousin Honoria. You know you get upset thinking about this. It happened so long ago—you ought to be able to forget."

"Nathanial won't let me forget," Honoria said, though she sounded quieter now.

"All of this happened years ago, when Amelia was a child. It can't matter now," Charles said coolly.

"What was Nathanial Amory like?" I asked. "Was he a good tutor?"

"I didn't get along too well with him," Charles said ruefully.

"That's because you were a little monster." I suspected that his mother wasn't teasing. "You never did anything anyone told you to, so Mr. Amory had his hands full. But he was a good teacher, and you learned in spite of yourself."

Honoria skipped over all this and spoke to me. "Nathanial was a gentle, thoughtful man—intelligent and gifted. He would have published more of his poetry—if only he'd sent it out. But he never thought it was good enough. His notebook, in which he kept poems and a journal, disappeared after his death. I suppose someone thought it valueless and threw it away. Fortunately, a few of his poems were privately published and I have those."

How strange, I thought, that Honoria should have turned to Porter Phelps after being in love with someone as brilliant and creative as Nathanial had apparently been. Once more I glanced toward the cabinet of china figurines that I'd noted earlier. If Porter had "collected" Honoria, who looked as tiny and delicate as one of those Dresden shepherdesses, how had he felt when he discovered her unsettling talents and individuality?

"No more talk about Nathanial!" Amelia insisted. "Molly, did you see the way Orva looked at you? I think she was stunned. I wonder if anyone told her you would be here?"

Apparently no one had thought it necessary.

"Tell me about her," I said. "Who is she?"

Charles answered readily. "Her name's Orva Jackson—her married name. She grew up on the plantation and married a man who'd also lived here all his life. He's dead now. She's always worked here, except for a short time when she was your nurse, Molly, and stayed at the house on South Battery. Your nurse and Amelia's. She was with you when you were taken. Even though I was a small boy, I remember the uproar. Someone put Orva out with an ether-soaked handkerchief and dragged her into another room to tie her up. Valerie was upstairs at the time. She came down to find you gone, and Amelia screaming. Of course, the police asked Orva a million questions that she couldn't answer. Afterward, the family wouldn't trust her to look after Amelia. She's worked out here ever since, and just about runs things. Mother gives the necessary orders, but Orva does most of the work—with a little extra help. Her daughter Katy lives in Charleston now and has gone into other work."

No wonder Orva had looked shocked when she'd seen me

today. I wanted very much to talk with this woman who had been my nurse, and I had to find an opportunity.

"You'll have to meet Katy," Amelia said. "She has been a friend of mine for many years. Nathanial Amory taught her too, along with Charles and Daphne, who's a little older. Katy is a children's librarian in the Charleston public library system. You'll meet her at the rehearsal tonight. We've invited some of the family. But Katy's in the play as well."

"We had to have a black maid in a couple of scenes," Charles said, "so we got Katy to audition for the part."

"It wasn't easy to persuade her to take the part," Amelia said. "She didn't want to do a stereotype role, but the play takes place during the War, and this was a character we needed. At least I've given her a real part to play, even if it's small."

"What does she think about her mother still working here at Mountfort Hall?" I asked.

Mrs. Landry answered quietly. "Orva is her own person. She does what she chooses to do, and she does it very well—with pride. Katy doesn't always understand. She belongs to a different generation, a different time."

Amelia seemed to be fidgeting a little, and when there was a pause she set down her fork and smiled at us all. "I can't wait any longer, Charles. I have to tell them!"

Her face had come to life with an expression that I'd sometimes glimpsed in my own mirror when happiness filled me—a look I hadn't seen too often lately.

"We've decided to move our wedding date, and we need to consult with everyone. We'd like it to be a month from now." She looked brightly at Charles and he smiled with warm affection.

"Such a short time," Honoria said.

Amelia turned to me, explaining, perhaps sounding a little uncertain. "I don't want to get married without you here, Molly, and I feel certain we can convince you to stay just that much longer."

"It took years for you to set the date and now you're in a hurry." Honoria sounded impatient.

"Everything can be arranged," Charles said easily. "We'll hold the wedding out here, as planned. You'll help us work everything out, Mother?"

Mrs. Landry looked quietly pleased. "Certainly. It will be difficult, but we can arrange it."

I felt trapped and unhappy. This feeling had more to do with my growing uncertainty about Charles than with the awkward position Amelia had put me in. Wasn't Charles everything I'd have chosen for a fictional hero? Though he was neither Rochester nor Heathcliff, he was certainly no Harry Lime.

Even as Amelia spoke, I knew he watched me surreptitiously, as though he were trying to solve some impossible riddle, and my uncertainty about him grew. I could only hope that he was right for my sister.

"I'm touched that you want me here for your wedding, Amelia, but how will your mother feel about this?" I asked.

"*Our* mother, honey. I expect she'll be so relieved to see me married that she won't mind a bit. She'd like babies around again."

My sister sounded calm and accepting when it came to Valerie, but I sensed less equanimity under her words. Perhaps this was what it meant to be an identical twin. What she didn't say I could feel. But there might be a dangerous difference. I could leave this place and these people if anything went wrong. Amelia was tied here by her love for Charles and her love for Valerie Mountfort.

"Porter will want to know about this right away," Honoria said. "Have you told him yet?"

Charles shook his head. "There hasn't been time. Amelia and I had breakfast together this morning, and we've just made up our minds." He reached out to cover Amelia's hand with his own, and she looked at him with so much love—so much vulnerable love—that I felt more anxious for her than happy. Yet a little envious at the same time. I had loved Douglas a great deal, but never like this. What Amelia felt for Charles was something I had never experienced, and the knowledge left me oddly empty.

By this time our luncheon plates had been cleared. Orva came and went unobtrusively, though I suspected that she missed nothing that was said at this table. Where did her loyalties lie? Somehow I hoped they were with Amelia, who might need someone she could count on.

The watermelon we had for dessert was sweeter than any I'd ever tasted in the North—vine-ripened and luscious. I enjoyed it more than most of the food we'd been served.

When we'd finished our coffee, Charles asked Amelia if she would take me back to Charleston. There were some things he needed to do out here for his mother, so he would drive home later.

We left the table and I saw my chance to ask Mrs. Landry about speaking with Orva Jackson.

"Since she was our nurse when Amelia and I were babies, I'd like to talk with her. Do you mind waiting a few minutes, Amelia?"

Amelia readily agreed, as though she sensed the purpose behind my words. When Evaline Landry went off to call Orva, Amelia and I sat down in a small sitting area on the land side of the house.

"I can understand why you want to talk with Orva," Amelia said. "But she doesn't really know anything about *that time*. She never saw whoever took you, and she's had enough questioning over the years."

"That's not why I want to see her," I said. "She can tell me what I was like as a baby. She can even tell me about our father and mother at that time. Things you can't remember."

A longing to know was growing stronger in me. A few things had begun to fall into place, but there was so much more to know, and Orva might be an important link.

I found myself waiting anxiously for her to come. Mrs. Landry could send her to me, but Orva would talk or not, as she pleased.

Six

Orva arrived promptly. I watched the black woman approach, her back straight under the stiff uniform, her face without expression. Nevertheless the gold earrings and the half moons that held back her hair indicated that this was a woman with a good deal of pride—the uniform only a disguise.

"You wanted to see me, ma'am?" she asked as I rose to greet her.

At once I knew that I didn't want this to fall into an exchange between mistress and servant.

"Please sit down, Mrs. Jackson," I said. "I hope you'll talk with me a little."

She glanced at Amelia, who smiled and nodded. "Please, Orva. My sister has some questions that won't be disturbing."

When she'd joined me, I spoke to Orva directly. "You must have been shocked to see me at the table, Mrs. Jackson. Someone should have warned you that I was coming."

"Mr. Burke told me, Miss Cecelia. But I was surprised anyway when I saw you."

Once more I had to explain. "That isn't the name I grew up with. My name is Molly Hunt."

She bowed her head, waiting, and I tried to reassure her. "I don't mean to ask questions about when I was stolen. It's just that there's such an emptiness behind what happened before I came to my adoptive parents. What was I like as a baby? I don't think I can ask Mrs. Mountfort about this—it might be too painful. You are the one who knew me best, aside from my birth parents."

Relief seemed to sweep through her, as though she'd expected something else from me. Her smile was suddenly warm, friendly, and she hurried into a flow of words, the cadences of her speech musical.

"I remember real well, Miss Molly. You were the one who cried the most. You sure let us know if you didn't like something. Miss Valerie didn't have enough milk, so you both had bottles early, and you had a fine appetite. If you'd been nursing, poor Miss Amelia would have got what was left. You weren't a good baby. Only your mama could quiet you. You wanted her to hold you all the time, and you'd sniff at her as if you loved the way she smelled."

Roses, I thought, and looked at Amelia. My sister had turned away, as though it hurt her to hear this. "I'll leave you to talk together," she said, rising. "There's something I want to see Evaline about before we leave."

"She's upset," I said regretfully as Amelia walked away. "Why should what you were saying bother her?"

For a moment Orva hesitated, then seemed to throw natural caution aside. "You are the strong one—you always were, Miss Molly. I can feel it right now. Could be your sister's a little afraid about what you might do."

"I don't think I'm going to do anything. Certainly not anything that might alarm Amelia."

"You're still wondering how long you better stay, aren't you, Miss Molly?"

"I don't like some of the undercurrents I've been feeling. But I'd like to stay a little longer so I can get to know Amelia better. And, of course, now she's moved her wedding up because of me."

Orva bowed her head without comment and waited for me to go on.

"I keep telling everyone that my real life is back home in the North," I said.

She answered softly, almost under her breath, as though she wanted no one else to hear. "Your *real* life is here with your sister, Miss Molly. When she was a little baby I might have given her what she needed most. But after what happened to you they sent me out here."

"What did she need, Mrs. Jackson?"

"Call me Orva, please. That little ol' baby needed a whole lot of loving. That's what she never got enough of."

"I don't understand—Amelia must always have had a loving family around her."

"I suppose that's the way it would look to an outsider—no offense meant, Miss Molly—but Miss Valerie couldn't help the way she was, even though it wasn't fair. She loved you most because you asked for the most. And when you were taken away, she couldn't settle for anything except to get you back. She messed up her whole life because of the craziness that got ahold of her. When Mr. Simon was alive he understood, and he tried to make it up to Miss Amelia. But when he died she was all alone."

At least I had gone to loving adoptive parents. "Now she has Charles Landry. A husband who loves her could make up for everything."

"That's for certain," Orva said, and then raised her eyes again to look straight into mine. "You and your sister are maybe too much alike in a lot of ways. But it's the ways you're different that can be worrisome."

"Worrisome?"

"I'm sorry, Miss Molly. Maybe that's not the right word. My daughter Katy gets after me about words all the time. She don't want me to talk in the ol'-fashioned way. So sometimes I get things wrong."

I didn't think she had said anything she didn't mean. "How are we different—my sister and I?" I asked.

"You still want the most. Miss Valerie used to be like that— before everything went wrong. She can still spit some pretty hot fire when she gets riled. *You* try for things harder than Miss Amelia. I can feel that, but you don't go all crazy-like the way Miss Valerie can. Maybe you need to watch out around your mama. Maybe she's not sure about you."

"How can you see all this just from taking care of me for a few months when I was a baby?"

"Babies know who they are. Some of them do. Your sister needs you a whole lot, Miss Molly. Maybe you owe her."

"I didn't even know I had a sister until Charles Landry recognized me when he saw me in New York. That was a million-in-one chance."

"I don't think so, Miss Molly. I think it was all meant to be."

"You sound like Honoria Phelps."

Her smile agreed with me. "Miss Honoria has powers. I don't have anything special. Just a feeling sometimes. And maybe it's better if I don't mix into white folks' affairs."

Perhaps she could say this to me because I was an outsider—not one of her own "white folks."

I ventured a question. "Are you sure you don't remember anything special about that time when I was a baby? Anything that would help me to know better what happened?"

Her eyes were a deep velvet brown, large and widely set. Unexpectedly, they swam with tears. "I blamed myself for what happened more than anybody else ever did! If I'd just locked the downstairs door—but we didn't lock doors in the old days. So those men walked in and did what they came to do."

"Men?"

"I know there was two because I heard them talking. One of them grabbed me from behind, while the other stayed out of sight. So I never saw what they looked like. They didn't talk like gentlemen. They sounded—different. From New York, maybe? I only heard a few words before that smelly handkerchief came over my face."

"What did you hear?"

"One man said something about a jackpot, and the other one told him to shut up. There wasn't no more I could tell the police."

She was silent, and I sensed that thoughts were tumbling through her mind—re-creating something that perhaps she hadn't told the police.

"There is something else, isn't there?"

106

Her smile had a downward twist. "You're still like little Cecelia—you stick in there for what you want. But the what-else wouldn't have done the police any good, so I never talked about it before."

"Will you tell me now, Orva?"

"I reckon I will, though it won't do you much good neither. While I was out under that ether stuff, I had a dream. A real bad dream. Mr. Nathanial was still alive then, and he was teaching the little kids. Mr. Charles and Miss Daphne, and my Katy too. In the dream he came and talked to me, and he sounded real scared —asking me what he should do. Should he tell, or shouldn't he? In the dream I saw him down on the dock out here at Mountfort, and he was getting into a boat. I tried to tell him not to, but he couldn't hear me and he paid me no mind. He just went right ahead and rowed out on the river. After that the dream was all a jumble and I can't remember what was happening, till a policeman began shaking me. Most times dreams go away when you come awake, but that one never did. And in a little while, when Mr. Nathanial drowned, I knew I'd dreamed true."

"How long after that did he die?"

"Only a few months. That was bad, because maybe I could have stopped what was going to happen. Only I never tried. And there's no use telling you this now—don't know why I have."

She rose and started away from me down the hall. I couldn't let her go, and I went with her, talking to her as we walked.

"Orva, I suppose you know that Honoria thinks Nathanial has come back to Mountfort, and is speaking through her? Even though only the little cat is supposed to see him."

"Not only the cat. I saw him one time. It was a real misty night. It seemed like I just had to go down to the dock. He was getting into a boat, and I called out to him—just the way I did in my dream. Only of course he didn't hear me then either. He got

107

into that boat and rowed out into the mist and disappeared. It scared me real bad, and I ran back to the house."

"Honoria thinks someone damaged the boat so that it sank." Orva nodded. "But why?"

"Maybe he knew something bad about the kidnapping, Miss Molly. He was here in this house where he could pick up a lot of what was going on. Maybe he was listening when he shouldna been. Miss Honoria used to work here as a docent, and Miss Valerie loved it out here. She lived here when she was a young girl. Of course, Mr. Porter and your father were out at the Hall all the time too."

"But what could any of them have known that Nathanial might have overheard? Wasn't it thought that some ring was operating that stole babies?"

Orva began edging away from me. "Don't pay me no mind, Miss Molly. Sometimes I talk as crazy as your mama."

"Is my mother crazy?"

She shook her head vehemently. "That's just a way of talking. Your mama is sane as anybody."

I tried another road. "How much do you know about the circumstances of my father's death?"

That seemed to alarm her. "I don't know anything about that. Mr. Simon was a real good man. He loved Miss Amelia and you more than anything—except maybe your mama."

"Could he have known something—that is—"

"I told you—I don't know anything about that. He didn't die until ten years after all the bad trouble." Her hands were visibly shaking and I tried to reassure her. "Thank you for talking with me, Orva. I didn't mean to upset you. I'm looking forward to meeting your daughter tonight at the rehearsal. I understand she's in Amelia's play."

"That Katy!" Her eyes lighted. "She's a spunky one. Like

you, Miss Molly. I'm glad she got away from here—even though I never will."

"I don't think you'd stay anywhere you didn't want to be."

"Maybe not. Maybe there's still unfinished business to attend to around here."

We were walking along the hall together when she suddenly stopped and reached for my right hand. Slowly she turned it over and stared at the strawberry mark.

"They're not the same—those marks, Miss Molly. I remember from when you were a baby. Miss Amelia has the bad sign. Maybe that's why you have to stay. If you go away, maybe something will happen to your sister that you coulda stopped. But if you stay, it could be you're the one in danger. You or her—one or the other. They never needed both of you."

"What do you mean—*they?*"

"I told you, Miss Molly, you can't pay me no mind. You'll stay awhile," she said. "You've got enough fight in you to stay." With that she dropped my hand and rushed off down the hall, as though her own words had frightened her. I wondered if she'd had some vision about me that she didn't want to share, and a chill touched me.

From down the hall the little gray-and-white cat ran toward me. She greeted me with a single mew and rubbed herself against my ankles. I picked her up and she rested her paws on my shoulders, purring.

Suddenly voices reached me from the bedroom that had belonged to Nathanial Amory—and perhaps still did. At the same moment Amelia, who had been waiting in a side room, came out to join me. "Did you upset Orva, Molly? She sounded pretty excited when she ran off."

"Perhaps, but I didn't mean to upset her. She told me a few interesting things about—"

Amelia stopped me. "I don't *want* to know! Father always said, 'Today is the only day that matters,' and I believe that."

I didn't know whether she was right or not. It seemed that the past might be playing a larger role in the present than she thought. At least I could look at her wrist now, as I hadn't done before. I held out my hand with the strawberry mark showing.

"I'm curious," I said. "How much are they alike?"

This didn't trouble her, and she held her hand beside mine. The birthmarks were smooth and flat on our skin—only a reddish pigment. Amelia's mark was larger, and there were shadings where the pigment had broken up, as it had not on my wrist. On my sister's wrist the markings bore a faint resemblance to a skull. Orva had spoken of a "bad" sign. Was this what she meant?

"They aren't at all identical," I said.

"And that makes sense," Amelia answered. "Sometimes we seem so much alike—sometimes so very different. Never mind. In many ways we are the same person. Let's find Honoria and start back to the city."

We found Honoria in Nathanial's room perched on cushions before a small desk, her legs dangling. Orva stood talking to her, and I wondered how much she had revealed of our encounter. At a window Garrett Burke stood looking out toward the river. When he heard us come in, he turned, watching.

Almost at once, Orva slipped out of the room, acknowledging Amelia and me with no more than a quick nod. Honoria returned to what occupied her—a spread of tarot cards across the desktop. She bent her head above them, and then looked up at me.

"I've been casting for you, Molly. There's one card that keeps coming up." She touched a card that lay before her—the picture of a skeleton with a scythe. I knew nothing about tarot, but this picture hardly filled me with confidence.

110

Honoria nodded. "Yes, it's the death card. But don't be alarmed. Most of the time it only means change—something entirely new in your life. An upheaval, perhaps. Perhaps the death of your past life."

"My past life, as you call it, is quite healthy, thank you."

Garrett changed the subject abruptly. "Too bad, Amelia, that you couldn't put twin sisters into your play. That would make for nice complications and mix-ups. Your Confederate soldier in love with one sister, and the Union boy with the other. Only who would know which was which if the sisters chose to change roles?"

Miss Kitty suddenly dug her claws into my shoulder, and I let out a yelp as I hastily put her down. She sat on her haunches, ignoring me, and licked the pink pads of one paw so she could give her face a good scrubbing. I never found it flattering—the way cats always washed themselves energetically after contact with humans. At least she and Garrett had distracted me from thinking about the tarot card Honoria had chosen for me.

"Miss Kitty felt something just now," I said.

Honoria looked around sadly. "I wish *I* could see him." She sighed. "Never mind—perhaps it's better that I don't."

Better for her present life with Porter, I wondered?

"Can we go back to Charleston now?" she asked Amelia. "Porter brought me out early this morning, but I'm counting on you to give me a lift back."

She shuffled the tarot cards together, wrapped them in a silk cloth, and put them into a plain pine box.

"They mustn't be contaminated by outside contact," she explained. "I'm the only one who handles this pack."

Garrett spoke as he moved toward the door ahead of us. "Thank you for your time, Honoria. We'll talk about Nathanial again. I've just come to that period in my writing, and I'd like to put down what really happened."

"Nobody knows what happened," Honoria told him, looking quickly around the room. "So don't ask me."

I had the feeling that he would ask her anyway. He had paused in the doorway and was looking back at me, so that I felt again that he searched my face in some special way, just as he'd done yesterday in Daphne's store.

"I hope you'll come to the rehearsal tonight, Molly. I'll make my earlier transgressions up to Charles by dying as dramatically as I can."

"You'll die as I tell you to! I won't have you hamming things up," Honoria said crossly. "I'm not sure if Charles can even handle a sword tonight—after you damaged his wrist."

"Why are you supposed to be fighting Charles?" I asked.

Garrett grinned. "For love of fair lady, of course." He waved a hand at Amelia. "Anyway, that was only a tap I gave Charles. He wasn't really hurt. I suspect he dropped his sword on purpose, because I wasn't following the script—and maybe I scared him a bit. I'll behave tonight—I promise."

I looked after him critically. He was definitely not the heroic type. Garrett returned to the room he'd made into his office and we all went downstairs to Amelia's car. Honoria sat in the backseat with Miss Kitty, while I sat in the front beside Amelia. The carrier was one that allowed its occupant to look out at the world, and Miss Kitty's perked ears were alert and interested as she stuck her head through the opening.

As we passed what had been Slave Row, I saw Charles outside the Landry cottage working on a shutter. Amelia waved at him, and he looked after us, smiling.

"Let's stop at the Gadsden Inn when we get to Charleston," Amelia said as we sped down the avenue of moss-hung live oaks.

"I want you to move into our house right away, Molly. That's where you belong, and Mama needs to get used to having you there. I don't think she quite believes it's in you yet."

I gave up my resistance. If I was ever to find my way through this maze, I had better be close to Amelia.

"I'll come with you," Honoria said to me. "I can help you pack, and there's something I need to show you at the South Battery house."

I knew she meant the mysterious letter, and began to let my anticipation grow. In a little while I'd have read the words Simon Mountfort, my father, had written to me all those years ago.

The drive back to Charleston didn't seem as long as the drive out. We crossed the bridge and drove down the peninsula to Hasell Street. When we'd parked the car in front of the inn, Honoria and Amelia came up to my room with me. Packing didn't take long, since I'd brought only one suitcase and a big tote bag.

Honoria moved around briskly, fetching my toilet articles from the bathroom and handing them to me to pack. She seemed bright and energetic, as though a source of new energy moved her, and I recognized uneasily that it had to do with me.

Miss Kitty waited for us in the car, its windows open against the warmth of the day—though the enervating humidity of true summer still lay ahead. In the old days the Low Country had been a place of malaria and other summer illnesses. Now, with screens and air-conditioning, people could live in the city the year round.

The trip from Hasell Street to South Battery was several blocks, and Amelia was able to park in front of the house.

Honoria nodded knowingly. "You can always arrange for a parking place ahead of time, you know. Just concentrate very hard on what you want and it will be ready."

Amelia smiled. "You'll need to get used to Cousin Honoria's little miracles, Molly. They happen all the time."

No one came to greet us at the door, and Amelia used her key.

I thought of what Orva had said about nobody locking doors in the days before I was kidnapped.

Honoria carried Miss Kitty in with us, and let her out of the carrier. Completely at home, she ran ahead up the stairs and leaped on top of a bookcase, to watch us climb to the second floor.

"We still have a small staff out at Mountfort Hall," Amelia explained. "But not here in town. Mother and I enjoy cooking, and of course someone comes in to clean, so we get by nicely without any live-in help. Times have changed from the days of our grandparents. I have a room ready for you, Molly, so let's get you settled."

Honoria and Miss Kitty followed us up a narrower flight to the third floor. Bedrooms ranged around a small central hall, and at the far end, where shuttered windows would have looked out into the neighboring house, a partially screened section was visible. I glimpsed a few trunks and boxes, and one object that caught my eye—an old-fashioned hand-carved rocking horse. It had been stored there for some time, but obviously it had once been loved by generations of children whose hands had given it a special patina.

Amelia saw my interest. "All the Mountfort children grew up with Applejack. Great-grandfather Samuel Mountfort named him when *he* was a little boy out at the plantation. He thought Applejack was a pretty name, and it stuck—no matter what comments grown-ups might make."

Honoria gave the rocking horse a sharp, humorous look, as

though she expected something from it, and Amelia smiled. "Our haunted rocking horse."

She didn't explain, however, and when my bags had been set down in the small bright bedroom I'd been given, Honoria stopped me from unpacking.

"Let it wait, Molly. I have an appointment this afternoon, and there's something we must do first. Amelia, dear, sit down and stop fidgeting. Your mother is probably napping, and you can look in on her later. First, I have something to tell you both."

Amelia caught the solemn note in Honoria's voice, and sat obediently in a small flounced chair. I chose the dressing-table bench, and Honoria, who was the one really fidgeting now, flitted around the room as she talked.

"I've never told you this, Amelia, there was no point, but two days before your father died he gave me a sealed letter that was never to be opened by anyone other than Cecelia Mountfort."

"Cecelia?" Amelia echoed. "But how could he—?"

"I'd told him again and again that your sister would be found, honey. Perhaps he believed me, and he wrote a letter for me to deliver if ever the time came. I suppose he had a premonition about his death. So anyway, now is the time. I put it in a very safe place, where no one would ever look, and now we'll retrieve it."

Honoria's flitting took her out into the hall, and to its far end, where the rocking horse waited beyond the screen. When Amelia and I hurried after her, Honoria waved a dramatic hand at the toy horse.

"Applejack has kept Simon's secret all these years! Perhaps it's the presence of the letter that has haunted him."

Miss Kitty prowled after us, as though she stalked some prey. No one paid her any attention, and she chose her own way to make us notice by springing onto the back of the rocking horse, to set it moving gently. Honoria had no time for her now and she plucked the little cat off Applejack and handed her to me.

"Hold her for a minute, Molly."

Miss Kitty put her claws into my shoulder and clung, but I endured this discomfort as I watched Applejack and Honoria. The horse had probably been made on a hand lathe, its body a smoothed, rounded oblong of dark wood. The head was set into one end, while the wooden stub of a docked tail protruded at the other. The head was flat on each side, with no modeling; a strip of once-varnished bentwood formed the mane and was painted with brown scallops to indicate hair. Straight boards fastened to the rockers formed the legs, and the whole was put together with round wooden pegs of various sizes. Two painted brown dots formed eyes that seemed intent on something far away that we couldn't see.

I scratched Miss Kitty's ears to keep her contented, and she drew her claws back into their pads and turned her head, watching every move Honoria made. Applejack's stubby tail had been fitted into a slot, and with a mighty tug Honoria removed it, leaving a square open space where it had rested. Into this slot an envelope had been thrust, folded many times so it would fit. Miss Kitty, always curious, leapt from my shoulder to Applejack's back and set him rocking again while she examined the empty slot where the tail had been. No one but Honoria would have chosen so unusual a hiding place.

The writing on the envelope Honoria handed me was addressed to Miss Cecelia Mountfort, and the flap had been closed with sealing wax, now cracked and broken.

Amelia sat down on a box, trembling, and Honoria touched her hand to quiet her as she spoke to me.

"Go into your bedroom, Molly, so you can read the letter

alone. Amelia and I will wait for you in her room across the hall."

I took the envelope into the bedroom, feeling vulnerable and a little frightened. When I opened it and read the words Simon Mountfort had written, everything in my life might change, and I wasn't sure I was ready for that. Nevertheless I broke the cracked red seal and took out three creased sheets of notepaper that bore the Mountfort crest.

Before starting to read, I glanced down the pages at handwriting that might have been familiar to me if I had grown up in this house. It continued boldly, line after line, until the bottom of the third page, where it seemed to waver into uncertainty. The final signature was again strong, however. I went back to the salutation and began to read.

My Darling Lost Cecelia:

Honoria believes that you are alive somewhere and I trust her. She is sure you will return to Charleston someday. Sometimes Honoria sees what the rest of us cannot. She tells me you will be a grown woman by the time you read this, and you will have a life of your own. Yet the blood of an old family flows in your veins, my darling girl. This may be hard for you to accept, since you have grown up elsewhere, but you do belong here.

Even as a baby you were strong and sure of yourself. Amelia, on the other hand, is a gentle, loving child. A child too easily hurt. Your loss has made a difference in her life that you may never understand. I fear I will not be here when she needs me, but perhaps the time will come when she will need you—and you *will* be here.

All is not well here. I have lived with an uneasy conscience for too many years, but I am convinced that I cannot mend anything now. Let me just say that I have been false to my integrity, both as a judge and a gentleman of the South. I have been told that my heart is not strong, so I am writing this before it is too late. In endeavoring to protect the Mountfort name I am as guilty as the man I am protecting.

I love your mother devotedly, but I can no longer reach her. Perhaps you will be able to.

When you return to Charleston, my darling Cecelia, it will be as a stranger to your own family. You cannot know how much you were loved unless I tell you in this letter. Your mother loved you too well—and your loss nearly killed her.

The past has a way of turning into the future. According to Honoria, that's what karma is—cause and effect. As we sow . . . I have reaped my own ending, since even silence and the fear of action are action and cause. Wrong, once done, must sooner or later surface and be paid for. Though perhaps not always in this life.

Your return may cause muddy depths to surface danger-ously. If I am wrong, and everything remains quiet, then regard this letter as an expression of what may only be foolish anxiety. Be gentle with your mother—she has been damaged most of all.

As a way of attempting to make up to you much of what has happened, I am leaving you Mountfort Hall. No one knows of this decision except my attorney and now you. If you do not return to read this letter, my dear daughter, then my attorney will never divulge my wishes and Amelia will inherit Mountfort Hall.

After my death—whenever it comes—my dearest wife and my beloved Amelia will receive the letters I have written to them. My words will say nothing of matters I touch on here. I will place this letter in Honoria's hands for safekeeping. I know she will hide it safely, so no one can find and destroy it. I cannot say more to a daughter I do not know, but whom I somehow trust.

For this reason I must set a heavy burden on you. Whoever is responsible for your kidnapping and Nathanial's death must be exposed and not allowed to wreck other lives. I have no proof, so I cannot guide you. I only know that I have acted wrongly, with terrible consequences I cannot mend.

Perhaps that Higher Power Honoria believes in will have brought you here for this purpose. I hope and pray you will know the truth and do whatever must be done to reveal it.

> Your loving father,
> *Simon Mountfort*

I sat for a little while with the pages in my hand, stunned by his gifts: the letter, Mountfort Hall, and the tangled web of crimes instigated so long ago. He had written a sad and baffling letter, expressing his fears but telling me nothing I could use. I was not sure whether I ought to share what he had written with anyone else. What might I stir up if I did? Yet I could not keep his words to myself.

More than anything at the moment, I wished I could see his face, look into his eyes. Perhaps I *could* do that. I'd been told there was a portrait of Simon Mountfort in this house. It was time for me to find it. Perhaps I could read more in his face than in his words.

Seven

Still carrying the pages of my father's letter, I went down the hall stairs quietly, so Honoria and Amelia wouldn't hear me, and stopped in the doorway of the Victorian drawing room I'd glimpsed when I came into the house. The portrait I looked for hung above the fireplace, and was lighted by its own small lamp.

Simon Mountfort was seated with the river side portico of Mountfort Hall behind him. He must have been a judge by the time this picture was painted, for he was not a young man. He'd dressed informally in tan trousers, with a dark corduroy jacket over a yellow sweater. One hand balanced a book resting facedown on his crossed knees. The other held a pair of horn-rimmed glasses that dangled from his fingers. He looked as though he had just put his book down and glanced up at a visitor —with not too welcoming an expression.

In a painted shaft of sunlight, hair touched with gray rose thickly above a fine forehead. The eyes were not fully open, as they might have been when he was young, and the mouth was straight, the lower lip fuller than the upper. No humor showed in either eyes or mouth. His expression was stern and rather distant. There was sadness here that matched the tenor of his letter, so the picture could have been painted not long before his death.

The man who had spoken to me lovingly in the pages I held in my hand was not to be found in the portrait. It was a terrible disappointment to me, telling me less than his letter. Yet pity stirred in me. He must have been a strong and powerful man until events forced him toward final despair.

I turned my back on this father I would never know and went upstairs to look for Amelia and Honoria.

My sister's door stood open and they both looked up at me— Honoria expectant, Amelia anxious. Until now I hadn't been sure whether I would show them the letter. But I couldn't keep it to myself. There was too much I needed to know, and I held out the pages.

"I don't know what to make of this, but I think you must read what he has written. You both knew him, so perhaps you can better explain it to me."

Honoria reached for the letter. "Let me read it first, since I must leave soon." She took it out into the hall, where she could be alone, and Amelia and I looked at each other uneasily. To avoid her eyes, I moved about the room.

It was a charming, feminine room that suited her, but was very different from my plainer style at home. The four-poster bed featured a lacy canopy from which mosquito netting might once have hung—before screens and air-conditioning. Rice-grain finials topped the posts, and several small fluffy pillows banked the head of the bed, their flowered material carrying out the rosebud theme of the wallpaper.

Amelia was watching me and I smiled at her. "It's a lovely room, and it suits you."

"What about the letter, Molly?" she asked. "Do you think I should read it?"

"Let's leave that up to Honoria," I said. "I don't know how to answer you."

"Whatever it says, we mustn't show it to Mama. She mustn't be upset—she needs time to recover."

"Recover from what? Has she been ill?"

"From the shock of your coming here."

"Perhaps it would be better if I could see her, spend some time with her. I should think she would insist on seeing *me.*"

Amelia shook her head unhappily. "Cousin Porter believes—"

"But *why?* And why must you all listen to him?"

"He's been like a brother to her, Molly. You don't know what it's been like. I could never make it up to her for losing you. Now that you're here, I can marry Charles with a freer heart. Once she accepts you, she won't need me as much."

I listened with a heaviness of spirit. There was nothing to do but hold her and I reached out my arms. She felt smaller and more fragile, even though we were the same size. I couldn't promise her anything—I was still too unsure about everything. But I tried to find words that might comfort her a little.

"Now that we've found each other, Amelia, we will always

belong together. Even when we're apart, as we may have to be, this feeling will connect us."

As Amelia clung to me, Honoria returned with the letter in her hand, and smiled. "Good! I knew this would happen between twins as close as you are. Amelia, I think you must read your father's letter. But don't show it to your mother—she has enough to deal with right now. Later, perhaps. Molly, will you come down to the door with me, please?"

Amelia took the letter almost fearfully, and I didn't look back as I followed Honoria.

Miss Kitty had vanished, and after calling her a few times, Honoria left the carrier by the door and we went outside to stand at the top of the steps.

"I wanted to talk to you about Simon's letter, Molly. The gift of Mountfort Hall is an amazing show of love and will upset some people a great deal, but what is meant to be will be. He must have been terribly sad and concerned when he wrote this letter. Even guilty. It's true he had a bad heart, and that was what killed him. So he tried to reach out to the daughter he would never live to see again. But what he wrote was too full of his own confusion and self-blame to do you much good. Did you know Orva Jackson found him the day he died? They were good friends, and that was very hard for her."

"Perhaps I'll talk to Orva about this the next time I see her. I liked her a lot, and I'd also like to meet her daughter."

"That's easily managed. The County Library, where she works, is several blocks away, so you'd better drive. Ask Amelia if you can borrow her car."

I held Honoria a moment longer. "Why can't I see Valerie?"

"As far as I am concerned, you can see her anytime. But Porter doesn't think it's advisable yet. So you'll have to talk to him."

"But *why?*"

"Maybe because Valerie makes up scenarios in her own mind and expects others to act in them. It's better to wait until she can make up her mind *sensibly.*"

I must have looked as impatient as I felt, for Honoria put a hand on my arm. I'd noticed her making that gesture with others, and I felt subtly quieted.

"Take it easy, Molly. You need time too. Time to digest who you are. You can't take it all in with one big swallow. We'll talk again later. Now I must hurry along to my appointment. It's only a short walk. 'Bye for now. And look after your sister."

For just a moment I wished someone would look after me. But my father on Long Island already belonged to another life, and whatever I needed to do, I must do myself.

When I rejoined Amelia she handed me Simon's letter. "Thank you for letting me read it," she said politely. "I must go see Mama now. She shouldn't be left alone when she's upset. We won't tell her about this letter yet, Molly. Can you amuse yourself for a while on your own?"

The letter had clearly shaken her, but it had also caused her to withdraw from me.

"I can manage," I told her. "Don't worry about me. Honoria suggested that I might drive over to the library, since I'd like to meet Katy Jackson. May I borrow your car?"

"Of course—a wonderful idea! The library is over on King Street and easy to find. Tell Katy hello for me. I'll see you later."

She gave me the car keys and a key to the house, and hurried toward Valerie's room, eager to escape from me. When I entered my cheerful little bedroom, I found Miss Kitty asleep on the bed. She heard me and gave her tiny mew of greeting, rolled over on her back and stretched, offering her long white belly for stroking. Such trust was irresistible and I obliged for a moment.

124

"You were hiding, weren't you, kitty? Go back to sleep now and I'll see you later."

She rolled herself into a ball and tucked her tail around her body, going right to sleep, though her tail twitched and flipped, speaking its own wide-awake language.

I went downstairs to where Amelia's blue car waited at the curb, but I didn't get into it at once. Across South Battery and the park I could see gulls wheeling above the wall, and I stood for a moment watching. A scent of the river came to me, pungent, yet not unpleasant as I grew accustomed to it.

When I got into the car I found a map in the glove compartment and studied it. The library wasn't five minutes away, and I was able to find it easily. A statue of John C. Calhoun dominated the area, his cloak blowing in a perpetual wind as he surveyed his city.

The entrance to the library was on the southwest corner of the building. I went inside to the desk and was told that I would find Miss Jackson upstairs. I climbed a long flight to the second floor and entered the reference room, where I found Katy sitting at a desk near a window. She wore a creamy cotton blouse the color of magnolia petals and a bright printed skirt in a geometric pattern. She had none of her mother's angularity, but was more gently rounded and not as tall. Her skin was dark, and she had used makeup discreetly across her high cheekbones, with a touch of dark red lipstick. Her black hair formed a rounded sculpture over her forehead.

"I'm Molly Hunt—" I began, and she looked up in quick recognition, her smile warm.

"I know who you are. Though for just a minute I thought Amelia had cut her hair. My mother phoned to tell me about you."

We shook hands in mutual liking, and she went on. "I'm glad

125

you stopped in. I expected to see you at the rehearsal tonight, but we'll be too involved to do much talking then. Can you sit down for a moment while it's not busy?"

She led the way to a table, where we could talk quietly in the empty room.

"You've known the Mountforts all your life, haven't you?" I said. "I'm still trying to get used to a pretty astonishing turn of events in my life, and I'm anxious to learn more about them."

She nodded. "It can't be easy to be both North and South in one body. Especially when you're not very well acquainted with your southern half. I lived out at Mountfort Hall when I was young, because my mother was more like part of the family. Of course, I knew all the young people—they're still my friends. Tell me, how can I help you?"

"There are so many pieces I'm trying to put together. I know how my father died, but I've just been told that your mother found him. Do you know anything about that?"

"Not much. Mama never wanted to talk about it, because she felt so sad about his death. Everybody liked Mr. Simon. But twenty years ago we were all children and nobody told us much. When he died Mr. Simon was sitting at the piano in the music room playing something from Debussy—a piece your mama liked real well."

Her words set me back in that room with the shrouded furniture. I wanted to hear the music he had played, and I had to learn what it was.

I was curious about Katy Jackson, as well as about the past. "Where did you go to school?" I asked.

Her answer surprised me. "I went to Stony Brook University on Long Island. I've often crossed the island to Bellport, where you're from, Miss Mountfort."

"I'm Molly," I said. "But you came back to Charleston—you didn't want to stay in the North?"

"I feel comfortable here. There's more prejudice against blacks in New York than I expected. Though it's a different kind from what we still meet here in some places. People have better manners here. And they smile at you."

Talking with Katy had a calming effect on me. She belonged to the present and I felt I could speak to her more openly than to anyone else I'd met since I'd arrived here.

"And I feel more comfortable in the North," I said. "I'm having trouble digesting a life that's totally different from the one I know. I'm a Mountfort without any of the traditions that are second nature to the family."

"Lucky you! I still have to live with some of those traditions because of my mother. She says you've already met the Mountfort ghost."

" 'Met' isn't exactly the word. I understand that Nathanial Amory was your tutor too?"

"And a very good one. We all loved him and his death frightened us and made us sad."

"How did it frighten you?"

"It was too sudden and strange. I think there was a lot of hushing up about what happened. Nobody would talk to us children about it. Miss Honoria carried on like crazy, and my mother was full of portents and warnings. She can be like that sometimes."

"Do you suppose what happened could have any connection with the present?"

"If that boat was damaged before he took it out, maybe it does."

"But the police—?"

"Of course they investigated, but the boat was never found.

Some of us wondered if somebody made sure that it wouldn't be found. There might have been a pretty big scandal, and that would have meant disgrace to the family." Katy sounded wry. "The police put it down to accident, but my mother doesn't believe that it was."

"What do you mean?"

"She believes that every event, every deed, perhaps every thought we think, weaves threads into a life tapestry that we're fated to follow. Without a crystal ball, we can't even know whether what happens is good or bad when it occurs. We can only see the significance when we look back from the distance of years. Sometimes, she says, good can come out of terrible happenings."

At least, finding Katy seemed a good event in my life, and I opened up enough to tell her about Simon Mountfort's letter, though I avoided any mention of his gift to me.

She listened thoughtfully. "About all you can do is try to help your sister."

"Of course. But how? Sometimes I think I'm getting to know her, and then she moves away from me. Is she afraid of something, Katy?"

Orva's daughter met my eyes gravely before she spoke. "Could be she's afraid of you."

"Of *me?* How could that be?"

"Maybe I shouldn't have said that. Anyway, she was fearful enough before you came, and I don't really know why. At least you're there now in the South Battery house, so perhaps you can get her to talk to you."

I didn't know where to go with this and tried another direction. "I'd like to know more about Nathanial Amory."

"Would you like to meet him?"

That startled me, and I watched as Katy went to a shelf and took down a slender volume to bring to me.

"These are the only poems he had published. Thanks to Honoria, they appeared after his death. If you'd like to borrow them, I'll check this book out under my name. We kids were all happy to see those lines he'd read to us printed in a real book. His picture's there on the back."

I turned the book over and studied what must have been an informal snapshot of a slender young man, fair-haired, with wide dark eyes that seemed to look into mine. An eerie effect after what had happened out at Mountfort Hall. He wore a cardigan and light trousers, and carried an armload of books, his smile directed at whoever stood behind the camera.

"Honoria took that picture. She caught the special way he had of looking at people—as though he cared about everyone. We missed him a whole lot after he died."

And of course Honoria had cared about him most of all. "I wonder how Honoria came to marry Porter Phelps after Nathanial?"

"Nobody stands against Mr. Phelps, Molly. If you're here long enough, you may find that out."

While I was wondering about the formal manner in which Katy spoke of Porter, she looked away from me toward a man who had just come into the reference room, and said she'd see me tonight. I thanked her for the loan of Nathanial's book and went down to Amelia's car.

For a few moments I sat leafing through the pages, reading lines here and there. These words were all that was left of a man who had been very much loved by the young people he had taught, and by one woman who had never forgotten him. I wished I might have known him—and not as a ghost!

The book in my hands seemed to fall open of its own accord

129

to a poem entitled "To Nora." The lines had an old-fashioned ring as I read them aloud, as though the writer had absorbed from a literary past and rejected present fashions in poetry. It was a love poem, and a sad one, the words filled with rain and tears and the scent of magnolias. The line between sentiment and the sentimental could be slight, but I had no doubt that these lines had come from the heart of the writer, and that the poet was speaking of a forbidden love. Nora? Honoria? An exquisite young Honoria? But why forbidden?

I put the book into my handbag, not ready yet to return to the house on South Battery. For a little while I would explore Charleston's Historic District on my own.

Later, when I looked back on my course of action, I thought again of that destiny both Orva and Honoria seemed to believe in. How else could I have been led toward a "chance" meeting at my publisher's office that would open up all sorts of possibilities?

At that moment, however, when I turned innocently to a further exploration of the area, I still thought I was moving of my own free will.

Eight

Again, the map gave me my direction and I drove down Meeting Street and found a place where I could park. I knew about the Market and I planned to do some exploring there. On foot I could move as I pleased.

The character of the Historic District was becoming familiar by this time. Charles had told me that once a fire had destroyed a third of all the buildings in this area. The siege and bombardment of Charleston by Federal troops had left a city in ruins.

There had been hurricanes and tornadoes as well, and a disastrous earthquake—the worst ever to hit the East Coast. Yet walking along these sunny streets, I saw nothing to indicate any of this, except for an occasional earthquake bolt, which might or might not be real, since sometimes newer buildings adopted the rosettes as decoration.

Charleston, I suspected, would always right itself, count its blessings, repair its wounds, and move into the future. The city was one of America's treasures and I felt a new and unexpected pride of belonging. Perhaps something in my blood remembered, after all. It would be satisfying to use this in one of my novels, and I made mental notes that I would later transfer to paper.

From a picture I'd seen, I recognized the great Market Hall building—an impressive Roman Revival structure that had been set high above its surroundings. Around its top ran a frieze of sheep's and bulls' heads, indicating that this was once a place where meat had been sold. Now the second level had been turned into a Confederate Museum, while the long arcade on the ground floor underneath housed shops and stalls for goods of every kind.

I wandered as I pleased, pausing here and there to examine what was offered. When I reached the far end, I stopped to watch basket weavers at their intricate work. These beautiful creations— containers and mats of all sorts, woven of sweet grass, palmetto, and pine needles—were spread out on floor coverings. The art of weaving such baskets had been handed down from African ances- tors and was unique to the Low Country of South Carolina. I would want several of these to take home, but would return another time to pick out what I wanted.

"Home" was still the place where I'd grown up and would eventually return. When I got back to the house on South Bat- tery, I would telephone my father and let him know some of the things that had happened to me during the past several days. For now, I would continue to explore, with no need for direction or purpose.

When I came to Charleston Place—a newer addition—with its enclosed shops and architecture adopted to suit the area, I found the entrance to the Omni Hotel and went inside. A small seating oasis near the door offered me a place to rest and watch passing visitors. The wide corridor led past a complex of expensive shops I might explore later. The spot where I sat was opposite the magnificent twin arms of a staircase that rose to the balcony above. Centering over the space formed by curving steps hung an elaborate chandelier of glass and metal. On the floor beneath, large squares of creamy marble, patterned with rose-colored diamonds, covered the expanse, and huge white pots of seasonal plants and flowers had been placed about the lobby area beyond.

There was a constant stream of people passing by to visit the shops, or coming from invisible elevators in the vicinity of the hotel desk. I could sit here quietly and let everything flow away from me—all that had disturbed me since I'd come to Charleston. The encounter with Valerie Mountfort had put me off especially, though there was no question about my being drawn to Amelia.

After a time I got up to explore the hotel spaces beyond the twin arms of the staircase. At once I came upon a secluded sitting area occupied by a man and a woman. Daphne Phelps and Garrett Burke sat close together, leaning toward each other, talking quietly. As I hesitated, wondering whether to speak or just to move quickly away, Daphne handed Garrett a small box, and for some reason I stayed to watch. They didn't see me at once, intent as they were on their own exchange.

Garrett opened the box, glanced inside, and put it away in a pocket. At almost the same instant, they both looked up and saw me standing a few feet away. For a single unguarded moment

133

they appeared so startled that I knew this was a clandestine meeting. That made no difference to me, except that it was too late for me to escape.

Garrett stood up and said, "Hello, Molly. Have they let you out on your own?"

"You make it sound as though I've been a captive," I said, with more of an edge to my voice than I had intended.

Daphne twisted a lock of her straight red hair, a large jade ring on her hand shining green in the lobby lights. The grin she gave me had a wry twist. "Hi, Molly. You might as well know that Garrett is an enemy spy and I am a Confederate agent. Any comments?"

"I won't give either of you away," I promised.

Daphne left her chair. "Whatever you're thinking, you're wrong. There may be devilment afoot, but we're not behind it. See you later, Garrett. I need to get back to the shop. I'll leave you to deal with Molly."

She went off toward the outside door by which I'd entered, leaving me thoroughly ill at ease. If Daphne hadn't made so much of this, I'd have dismissed their meeting as none of my business, and thought nothing more about it.

Garrett stood up, easy enough in his manner. "It's nice to see you, Molly. Will you have tea with me? The Palmetto Court, nearby, is pleasant. I'd like to talk with you."

I wasn't sure at this point that I wanted to talk with him, but I could find no excuse to escape. We entered from the corridor, and were shown to a table in the open-air court. A bright blue umbrella shaded us from the sun, and palmetto palms rattled their fronds above us in a slight breeze.

I'd never felt entirely comfortable with Garrett Burke. From the first time I'd met him in Daphne's shop, he had seemed to

134

stand back and study me quizzically, so that I wondered what sort of judgment he was making.

At first neither of us had much to say. Tea was served with fingers of toast and little cakes, and I sipped and munched, wondering what to talk about. Perhaps I would just plunge in and see what happened. I could hardly do much harm, since Garrett was an outsider—like me.

"Do you know what my sister Amelia is afraid of, Garrett? Something seems to be worrying her, and I'd like to know what it is."

"Don't try to take on more than you can handle, Molly."

"But I need to understand what's happening. My father wrote a letter to me shortly before he died, and Honoria gave it to me this afternoon. Apparently Honoria had assured him that I would return. It's a strange letter, filled with hints and telling me very little."

"Do you care to tell me what he said? Or, better still, show me the letter?"

For a moment I hesitated, and then gave it to him. After all, Garrett was the Mountfort biographer, and everything that concerned Mountfort Hall and the past would interest him.

He read Simon's words slowly, carefully. I watched, but couldn't interpret his expression.

"Mountfort Hall is an impressive gift and a dangerous one. This may tell you more than you realize, Molly," he said as he handed the letter back. "The big question is what Simon could have done that gave him such a guilty conscience."

"I'm not sure I want to know—except as it might affect Amelia," I said too quickly. "Perhaps knowing would only create more pain for both Valerie and Amelia. Perhaps it's better to ignore some clues and not dig too deeply."

"If it affects the present, how can you let it go?"

I shook my head unhappily. "All I feel now is confusion. I'd rather be writing a story. My main character always knows what to do, how to take charge. *I,* on the other hand, feel helpless."

"Your characters get their motivation and strength from you, so you can't be that helpless."

His words startled me. My adoptive father had never thought much of my ability as a writer or an independent woman, and it had colored my opinion of myself.

Garrett went on. "You haven't been exactly timid in coming here. So maybe you should step back and take another look at yourself. You may have more in common with one of your own women characters than you realize. It could be you're the one who will pull this whole tapestry of deception apart. Then we can see what lies underneath the pretty stitching. Perhaps the Mountforts will breathe a lot more comfortably and stop fearing the past when the truth comes out."

Something always carefully guarded about Garrett's manner had disappeared, allowing anger and a deeper passion than I'd realized was there to surface.

I tried to speak quietly. "I don't want to pull any loose threads. I only want to see Amelia safe and happy."

"Then won't she need something stronger than old deceptions under her feet?"

"Tell me what you mean."

"I really don't know. Working on the Mountfort story, I come across dark corners that tempt me to probe. And maybe even scare me a little. Porter would just as soon have me skip along and gloss over anything that might be too revealing. He can't be happy about having you come here to complicate everything."

"What if you are one of the dark corners?" I asked.

He seemed amused. "Do you think I'm working on *my* story?"

136

I began to wonder about Garrett Burke. Where had he grown up, gone to school? Who were the women in his life? Was Daphne the woman in his present? I remembered now the way I'd seen her look at him.

"Stop taking me apart." His smile mocked me. "I'd rather stay an interesting puzzle. What do you think about your sister's coming marriage to Charles Landry?"

"She's certainly in love with him. Though judging by that so-called duel you fought today, I don't think you're crazy about him. Why not? Does he really love my sister?"

"You'll probably find that out for yourself—if you stick around and don't run away from what might frighten you. The women in your stories don't run away, do they?"

"They're courageous in a way that I'd like to be. *I* might very well run."

"First try to find that thread to pull, Molly."

"I think I'd better get back to the house before they start worrying about me."

He paid no attention. "Would you like a glimpse into one of those dark corners, Molly?"

When I didn't answer, he took something from his pocket and held it out to me. It was the small box I'd seen Daphne give him a little while ago—a jeweler's box with a hinged lid. Inside on a nest of cotton rested a tiny object made of coral and silver. The pink coral had been skillfully carved into the form of an open lotus blossom, each petal intricately formed, the whole set in a silver backing. When I took it out of the box, I saw it was a clip earring.

"What's the significance of one earring?" I asked.

"That may be the whole point. What happened to its mate? Daphne says this is probably the work of one of Charleston's finer jewelers. Made years ago. It came into her hands in a rather strange way when she was a little girl. She kept it as a secret treasure, and forgot about it until recently. Something made her remember, and she brought it to me and told me the story. It may even be a link in one of those dark mysteries. Perhaps she'll tell you the story sometime. I'm not sure she'd want me to."

"Then why did you show it to me?"

Watching him, I saw that a deep vertical line in one cheek came from drawing up one side of his mouth in a wry, even cynical grin. It was a look that made me nervous.

"Could be," he said, "that I like to stir things up, Molly-Cecelia. Now that the earring has surfaced, let's see what will happen. I'll walk you back to the house, if you like."

"I have Amelia's car," I told him. "It's parked on the other side of the Market."

Garrett came with me and on the way I told him about meeting Katy Jackson at the library. When we reached the car, I picked up Nathanial's book of poems from the front seat and showed it to him.

"Of course you've seen this?"

He took the slim volume from me thoughtfully and began turning the pages. "Yes—there are copies in the library out at the Hall. You might read the lines on page twelve, Molly, and see what you make of them."

"We always seem to come back to Nathanial," I said as he handed the book back to me. "Have you come across anything about his death in your research?"

"That's one of the dark corners. It's strange how involved I've become with the Mountforts and everyone who has touched their lives. The figure of Nathanial Amory interests me, but I'm not sure I can report objectively anymore. His story seems especially tragic."

With Garrett, I was always aware of a natural restraint, and I suspected that he had discovered more than he was ready to reveal.

"You *have* come across something, haven't you?"

"Not really. Of course, there's always the puzzle of Honoria. She's one of the enigmas in the picture."

"Because she hoped to marry Nathanial?"

"I doubt that. Apparently he never made it a secret that he had a wife back home."

"Really!" I wondered why no one had mentioned this to me. "Is it true that he came here because of some distant connection with the Mountforts?"

"So Porter claims. Probably an illegitimate connection. Which would hardly have mattered by Nathanial's time. Porter would like to leave Nathanial out of the story entirely."

"Because of Honoria?"

"It's possible."

"Are you going to do as Porter wishes?"

Garrett didn't answer. He was studying me again in that way I found disconcerting.

"I wonder if Nathanial called Honoria Nora?" I said.

He knew I'd read the poem, but he shrugged and opened the car door for me, ending any further talk. "I'll see you at the rehearsal tonight, Molly. Be sure to go backstage when you're at the theater. There's a whole mysterious world back there that should interest you as a mystery writer. See you later."

His departure was abrupt, and I knew he wanted to stop my questions. He hadn't been unfriendly, but he could pull down some sort of curtain that prevented me from going any further than he wished.

I watched as he went quickly away, not with Charles's long, rather graceful stride but with a spring to his step, as though life interested him endlessly.

I opened Nathanial's poems to the page Garrett had mentioned. The title seemed to spring at me: "Ode to a Pink Lotus." The lines described a delicate flower carved in coral and set in gold. At once the darkness of this particular corner seemed to deepen. Why an ode to a woman's earrings? And why gold, when the real earring I had seen had been set in silver? Was it simply poetic license?

I drove back to South Battery and parked Amelia's car near the house. When I opened the front door my father's portrait drew my attention, and I stood in the drawing room doorway to study it. The man in the portrait had something to tell me, I felt. Something he wanted me to know.

A sound to my left made me turn. Valerie Mountfort sat across from the portrait, her hands folded in the lap of her long rose-colored gown. Her fair hair hung in a braid over one shoulder, and she sat very still, watching me.

"I've been waiting for you, Cecelia—if that is your name. Amelia has gone out, so we can be alone. I've been wanting to talk with you when no one else was present."

She was the one person who had a right to call me Cecelia. I sat down and waited for her to go on, suddenly tense and unsure of anything.

"I would like you to understand something," she began. "That is, as far as I can understand it myself. Simon told me once that I was trying to live with an illusion that could destroy me, and that was damaging Amelia. Perhaps he was right, but I could never seem to help myself. Cecelia was the baby I loved most. In my mind I built a life for that baby. I watched her grow up in my imagination. We were friends, as Amelia and I have become friends. Honoria has always said you would return, and I believed her. But I suppose I also believed in my own fabrication, and I expected the Cecelia who came back to me to be my make-believe daughter turned to flesh. A delusion, of course—though one it has been hard to give up."

I could understand about delusions—illusions—though mine were usually confined to my books. Now I wanted to offer her some reassurance that might lessen her difficulty in accepting me.

"Of course, we're strangers now, but that will begin to change when we get to know each other."

The look she gave me rejected such banality. "It's as if I've lost my daughter twice. Once as my baby, and now again when you are someone I don't know. Even your accent is wrong for any daughter of mine."

"A Yankee with southern blood?" I tried to smile, to lessen the tension that seemed to be growing in Valerie Mountfort. I could understand why everyone tried to protect and spare her. There seemed a fragility about her—as though a mere gust of wind might blow her away.

She sat a little straighter, and some spark lighted her beautiful eyes, surprising me. I remembered that someone had told me how lively and adventuresome she'd been as a young girl. Hadn't she and Charles's mother run off together on some escapade when they were girls?

"Never mind," she said. "It doesn't matter anymore. I know now that I can never recover my lost baby. And I don't want a substitute." She stood up, one hand touching her long fair braid. Her smile seemed bright and artificial, reducing me to a guest who must be courteously treated. When she moved, the faint scent of attar of roses reached me, bringing with it a sense of comfort, of safety that had no basis in reality. Some infant memory pressed into the baby she had held in her arms?

"There is one thing you could do for me," she said.

"Of course. Just tell me."

"Amelia said there was a letter that Simon wrote to you all those years ago. Will you let me see it?"

I was reluctant to let her read the letter. She was much too uncertain a quantity, and I had no way of knowing how she might react, but there seemed no way to refuse her. Once more I took the letter from my handbag and brought it to her. She switched on a lamp and began to read. Tears spilled down her cheeks as she read. I had no comfort to offer her, no words that might be useful.

When she'd read through to the end, she refolded the sheets and returned them to the envelope. "This is an illusion too, Cecelia—just another fantasy. Simon took blame for what others did to him. This guilt he carried had no basis in fact. I'm afraid he was often weak and ineffectual."

Her words disturbed me. I had pictured a loving marriage, but her tone of voice was bitter, unforgiving. Unforgiving of what?

Once more I went to stand before the portrait of Simon Mountfort where it hung above the mantel. "I can't find my father in this picture. His letter makes him more real to me. I wish I could have known him as he really was."

She came to stand beside me. "There's very little of the Simon I knew in that portrait. I never really liked it, though he did. The artist gave him a strength he never possessed in life."

I knew that strong, willful people had a tendency to dismiss as foolishly weak those who were gentle and considerate. Instinctively, something in me moved closer to my father, and away from Valerie Mountfort.

Abruptly she turned her back on the portrait, dismissing Simon from her life, and gave the letter back to me. "Of course Mountfort Hall must belong to Amelia—not you."

"I agree," I told her, but she went on as though the matter would be easily solved.

"Amelia tells me you are going to the rehearsal tonight, but I'm going to wait until I can see the real production. I've read her play and I think she has created something quite special."

"It's interesting that Amelia and I both like to write," I ventured.

Valerie shrugged. "Amelia gave me a copy of your new book, but I'm afraid it's not for me. I don't care for mystery stories. They're too disturbing and unsettling."

Especially when one lives in the midst of an unsolved mystery, I thought, and wondered if she turned away from that too.

"Did you like Nathanial Amory?" I asked on sudden impulse.

That seemed to trouble her. "No! No, I don't think I ever did. I told Simon that I didn't want this—this outsider teaching Daphne, or young Charles, who was practically our ward. However, Simon thought Nathanial would bring a broadening element into the children's lives. Certainly, his credentials seemed excellent."

"Why didn't you like him?"

"I didn't know him, really."

Because she was too lost in her grief over a stolen daughter? But she must have known him for some time before that tragedy happened.

"Of course, I regretted his shocking death," she went on. "But I wasn't sorry to have him removed from our lives. Of course, Simon was dreadfully upset. I think he never got over Nathanial's death—though it wasn't as if they'd been close friends. Simon blamed himself for too many things that were never his fault. He made me impatient at times. I hope you'll forgive me, Cecelia, but I'm beginning to feel tired. I was ill not long ago and I must take care of my strength. When Amelia comes home, will you please tell her I would like to see her?"

"Of course." I watched Valerie Mountfort as she went toward the door, and then asked one more question. "Did you ever own a pair of earrings made of coral—with the coral carved in the form of a lotus blossom?"

This seemed to surprise her. "Yes—I still have them. Simon ordered them made for me many years ago. I haven't worn them in years. How did you know about them?"

No suitable explanation came to me. "Katy Jackson showed me a book of Nathanial's poems when I stopped at the library to see her. One poem was called 'Ode to a Pink Lotus,' and I understand he was describing a pair of earrings. They sounded unusually beautiful and I was told they belonged to you." This was partly fabrication. I didn't want to admit to seeing the earring set in silver.

"They are beautiful. I'll show them to you sometime."

She went out of the room, her back held straight, with no drooping of her shoulders. Looking after her, I could feel nothing for the mother who had borne me. We were strangers in every way, and probably had very little in common to draw us together. So much for old fantasies I'd built about my "real" mother—and that Valerie had built about me.

I wondered idly if she would find *both* her coral earrings in her jewel case when she looked for them.

I waited until she had disappeared up the stairs before I started for my own room. Amelia stopped me by hurrying through the front door, and the sight of her shocked me. My sister had cut her hair. It hung loose just above her shoulders, as mine did, and had been curled under, copying my style.

She laughed at the look on my face, and drew me to stand before a mirror in the hall. The resemblance stunned me.

"What fun we'll have with this!" she cried. "Charles has said that with our hair cut alike no one could tell us apart. What tricks we can play!"

At that moment she seemed very young—a girl who wanted to play mischievous games. I wished that I didn't feel so dismayed by the resemblance. As if, somehow, I'd lost a piece of myself.

At least our expressions in the mirror were different, and Amelia mimicked my frown.

"What is it, Molly? I thought you'd be pleased."

"I'm pleased that I have a sister. But I don't want to fool anyone, or—"

"Don't be stuffy! Now I can become more like you. Confident and capable."

Those words hardly described the way I felt. "Until you open your mouth," I said. "No one will ever confuse our accents."

She heard someone coming up the outside steps and ran to a window. "There's Charles now! He's going to have supper here and take us to the theater. Let's begin, Molly. Watch this!"

She opened the door for Charles without speaking, and he gave her a warm smile. "Hi, Molly," he said, and turned toward me, only to be stricken with confusion.

Forcing herself not to smile, Amelia linked her arm through mine and we faced him together, even though I was reluctant to go along with this game. He hesitated only a moment, and then reached for Amelia, pulling her into his arms.

"You couldn't fool me for more than ten seconds," he said.

Amelia pouted her disappointment. "But how—"

Charles laughed. "Molly's the old lady. You're the child—a dead giveaway, Amelia."

I wasn't sure I liked that, but I felt relieved that the charade would fool no one for long. The differences between Amelia and

145

me went deeper than the surface, and anyone who knew either of us would easily tell us apart.

I'd forgotten something in my surprise over Amelia's hair. "Your mother wants to see you," I told her, and she nodded.

"I'll go right upstairs. I hope my hair won't upset her too much. Go on out to the kitchen and see what you can put together for supper—both of you."

Charles gave me his ready smile, and I was glad to be with someone who wasn't full of dark subterfuges, as Garrett Burke seemed to be.

"I'm glad you've come, Molly. You're good for your sister. But don't worry—there's no real identity crisis."

"What she did bothered me for a moment," I admitted. "I don't want to lose *me.*"

"No danger. I do wish, however, that Amelia were more like you. Oh well, come along and we'll see what's for supper, Molly. And you can tell me about your afternoon."

I edited as I went along, describing my walk through the Market, my exploration of Charleston Place—but without any mention of seeing Garrett and Daphne there. Then I retraced my steps and told him about my earlier meeting with Katy Jackson at the library.

"I understand you were all tutored together by Nathanial Amory, including Katy," I said. This was a subject I didn't seem able to leave.

"Right. Simon was always out in front with the civil rights movement. Kids don't start out with prejudice—it's handed to them by grown-ups. I'm glad your father could help us to avoid that."

"I remember something Douglas used to say—that prejudice means taking a stand against something you don't understand."

"The trouble is we don't always know what we don't understand. Well, enough of all this heavy stuff. Katy's mother will be there tonight, and so will mine. I've persuaded them to come and watch, since their kids are in the show."

Charles had led me away from the subject of Nathanial Amory, though this probably wasn't deliberate.

"How is your hand?" I asked. "Can you manage the duel tonight?"

"It's fine. I put on a bit of an act today to pay Garrett back. He was the one who got out of line, and I don't much trust him. But we'll do better tonight. Honoria will see to that."

"Why don't you like Garrett?"

Charles busied himself making sandwiches. "Who taught you to ask all these pointed questions, Molly? Is that the writer in you coming out? You remind me a little of your mother when she was younger and could be pretty feisty. Is this a throwback for you?"

"How would I know?"

"Well, I like your spirit and I like you. It's too bad you couldn't have stayed right here where you belonged. Just think how different things might be."

He gave me a searching look that I couldn't interpret. Just as I was beginning to feel ill at ease, Amelia joined us and fixed a plate for her mother. When she had taken it to Valerie and returned, we sat down to eat our informal meal.

Straight off, Amelia asked me a question, and her light-hearted mood had vanished. "Why did you show Mama our father's letter, Molly? It upset her badly."

"She knew about it and she wanted to see it. I couldn't avoid showing it to her. But she already seemed tense when we met. We talked about a number of things—as strangers might."

"But you're not strangers!" Amelia wailed. "Charles, help me on this—make her understand!"

147

Charles shook his head amiably. "You're on your own, honey. I'm sure Molly will manage just fine."

Amelia herself was not managing. I could sense a deep unease that sometimes bordered on fear. This was what troubled me. What was it that so disturbed my sister?

Perhaps tonight, if I were watchful, I might be given some direction. There must be something I could do to help Amelia with whatever it was that troubled her.

Nine

The Mountfort theater fronted on a narrow street with an alley stretching back along one side. It had once been an enormous warehouse and was a perfect building to contain a theater. The original brick construction showed on the lower half bordering the sidewalk, while the upper half still wore stucco that had been plastered over the brick. Two large arched doorways led into the lobby, and a colorful sign extended over the pavement in front.

On the sign, actors in fanciful costumes performed before an audience glimpsed in the background. The legend read:

STAGE CENTER PLAYERS
WORKSHOP

Charles opened a door, and Amelia and I stepped into the lobby, where photographs and playbills had been posted on the walls. The box office cage stood at one end, while two sets of swinging doors opened into the auditorium.

We entered through the left-hand door and I stood for a moment looking about in the dim light. Three banks of red upholstered seats, cut through by two aisles, sloped toward the brightly lighted stage. On either hand the exposed walls were the original redbrick. As a theater, it had not been prettified, but would serve its purpose very well. Once an audience was in place and the lights went down, only the stage would matter.

It was a small stage, probably best suited to intimate scenes. There was no proscenium arch, but a simple white border that framed it like a picture. A plain green backdrop separated the stage from whatever lay behind, and flies vanished into darkness overhead. Up on the stage, Daphne, Garrett, and Honoria appeared to be arguing enthusiastically. Honoria was not only directing this play, she was also performing—in her own role as director.

Tonight she wore jeans that must have been purchased in a child's store, and a blue smock that hung below her knees. She had tied a scarf patterned in green-and-blue mosaic figures over her hair, and knotted it high to give her a bit more stature. There was no apron to the stage, no footlight area, and she came to the edge and stood looking down at us as we approached.

"You're late, Charles! We can't get into the next scene without you and Amelia."

Charles hurried up the steps at the left to join her, but Amelia's hand on my arm kept me beside her as we looked up at Honoria. I was aware of Orva Jackson and Evaline Landry in the front row, and of Katy in the wings, waiting to come on.

Honoria stared from Amelia to me. "My God! Which of you is which?"

Before we'd left the house Amelia insisted that in this first appearance as identical twins, we should dress as nearly alike as possible. She had loaned me jeans and a denim shirt like the ones she was wearing, and of course her clothes fit me perfectly.

Amelia smiled up at her sweetly and pointed to me without speaking.

"Then get up here," Honoria ordered, accepting the deception. "We'll talk about your hair later."

"Take another look, Honoria," Charles told her as he strode out on the stage. "They're not *that* much alike."

Honoria could move faster than anyone I knew. She sped across the stage to the steps and flew down as though she hardly touched them. When she stopped before Amelia, she was bristling with disapproval.

"Your hair was so beautiful, Amelia! How could you bear to cut it?"

"There wasn't time to wait for Molly's to grow," Amelia told her. "And I wanted to see if we really looked alike. Don't be angry."

Charles laughed in enjoyment of Honoria's confusion, and Daphne, who handled the props for the play, came to stand beside him, looking down. Even Katy stepped from the wings to see what was happening, and I was aware of Orva's arrested attention. Mrs. Landry's expression seemed guarded, as though she

151

avoided family arguments. Garrett remained apart, studying the script in his hands, though I suspected that he missed nothing.

"Charles was right," Daphne said. "If you keep your mouths shut, nobody can tell you apart." Her eyes danced with their own green light, and up there on the stage she seemed an impressive figure, nearly as tall as Charles.

I couldn't join in the fun. "I'll certainly open my mouth," I told Daphne. "I don't want to confuse anybody."

"Good for you, Molly," Honoria approved. "No tricks."

Garrett—never the handsome hero, shorter and stockier than Charles—looked up from the pages in his hand and caught my eye with an oddly sympathetic look. I wondered wryly if he thought we were aligned against southern forces.

"Never mind!" Honoria cried impatiently. "Do get up there, Amelia, so we can get on with this scene."

I sat beside Orva in the front row, while Amelia ran up to join the others.

Honoria returned to her director's duties. "This is the scene where Amelia has hidden the Union soldier, and you, Charles, come in right center, expecting to be greeted joyfully by your sweetheart—Miss Sunshine here—whose hair is now all wrong for her part."

Amelia didn't mind the jibe. She bent to drop a kiss on Honoria's cheek, and was rebuffed at once.

"Don't take liberties with the director! You can't get around me that way. I want to see you do a lot better with the dialogue than last time. You may be the author, but we still have to make you into an actor."

As they went on, I found that Honoria was the one I watched. She seemed to know everyone's part, and when one of the actors' attempts didn't please her, she would throw herself into the role and play the scene vigorously. She even caught

Garrett's northern accent when he was hauled out of hiding by the Confederate soldier. And she could mimic Amelia beautifully.

Once she stopped everything to lecture the whole company. "Stage Center doesn't usually put such amateurs into its plays. Charleston will come to see you because of the Mountfort name. You're family, in a sense, and they'll enjoy and forgive. But I'd like to see you give a good performance and surprise everyone."

After that, Charles and Amelia seemed to make more of an effort, though I wasn't sure about Garrett.

Katy, as the family maid, had a few lines when she first opposed Charles as he burst into what was apparently the parlor of a southern mansion. She delivered her lines pertly and made her own small impact, so that I hoped Orva was pleased. I couldn't tell by looking at her handsome profile, but she was pulled forward slightly in her seat and I felt sure she was enjoying herself.

Daphne dealt capably with props, and acted as stage manager, keeping well out of Honoria's way. There was no question about who was in charge, and after one of Honoria's outbursts, Orva surprised me by laughing softly. As I'd thought, Honoria, too, was performing.

Charles would look wonderful in a Confederate uniform— born to the part. Garrett, by contrast, as the Union soldier being hidden by the southern belle, played his role less gallantly. I could only hope that Honoria would whip him into shape before the actual performance.

The duel scene, to be fought with the type of swords officers had worn, was executed with gusto, and Charles managed all of his choreographed moves with natural grace. Garrett, far the clumsier of the two, at least behaved properly, and fell wounded at stage left as he was supposed to do. He looked over the edge of the stage at me and winked as the scene ended where the curtain

153

would come down on the first act. In the next scene Amelia was a delightful spitfire, excoriating Charles as a murderer, weeping wildly over her dying hero, and clearly enjoying a role that was far from her everyday nature.

"Good!" Honoria approved. "You're just right, Amelia. But, Charles, don't turn your part into a caricature. Play down the noble hero, or the audience will laugh. Besides, they won't be sure who the hero is when Garrett comes back in his spirit role. All right—let's take a break, and then we'll get into the first ghost scene."

I glanced at Orva next to me and the expression on her face revealed that she was having a very good time. Beyond her, Mrs. Landry unbent enough to give me a slight smile. I had noticed her staring at me several times during the evening, but every time I looked at her, she would turn her attention back to the stage.

"Charles will be fine," she said complacently, treating me to another one of her penetrating glances. "Of course, Amelia wrote the part for him."

"Of course," I said, wondering why I didn't like her.

I'd watched long enough and before Honoria called the company together for the next scene, I took the opportunity to slip out to explore backstage. Garrett had told me to be sure to see what was back there, so I ran up the few steps at the side and disappeared into the wings. Nobody would miss me, I was sure. At once I found myself in a dimly lighted and utterly confusing world.

Down a few steps, I passed a lighted dressing room and glanced in to see the room-long makeup shelf with a mirror covering the wall above it. Assorted chairs were pulled up to individual places, and makeup kits stood about on the shelf, probably belonging to actors in the current play. Tonight was their night off, freeing the theater for Honoria to call a rehearsal. I

154

glimpsed a woman's wig on a stand, and a pair of high-heeled red satin slippers tossed on the floor. The men's dressing room was probably on the other side.

A narrow aisle led to steps that descended to a lower level. It was here that I became aware of the enormous area that spread out backstage. The theater itself occupied only a tiny corner of the whole. Overhead everything disappeared into murk, lighted only by an occasional bare light bulb, hanging down on a wire.

At once I was a writer, my imagination caught by this fantastic scene. How I would use it in a story didn't matter at this point. What counted was the strong sense of excitement that set my imagination to work. A fiction writer needed to retain a childlike wonder over anything that was new and different, and I had no trouble in achieving a sense of delight in the scene around me—a rich setting for a mystery novel.

This entire area was a world inhabited by props—anything at all that might ever be used in a play—or had been used and saved for next time. Aisles crisscrossed in a grid pattern walled in by high shelves and cabinets. The "filing system," if any, seemed strange. Racks of garments—some modern, some period—stood near shelves of dishes. A cardboard box of men's hats decorated a small refrigerator. Two tall artificial palm trees, needing new fronds, leaned over an umbrella stand. A small iron garden seat, its fretwork painted a dingy white, stood next to an overstuffed armchair that had seen better days. One section of shelves held nothing but wigs, covered by a sheet of plastic.

Farther along, up a slope in the uneven floor, boards and ladders had been piled beside a long workbench. Whatever was needed could probably be built right back here.

On a cross aisle, leading more deeply into this dusky confusion, stood lamps of every variety—table lamps, desk lamps, standing lamps, and even a tall streetlight standard that would

155

simulate gaslight. Around another corner a lonely coffeepot tilted against an ancient typewriter. And over everything the high dangling light bulbs threw shadows that sometimes seemed to move without cause or reason. Because some errant thread of wind blew through this place? The air, on the other hand, was hardly fresh and I became aware of the mingled smells of dust and mustiness.

As I wandered about, I tried to make mental notes, but there was too much to absorb and I couldn't possibly remember it all. Perhaps I would return and snap a few flash pictures of whatever caught my eye. Instinctively I knew that anything at all might happen in this lonely, remote place. I paused to listen for the sound of wind and realized that I could barely hear sounds from the stage.

Turning into a new section, I came upon a medieval weapon —a long pole with an ax head set just below its tip. A halberd? It stood upright against an unattached door that led nowhere. I wondered if it would be useful to one of my characters as friend or foe. Certainly it would make an unusual weapon in the hands of a villainous character. When had the required bop-on-the-head been delivered by a medieval halberd?

So deeply was I into my story, with bits of action coming to life in my mind, that Honoria's sudden screeching rage from the distant stage seemed an intrusion. I would have to go back. Something was driving Honoria wild, and it would be interesting to see which one of her actors had so infuriated her.

When I found my way back to the wings, I could look out upon the stage, where Garrett Burke was playing his spirit scene. I stayed out of sight to watch Honoria's dramatic displeasure.

"You're a *ghost,* Garrett! You can't go clumping around like that. You'll have dim lighting to help you, and maybe we'll blow in a little mist, but if you go stomping around and bumping into furniture, you'll wreck the illusion."

Garrett's back was toward me, and its set suggested that he didn't take criticism well. I'd already felt that he didn't want to be in this play, and I wondered why he had joined the company in the first place.

From the wings Daphne spoke to him quietly. "Hey—take it easy, Garrett. She's right, you know."

His back seemed to relax a little. "Okay, Honoria—maybe I'd better resign right now. Find yourself another Yankee soldier."

Honoria changed her tactics at once. "It's too late for that. I'm sorry I got mad, Garrett. We're all wound up tonight, and I think you'll be fine when you begin to think about the character you're playing. You've just returned as a spirit, and you're not sure where you are, or what you are. You probably aren't even aware that you're dead. So we need a lighter touch and a lot more bewilderment. This is where Amelia's character sees you for the first time, and she's shocked and terrified. She can't forgive Charles for killing you, but how can she be in love with a spirit? Try to get the feeling of what's going on, Garrett. You've been doing research out at Mountfort Hall. So think of Nathanial. Amelia, it is Nathanial you've based your Union soldier on, isn't it?"

Daphne, watching from the wings, made a slight motion of rejection, as though Honoria's words upset her. But Amelia answered readily.

"That's right. The way you seem to evoke Nathanial's spirit gave me the idea. Let your imagination go, Garrett, and pretend a little."

Garrett wasn't smiling and he didn't look cooperative. "Sorry," he said, "but I'm not in the right mood for ghosts. Can you let me off for now, Honoria? Go ahead with the scene between Charles and Amelia."

"All right—time out!" Honoria turned her back on him in

157

displeasure and spoke to Amelia. "Get those stars out of your eyes, honey. You're not sure about Charles yet, and you're stricken because of what he's done. You've been half in love with your Union soldier ever since you hid him in the house—so don't fall into Charles's arms. Do it the way you've written it. Your own dialogue lifts the scene out of the obvious."

Garrett came off the stage, moving so quickly that he bumped into me. At once he grabbed my elbow.

"Let's get out of here. I've had enough."

"I'm not going anywhere," I told him, retrieving my arm. "I came to watch, and that's what I'm going to do."

"You can come back to this drivel in an hour, if you like. They'll still be here. I want to show you something."

All that male impatience, and especially his dismissal of Amelia's writing, rubbed me the wrong way. Nevertheless my writer's curiosity was surfacing and I wanted to know what Garrett was up to. He was part of the puzzle I'd begun to feel driven to solve. When he strode through the dim backstage area toward the stage door, I followed him.

At least he waited for me at the door, and guided me down the few steep steps to the alley. The passageway, narrow and partly walled, opened to cross streets at either end. Vines grew over brick walls, and tree branches threw moving shadows in a light breeze. Through thin haze a half moon bathed the entire scene in an unearthly patina. A scent of flowers came to me, and the smell of river and sea.

Garrett put his hands lightly on my shoulders and turned me about. "Look up," he directed.

I tilted my head back to see the lighted spire of a church reaching magically into the sky. The garnet night glow of the city back-lighted the brighter steeple. Blank windows circled a spire that pointed toward the moon, and shadows sculpted the whole, giving it mysterious form.

"That's St. Philip's," Garrett said. "More Charleston history. John C. Calhoun is buried in the churchyard there, and in more recent times, DuBose Heyward, who wrote *Porgy.* Just let yourself feel what's there."

The high golden spire seemed to shed tranquillity upon the lower roofs of the city. It stood so far above troubled human emotions that the sight of its serene beauty lifted my own spirits. The moment seemed both exalting and quieting at the same time. This was a gift I would never have expected from Garrett Burke.

"Thank you," I told him softly.

His own anger seemed to have stilled, and whatever disturbed him had subsided for the moment. He dropped his hands from my shoulders, satisfied that I had seen what he wanted me to see.

"There's a café on the next street where we can have coffee, if you care to join me, Molly. Then you can go back to the theater."

Dreamily, I went with him in the direction of the far cross street, still caught up by an enchantment I didn't want to lose. We followed the uneven bricks of the narrow alley, and I was aware of old trees, and of lighted windows beyond walls on either hand.

"This is Philadelphia Alley," he told me as we walked along. "Real duels used to be fought here—though usually with pistols."

It was easy to imagine the dramas that had been played in this shadowy place.

We crossed the street where little traffic passed at this hour, and went up a few steps to the café. Inside were small round tables with marble tops, and old-fashioned ice cream parlor chairs set around each one. We chose a table where we could look out at the street. Garrett ordered Key lime pie and coffee, while I asked only for coffee. When we faced each other across the little table, I no longer felt that I had any sure knowledge of this man. He seemed filled with emotions I hadn't expected, and I didn't know how to deal with either his anger or his gentleness.

"You look disembodied," he told me.

"That's a good word for what I've been feeling ever since I came to Charleston. I'm no longer sure of who I am, or where I belong. I seem to be floating between two worlds, and I don't like that feeling. Before I left the South Battery house, I phoned my father—my adoptive father—but I felt strangely alienated from him. Since my mother died he's begun to slip away from everything around him. Yet I haven't any feeling of being Simon Mountfort's daughter either. I don't like drifting. I want to take hold of something solid."

"Amelia is real enough," Garrett said. "If you're beginning to care about her, that's a start."

"I believe I am. And I don't want to leave until I understand what is happening to her. If she's in any sort of trouble, perhaps I can help a little."

Our orders came and I sipped hot black coffee and let it warm me all the way through. My chill had nothing to do with the Charleston evening.

"I'm a good listener," Garrett said. "If you care to talk."

"There isn't anything to tell you, really. That's the trouble. The way I feel, I could almost play the Yankee ghost. But, Garrett, Amelia hasn't written drivel, as you called it. The right actors could bring her words to life."

"I know. That was the wrong word to use. I like Amelia. I just don't like the direction she's taking with Charles."

"With a Confederate soldier."

He grimaced. "Don't tease me! I'm concerned for your sister."

"Because she's in love with Charles? Can anyone be too much in love? I think I envy her. Why don't you like Charles?"

160

He grinned at me—an easy grin, with tension gone. "Maybe I'm envious too."

"Because you're attracted to Amelia?"

"I'm fond of her and don't want to see her hurt. Perhaps I'm envious of the way everything has been made easy for Charles."

"He wasn't born with any silver spoon."

"Maybe not, but he's had a lot handed to him. And now he'll be one of the Mountfort clan, which, I suppose, is what he's always wanted. His mother has wanted that too. And she's been looking forward to being more than the docent at Mountfort Hall. Of course, your father's bequest has put a kink in those plans."

There seemed a sadness in his voice that puzzled me. I couldn't really believe that he was envious of Charles Landry. Garrett seemed too much his own man.

"I've been ignoring that part of his letter. It shocked and pleased me, but I don't *want* Mountfort Hall."

The little café formed a square of light above the street. Only one other table was in use, so the room was quiet. I looked out the window and down the alley through which we'd just come. St. Philip's spire still floated in a golden haze at the far end. Garrett, too, looked out toward the lighted steeple and began to speak almost dreamily.

"Honoria believes in destiny. You've heard her. She thinks you were brought here for some special purpose, Molly. Your father's letter seems to confirm that premise."

"I don't accept that! I want a destiny of my own. I'd like to find the right path for myself through all of this, but how can I? I'm an outsider."

"Not to your sister. Have you seen the way she looks at you sometimes—with so much loving trust?"

"I'm not sure I want that."

161

"You've already begun to take hold. Just step carefully and stay alert. Be sure people don't mistake you for her, now that she's cut her hair."

I didn't understand his meaning, but I felt too content to ask. I'd finished my coffee, and Garrett had eaten the last of his pie. "Thank you for this—respite," I said. "Now I'd better get back to the theater."

A few minutes later we walked through the alley again, between walled gardens and the piazzas that overlooked them. When we reached the stage door, he put a hand lightly on my arm.

"I won't go in, Molly. I've had enough for tonight. Thanks for coming out with me. I'll walk back to my place—it's not far away."

Our parting seemed oddly formal in contrast to that almost intimate moment when he had shared the view of the church spire with me. We said a polite good night, and he opened the stage door for me. Then he went off toward the street that fronted the theater. When the door swung closed behind me, I found myself again in that world of wild fantasy that existed behind the stage.

The great spaces seemed even darker than before, with those unshaded bulbs that hung from crossbeams shedding a feeble light. Overhead, all detail vanished into thick darkness reaching up to the distant ceiling. No sounds from the stage reached me, and I was suddenly uncertain of its direction. The aisle I'd followed had taken a couple of turns, and my sense of direction was gone as completely as though I'd never been here before.

I disliked the stillness most of all. Everything was too quiet and I recognized none of the objects around me. A row of smiling–frowning theater masks looked down at me from a high shelf as if enjoying my confusion, and mysteriously added to it. I wondered if the others had given up and left without me—though surely Amelia would have waited and looked for me.

At random I took another turn, assured myself that the rest of the company certainly wouldn't go off leaving lights burning and the side door unlocked. In a moment I would find some landmark I recognized and would reorient myself.

I passed a dressmaker's dummy on its stand, with a broom propped against it—nothing I'd seen before. The unaired, musty smell of the place pressed down on me, so that I longed for a breath of fresh air. But now I'd even lost the direction of the alley door. On the floor a basket of make-believe rocks blocked my way, and I stepped around it uncertainly. A nearby table held plates of cleverly modeled artificial food, and a red hot water bottle hung limply over the handle of a teakettle set on a bench. Two tall German beer tankards stood stolidly beside an empty bottle of French wine.

I rejected the unsettling notion that I had stepped into a madman's dream. These things had simply collected over the years, and no one had imposed a filing system that would make sense. It would all be perfect for a story, and I should start thinking like a mystery writer again. If the place felt a little creepy to me, that was fine—I must savor, remember, use. Was that really a footstep I heard not far away? If it was real, it was probably someone looking for a prop, not dreaming I was here.

"Hello!" I called out, but no sound answered me except for the creaking and whispering of an ancient warehouse. The building wasn't as silent as I'd thought. A board squeaked nearby—a sound that could only have been made by a foot. A secret foot, since the person hadn't answered my call. Suddenly I did what none of my heroines would ever have done—I panicked and

163

started to run. There was an aisle ahead of me, and it didn't matter where it led.

Three steps that led to another level came up suddenly and I didn't see them in the dim light. When I tripped over the bottom step, I tried wildly to catch my balance as I stumbled up, managing to reach the level above. There I fell forward with a tremendous clatter and went off into floating darkness.

I knew later that I'd banged my head on the corner of an iron wood-burning stove as I fell. I have no idea how long it was until throbbing awareness returned. My head seemed to contain a beating hammer, and I stayed still until the sensation quieted a little.

The crash of my fall had brought no one to rescue me, so I was still alone. The floor where I lay smelled dusty, yet slightly fishy. Under a table inches from my nose were cardboard boxes filled with seashells—uncleaned and definitely fishy.

At first I was too stunned to be frightened. The throbbing in my head took all my attention. Alarm came when I put out a hand to push myself up from the floor, and set it upon a long pole that stretched beside me, its ax head turned inward toward my face. For a moment I lay staring at the medieval halberd I had seen earlier leaning against a disembodied door that was now nowhere in sight. The same curious question formed in my mind, directed at the weapon itself: friend or foe?

I picked it up and used it as a staff to help me get shakily to my feet. It could be my friend for now, if I needed a weapon. Though why I should need one seemed fantastic. Behind me were the three steps I'd stumbled up. The halberd hadn't been used against me—I had banged my head in falling. Nevertheless, it seemed as though someone had placed it carefully beside me as I lay unconscious and had gone away without trying to help. Or perhaps that someone might still be out there watching me, listening? I remembered my earlier sense of a presence in this dim and silent world—and now I grew really frightened.

The scream that tore out of my throat wasn't planned or controlled. It simply happened. And it wasn't a single scream. I yelled my head off, so that if anyone was left in the building they'd hear me. Or, if some enemy lurked nearby, my shrieking might frighten him off.

It was Charles who found me, guided by the uproar I was making. He put his arms tightly around me. "Stop it, Molly! You're all right now. What happened?"

Clinging to his shoulder, I muffled the sounds I hadn't known I could make, and he patted me soothingly.

"We were waiting out front for you to show up, Molly. I'd just started down the auditorium to turn off a few lights when I heard you howling."

Screaming hadn't helped my head, but at least I stopped trembling when Charles held me.

"I'm sorry. I got lost back here, so I didn't know where anything was. I thought I heard someone and I panicked and started to run. That's when I fell up those steps and banged my head on the stove. All terribly foolish. I have too much imagination. Please get me out of here, Charles."

He led me to the darkened stage, then up an aisle through empty seats. I hadn't looked again at the halberd he had taken out of my hands and left behind. The thought of it only frightened me and I didn't tell him that I thought someone had left it beside me deliberately. When we reached the well-lighted lobby, the others crowded around me, and Amelia saw at once that I was hurt.

"Molly, your forehead's bleeding! Here—let me." She used tissue to dab at the blood, and someone brought me a glass of water and aspirin tablets. When I'd swallowed them I looked around, not trying to figure anything out, but just checking.

Honoria hovered anxiously beside Amelia. Katy and Orva stood back, waiting for whatever happened next. It seemed to me that Orva watched me intently. Apparently, only Charles had heard my screaming. It was his mother, Mrs. Landry, who made a sensible suggestion.

"Take your sister home, Amelia. Bandage that cut and get her to bed. You can see that she's had enough excitement for one evening."

Daphne Phelps, who had stayed outside on the street, came in and was told what had happened. Of them all, she seemed the least disturbed. "You ought to have better sense, Molly, than to go poking around back there when you don't know the place. It's lucky you didn't break your neck."

Charles said nothing about my suspicion that someone else had been back there with me, and I left that out, since what had happened was already beginning to sound like fantasy. Except for the halberd.

"I wasn't poking around," I told Daphne. "Garrett brought me to the side door, and I expected to find my way to the stage easily when I came in. But I took some wrong turns, and there weren't any sounds or lights to guide me to where I wanted to go. I got confused, and after I fell I panicked."

They all stared as though I'd suddenly grown two heads. "Garrett?" Honoria echoed. "Did you go outside with Garrett?"

"Yes. We had coffee at some little place, and he brought me back. He thought you'd go on rehearsing for some time."

"We tried," Amelia said. "But Garrett left such a hole in the second act that we gave up. We didn't know where you had gone."

166

"No professional actor would behave the way Garrett did!" Honoria fumed. "Maybe we *should* replace him."

Amelia slipped an arm around her. "You said yourself it's too late to make changes now, and besides, he was your choice in the first place."

"I'll talk to him," Daphne offered. "Of course, we can't make changes now. He'll work out—you'll see." She sounded fond and tolerant and the matter was left in Daphne's hands.

Honoria picked up my wrist and turned it so that the strawberry mark could be seen. "Molly, dear, I can feel it pulsing."

"That's my heart thumping," I said impatiently.

She shook her head, her eyes dreamy, distant. "It's begun. There's no turning back now. Something happened, didn't it, Molly? Something that threatened you?" She must have seen the rejection in my face, for she went on quickly. "Never mind. We'll talk another time. Evaline's right—Amelia must get you home."

But as we moved toward the street doors, Daphne stopped us. "Tonight we had an audience for the first time—even though we didn't give them much of a show. Before we go home and forget about it, we ought to know what they think. Katy? You were watching from the wings."

Katy, who was closest to the door, turned back. "What I've seen has caught my interest. I have a feeling that Amelia's writing is getting beneath the usual North–South clichés. And of course it's antiwar. I'm curious to see where she's going with this."

I didn't want to stand here listening to talk about the play, but Amelia needed to hear what was being said.

"Orva?" Daphne asked. "Tell us what you think?"

Orva was the tallest one there—taller than Charles—and she managed to convey more dignity than the rest of us. "Bringing back the spirit of that Union soldier can maybe stir up what's best left alone—like Miss Honoria is doing out at the Hall."

167

"Don't go spooky on us, Orva," Daphne said quickly. "It's only a play."

"And the play's the thing, of course," Charles said lightly. "Daphne, this isn't the time for impromptu reviews. Take Molly back to the house—she's about out on her feet."

But Daphne had one more question, which she directed to Evaline Landry. "Tell us what you think—please."

"For me it's not credible," Mrs. Landry admitted. She caught my eyes upon her and smiled slightly. "But then—nothing that has happened in the last few days is really credible, is it?"

All I wanted was to lie down somewhere and wait for my head to stop throbbing. Charles whispered in my ear, "Time to get you to bed." He pushed a door open and we went out into the pleasant coolness of the evening. I breathed deeply of those mingled odors that were beginning to smell like Charleston to me.

As we reached Charles's car, Orva spoke to me directly. "Will you be coming back out to the Hall pretty soon, Miss Molly? I've been thinking about things that happened when your daddy was a little boy growing up out there. I was some older, so maybe there's stories I can tell you." I thanked her and said I would come out when I felt better.

Mrs. Landry had driven Orva in and together they had picked up Katy, so they returned to her car. When Daphne went off on her own, Charles drove Amelia and me back to the South Battery house.

"We won't tell Mama what happened to you," Amelia decided. "She's already upset about my cutting my hair, and I don't want to add to her distress."

I didn't want to tell anybody anything. When we stopped in front of the house, Amelia kissed Charles warmly and told him she'd see him tomorrow. He gave me a strange long look, as though he wanted to tell me something before he drove away. Instead he ruffled my hair affectionately and left.

Once in the house, I hurried up to my room, undressed, and got under the covers. Amelia brought me a glass of hot milk with amaranth cookies, and sat with me for a little while. The hammering in my head subsided and I could listen to her sleepily.

"Garrett should never have let you come in the stage door by yourself," she told me. "He really behaved badly tonight. I can tell you how sick of him Charles is becoming. He even thinks Uncle Porter ought to fire him from the writing job he's doing about Mountfort Hall. Though I can't agree with that. I've read some of what he's written and he's really good. Anyway, it will all simmer down, and we'll do better with the next rehearsal. Even Honoria got out of hand tonight. Nobody should ever shout at Garrett. Not with that chip he wears on his shoulder."

I lay back on my pillow, pleasantly drowsy. "Garrett showed me something wonderful tonight. He took me into the alley outside the stage door, where I could see the steeple of St. Philip's floating above Charleston. The sight made me feel quieter and more peaceful than I've felt since I came, and I'm grateful to him."

"I know. Garrett can change from one minute to the next. Daphne will know how to handle him. She's closer to him than any of us."

I was practically asleep, and Amelia dropped a kiss on my cheek, and whispered, "Good night, sister." By the time she closed my door, I must have been deeply asleep.

The sound that wakened me was one I couldn't identify—a soft, regular movement that had a hard edge to it. Somehow I sensed that it was a familiar sound out of my childhood. It appeared to come from another part of this floor, and I knew I wouldn't get back to sleep until I'd identified the muffled, steady thumping.

When I sat up I saw that Amelia must have unpacked for me, since my terry robe lay over the foot of the bed, and my slippers had been set out. My head no longer throbbed and when I touched the bandage Amelia had placed over the cut on my forehead, I felt only a slight stinging.

I slipped into my robe and slippers and opened the bedroom door softly. The sound grew louder, and now I recognized what it was. On the far side of the house, where a screen shielded the area where trunks and boxes had been stored, the rocking horse, which had kept the secret of my father's letter for all these years, was thumping back and forth on the bare floor, as though propelled by some persistent rider.

Ten

The upstairs hall sitting room, on which several bedrooms opened, was illumined at this hour by a single table lamp. At the front it opened onto a small balcony two stories above the front door. I stood for a moment looking about, listening intently. I'd slept deeply for several hours, but I was wide awake now and both curious and uneasy. The other bedroom doors were closed and nothing stirred, so Amelia and her mother must not have heard what I had heard.

Since there was no sound now coming from anywhere, I stepped out on the balcony beneath the stars. On either side the splendid white houses of South Battery slept peacefully and regally in the glow of streetlights. The balconies of the houses in either direction repeated patterned white balustrades over and over. Along the near shore paths of yellow light floated across harbor waters. Somewhere behind me on another street someone was playing a jazz piano, clearly improvising.

For a few moments the night seemed to quiet me, and then the thumping sound began again. This time it didn't stop when I returned to the sitting room, and I could tell that it did indeed come from the screened area of the dark storeroom.

I moved quietly in that direction and found a light switch. At once the wooden rocking horse ceased its vigorous movement, slowing gently to a stop. No one rode its back, and no one hid among the trunks and boxes, except for Miss Kitty. I might have suspected her of rocking the horse, but she stood poised on the lid of a trunk with her fur puffed to twice its size. Even her tail bristled in alarm. Yet out at Mountfort Hall she'd seemed happy playing with Nathanial's "spirit." So whatever presence moved the rocking horse must have seemed inimical to the cat.

I shook myself impatiently, dismissing such nervous and exaggerated imaginings. But when something touched my shoulder, I almost screamed. I swung around to find Valerie Mountfort behind me, smiling apologetically.

"I'm sorry, Cecelia. I didn't mean to startle you. I heard the horse rocking so I came out—and here you were, ahead of me. But of course it stopped, as it always does when someone comes near it."

In her long white nightgown, with ruffled lace at her wrists, she looked like a beautiful ghost herself. Fair hair curled about her forehead in short locks, while the rest hung in its long braid down her back. In this light she looked amazingly young—younger than Amelia. As though life had been arrested for her somewhere in the past. As illusion, of course, since I'd seen her sad, worn look by daylight.

She perched herself on the rounded top of a low old-fashioned trunk, her knees pulled up under her voluminous gown and her hands clasped about them. Nearby, Miss Kitty relaxed, her fur subsiding.

This strange woman who was supposed to be my mother regarded me calmly. "Don't go back to bed right away, Cecelia. Stay a little while and talk to me. I've rested so much today that I'm wide awake, and I won't sleep now. It must be around three o'clock."

I was wide awake too, and I sat down on a stool, waiting uncertainly for whatever would happen next. Miss Kitty suddenly sprang past me and flew through the air to land on the back of the rocking horse, setting it gently in motion. Apparently whatever had alarmed her was gone, and the rocking horse was her friend again.

"Is it the cat who does this?" I asked.

"It happens when she's not in the house, and she could never rock the horse that hard. I haven't heard our visiting spirit for some time. Perhaps it's your presence that has brought it back—to see what you're up to, Cecelia? The horse really belongs out at the plantation, along with other family ghosts. I must have it sent out there soon."

She spoke calmly, as though she took such matters as visiting spirits for granted.

When I didn't comment, she went on. "How did you hurt your head, Cecelia?"

I touched the small bandage. "It's nothing. I was exploring the theater tonight. I got lost backstage in the storehouse of props

173

and fell over some steps. I banged my head pretty hard. Unpleasant, but not serious."

"How did the rehearsal go?"

"Not very well, I'm afraid. Garrett Burke upset Honoria, and when she got peeved with him, he walked out."

Valerie lowered her knees, her bare feet on the floor, and Miss Kitty stopped playing king-of-the-hill on the rocking horse and sprang onto Valerie's lap, asking for attention. When my mother smoothed her fur affectionately, the little cat began to purr.

"I wish she could talk," Valerie said. "Sometimes I think she knows more about what's happening than anyone else."

"What do you think is happening?" I couldn't call her either Mother or Valerie, and I felt disturbed by the spark that I sensed in her in these dark hours of the morning, as though a conflagration might be starting that I wouldn't be able to put out. Perhaps she wasn't as frail as everyone seemed to think.

She went on, quietly reminiscing. "Sometimes I make a comparison with the swamp at Cypress Gardens. We used to go there sometimes for picnics. Especially when the azaleas were in bloom. My mother was old then, but she loved that eerie place."

Her mother—my grandmother. The connection was there, if only I could find a way to pick up the thread and accept a past that still didn't seem real to me.

"The swamp can be utterly still," she went on dreamily. "Its green surface reaches like a carpet in all directions, with cypress trees growing out of it singly and in clumps. The green color is because of the duckweed that covers the surface and never shows a wrinkle unless there's a ripple of wind. Then it drifts and you can glimpse the black water underneath. On the surface it all seems still and peaceful—the way our lives used to be. When Porter and I were young, and Simon was—different. He was my first love, my only love. I looked up to him as I'd never done to anyone else. Until I married him, and found out what he was really like."

Once more I found myself shrinking from her criticism of my father.

Her voice quickened. "The swamp is quiet, smooth—until a storm blows up. Then it comes to life and roils itself over, as though the bottom were being dredged up and all its secrets exposed. Strange objects float to the surface that no one knew were hidden beneath all that peaceful green. Are you the storm, Cecelia? The storm that's causing hidden secrets to float to the top of our lives and reveal themselves?"

"If that's what's happening, it's not my choice," I told her. "Though perhaps what has been buried for too long *ought* to surface."

"No!" Her sudden vehemence startled me. "Let the swamp hide all that's ugly and shouldn't be revealed. Then we can be safe and happy again. I think that's what Simon wanted. I was often too impatient with him. I asked too much of him. I wanted my baby returned, and he couldn't give me that. If I hadn't been the way I was, perhaps he needn't have died."

She seemed to be of two minds, reversing herself.

"I've been told that he was ill. His heart."

Valerie steadied herself, grew quiet again—too carefully quiet. "Yes. He never told *me*. He didn't trust me enough. Perhaps he had reason not to trust me."

In spite of her apparent self-criticism, I wondered how aware she really was of her effect on my father. Simon's attitude might not have had anything to do with "trust," but might have grown out of a desire not to cause her pain.

She went on as though she mused aloud, stroking the cat absently. "I stopped loving him long ago. I was too young and I married an imaginary man. I'd thought of Simon as strong and

175

wise—like my cousin Porter—but, in reality, he was only weak and ineffectual."

Porter strong and wise? My sympathy was entirely with Simon Mountfort.

Abruptly, Valerie pushed the cat off her knees. Miss Kitty did a corkscrew turn in the air and landed on her feet, immediately sitting down to wash her face.

"I have an idea, Cecelia. You don't really want to go back to bed, do you?"

Mischief had touched her, and it made me all the more uneasy. "What do you have in mind?"

"Let's get dressed. Quietly, so Amelia won't suspect what we're up to. Amelia would stop us and I don't want that. We can take my car—it's only a little way to go."

"A little way to where?"

"It's a surprise. You'll see when we get there."

"At three in the morning?"

"That's the best hour. The time of dark bewitching! Don't be stuffy, Cecelia. Get dressed and I'll meet you downstairs."

Our roles had been reversed. She seemed the younger one now—a girl bent on some escapade. Yet if I awakened Amelia, I might never find out what Valerie intended. I needn't like or trust this woman to go with her. I just needed to be watchful. Of course, at that time, I had no suspicion of her trickery.

Miss Kitty came with me to my room, and observed me as I put on gray pants and a light jacket. She seemed to find my behavior interesting, but normal. I wondered what went on in her little cat brain. Sometimes she showed her own special intelligence, but she had no way to analyze or evaluate except by interest. Certainly I had no desire to go back to bed.

"Go to sleep, cat," I told her. "And don't inform anyone that I'm going off with my mother."

176

She gave me a slow blink, and curled up on the bed, closing her eyes, her tail wound under her chin.

When I went down, Valerie was waiting for me at the foot of the stairs.

"You took forever, Cecelia."

It was the first time I had seen her out of her frilly lounging clothes. She'd put on a swirly flowered skirt and a light pink sweater to protect her against breezes that could sweep up the peninsula from the ocean. What startled me, however, were the clip earrings she had chosen to wear—coral carved in the form of a lotus and set in gold. Duplicates of the single earring I'd seen earlier today, except that the one Garrett had shown me was set in silver. Apparently, whatever the mystery of the single earring, it had nothing to do with Valerie Mountfort, whose earring set was intact.

She touched one ear with a finger. "You wanted to see them, so I put them on."

"They're beautiful," I said, and let it go at that.

When she opened the front door and ran down the steps to the sidewalk, I followed more slowly. A passageway led along one side of the house to where she kept her car in a rear courtyard. I got in beside her, aware of her strange excitement, and of that sense of mischief that still held and made me distrustful.

I had no map of Charleston firmly in mind yet, so I couldn't follow the turns she took—a fact that would be of no help to me later on when I might need to know where I was.

The streets were empty and quiet, except for an occasional all-night party going on. Even the gardens seemed more mysterious than by day, and were alive only to night creatures. Flower scents were sweeter than ever. From river to river, and clear to the ocean tip of the land, where the two rivers met, Charleston slept.

A few blocks along what Valerie told me was Broad Street I

177

saw an impressive building built squarely across its end, stucco over brick. Valerie turned the car toward the curb and parked in front of the building. Streetlights made it clearly visible and I saw high steps mounting on either hand to a white Palladian doorway.

Valerie's excitement held, and a strange eagerness drove her. I wondered if I could handle whatever might be about to happen. For now I could do nothing but go along.

When she got out of the car, I followed her up the right-hand flight of steps between iron railings. At a landing we turned up a longer central flight to the door of the building. As I went up, I glimpsed arched windows and a closed door set at ground level between the two wings of steps.

"Where are we?" I demanded, suddenly feeling very vulnerable.

She took a key from her pocket and waved it at me exultantly. "This is the Old Exchange Building—one of the oldest in Charleston. It used to open on the river, where ships could unload onto its stone floor. It was built while the town was still a royal colony. Such history here! I can't wait to show it to you."

She used her key to open the door, and laughed at my questioning look. "I still take children's tours through once in a while, and I've kept my key."

I looked nervously over my shoulder at the street, where nothing moved.

"We won't turn on any lights," she assured me. "Then if a police car comes by, they won't see a thing. Don't dawdle, Cecelia —come along."

In dim light from the street I saw the reception desk near the door, piled with brochures. The stone floor stretched out across the enormous room, worn and uneven.

"This is where trading used to take place, with ships unload-

178

ing back there on the river. All that began more than two hundred years ago, yet the old bricks and stones are still standing. Of
course the building was used for other purposes during the
Revolution. I'll show you later, but first we'll go upstairs."

I had no idea why she had brought me on this historic tour at
such an hour, and with such secrecy. An electric quality still
drove her, and I wished I knew what she intended.

Stairs opened on one side and we climbed to the floor above.
Again streetlights threw patches of yellow through the windows,
so nothing was completely dark. Here the bare floor was polished
wood, and two fireplaces gleamed white in the dim lighting.
Graceful white columns, whose scrolled tops supported the ceiling, stood out from the walls around the great room. Above twin
mantels hung portraits that Valerie said were Queen Henrietta
Maria and King Charles I of England (the father of Charleston's
namesake). All this would be lighted by the marvelous overhead
chandeliers for a party. It was a ballroom, undoubtedly. But why
were we here?

Valerie flung out her arms as though she moved to unheard
music. "What wonderful parties have been held here in the Great
Hall! What splendid dances! How many times Simon and I have
danced in this very room! This is background you need to know
about, Cecelia."

Why did I suspect that this was not her reason for bringing
me here?

As I watched, her arms accepted an invisible partner and she
moved into the steps of a formal waltz. I could almost see her
swirling skirt change into a ball gown of satin and lace as she
danced with her tall husband—perhaps in that distant time of her
youth when she had loved him dearly. Or loved what she thought
him to be? And what about Simon? Had she been what he
wanted and expected?

My mother and father, I told myself, and began to believe a little in this fairy tale. As I watched, I could almost hear the music. Not Strauss. Cole Porter perhaps, or Irving Berlin. She dipped and whirled and I knew that a strong arm supported her. The room was peopled in my vision with a throng of dancers.

She whirled to a stop, applauding the invisible orchestra, and came running back to me, light as a young girl.

"I've always wanted to do this. I've wanted to dance once more in this room with my own partner. Usually I'm herding schoolchildren through and trying to make them understand how real history is. The Federal Government was going to sell this building at one time, and it could have been torn down. Can you imagine? Back in 1913 the DAR got the United States Congress to deed the Old Exchange to be held as a historic memorial in perpetuity. Of course, I am a Daughter of the Revolution, and so are you, Cecelia. Our Daughters of the Confederacy came later."

I knew very little of what the DAR stood for today, but the sense of connection with history mesmerized me. Maybe this was why my mother had brought me here.

"Now I'll show you the real treasure this building holds," Valerie ran on. "This is the dark time before dawn when you can really experience what is hidden here."

She hurried toward the stairs and as I looked to where they descended to the bottom floor, I held back. "Is it necessary to go down there?" My alarm suddenly increased again. Her words about the "dark time" and something hidden were far from reassuring.

"Of course, Cecelia!" She ran down the steps ahead of me. "There's living history here. Don't you want to know where you came from?"

I came from an old white house on Long Island—a place that carried no history of intrigue and war and murder. Did I need this eerie world into which Valerie Mountfort was leading me? Nevertheless compelled, I followed her down.

When we reached the brick floor at the bottom, she tapped me on the arm. "Step carefully—these bricks are very old and uneven. They've been worn down by centuries of feet. This is the dungeon, Cecelia."

The area smelled dark and warm and shut in, though probably by day there would be air-conditioning for the comfort of tourists. Blind in pitch darkness, I groped until Valerie switched on several lights that hung about the cavernous space. Illumination remained dim and shadowy, so that for a moment I thought we were not alone. Then I realized that former happenings in this place had been depicted with small dioramas of life-sized figures in costumes from the past.

Valerie was playing her role of tour guide now. "Isaac Haye, a patriot of the Revolution, was held here before his execution by the British. There were common criminals, as well—the pirate Steve Bonnard, among others. I've always thought it strange that I've never felt a sense of the dead in this place. Honoria says that's because life was so miserable here that they'd rather do their haunting elsewhere. Just the same, if we are very quiet and listen, we may hear the human cries that were impressed on these walls and pillars and arches. Cries that will echo forever!"

I tried not to listen to the silence. She hadn't told me her reason for bringing me here, but I still felt too vulnerable and alarmed.

She'd brought a flashlight, and when she cast its beam forward I saw the intricacy of groined brick arches rising from the pillars, intertwining overhead. The very artistry of the arches gave the place a terrible beauty.

"Take my hand and we'll go up on the bridge," she directed.

181

Her hand was hot when I touched it, as though she burned with some blood fever that drove her.

I stepped with her onto a runway built over the remnants of an ancient brick wall. Valerie swept it with her flashlight beam and continued her patter.

"Charleston was the only British walled city in North America. The Old Exchange Building is built over what's left of the seawall. You can see a section of the old wall down there below us. Bits of that wall crop up in other parts of historic Charleston."

Even as her words sounded reasonable and informative—words she could probably say in her sleep—something ran beneath the routine pattern, and I heard a tremor of anticipation that upset me. But when I tried to persuade her to return upstairs and leave this unhappy place, she dismissed my words carelessly. Leaving was not in her immediate plans, and I had no intention of leaving her until I knew why we were here.

We wandered into another part of the great dungeon, where lifelike figures played out more tragic prison scenes. Great brick arches collected menacing shadows that seemed to move as Valerie's flashlight moved. Suddenly I'd had enough. I would go no farther into what had begun to seem like a maze. Any sense of direction I might have had was lost, and I no longer knew where to find the stairs. I stood with my back against a brick column, trying not to see the suffering displayed by a ragged figure a few feet away. Suffering that had once been horribly real in this place.

"I'm not moving another step until you tell me why you've brought me here."

A chuckle of amusement escaped her lips before she became serious again. "You can't call me Mother, can you?"

"I'm sorry—" I began, but she broke in quickly.

"Of course you can't! You can't use that word because I'm not really your mother. And you aren't really my lost Cecelia. I don't know why you came to Charleston—or perhaps I do. You knew there was an inheritance involved, didn't you? An inheritance you would share with my daughter, Amelia. Simon took care of that in his letter to you and in his will. If you returned within a period of thirty-five years, you were to share equally with your sister. If Amelia were dead, you would receive it all. The amount has been growing all this time, so this might put Amelia in jeopardy. Though at the end of the period of restriction if you hadn't claimed your share, what has become a fortune would revert to her. Which might put *you* in jeopardy."

"I don't know anything about this . . ." I began.

"But of course you *are* an impostor," she went on, paying no attention. "You fooled Charles and some of the others, including Amelia. But I was never fooled. The likeness startled me at first—even shocked me. But I was able to go behind that with a mother's true feelings. You aren't my darling lost baby, and I mean to make you so sorry you came that you will go away and never come back. Tonight you'll have a taste of the punishment I can manage for you. Just a hint to show you what the real thing might be like."

Her delusion was complete and I realized there was no way I could reach her. I wondered if it had been her hand that had placed that halberd beside me backstage at the theater—even though she was supposed to be home in bed.

I knew I must escape and find my way to the stairs, then I could reach the street and get help. If only I didn't feel so lost and confused. This was worse than losing my sense of direction at the theater, where at least there had been adequate light.

Valerie gestured with the beam of her flashlight. "There's a barrel over there, Molly Hunt. You might as well sit and be comfortable. You won't have more than a few hours to wait before the building opens and someone finds you. Perhaps you can even catch up on some sleep."

She meant to leave me here, and I couldn't let that happen, but even as I reached out to grasp her arm, she touched a switch that extinguished the lights around this cellar area. At the same moment she turned off her flashlight and moved out of my reach. I hadn't noticed the location of the switch, since it had all happened so fast. Once more, her beam flashed across my face and then went off for good.

Valerie Mountfort, who knew this place by night and day, ran away from me, her feet sounding on the bricks and echoing among the arches of the ceiling. Echoes seemed to come back to me from all sides, so I had no sense of the direction she had taken.

When all the sound died away, the silence seemed as dismaying as the darkness. I couldn't hear her feet on the stairs, or on the heavy stone floor overhead. I knew she would return to her car and drive home, leaving me here without the slightest qualm.

I made myself be quiet. Primitive fears would be my worst enemy here, and I must keep my imagination from taking flight. I was disoriented—that was all. There was nothing to harm me. I groped my way to the barrel she'd shown me, and sat down to think about my circumstances. I might even entertain myself by thinking like a writer. I must stop the shaking that was affecting my limbs. This experience would work wonderfully in a mystery novel, but I didn't care for it in real life.

Perhaps, after all, I could remember the direction of the stairs. I would simply open my consciousness, ask for help—and let myself be guided. I sat very still, trying to relax every part of my body, waiting for some—enlightenment?

All around me the silence pressed down with the weight of those mysterious arches. Nearby something rustled and crept across the floor. Mice—rats? Once ships beyond the seawall had unloaded their wares and brought them into this building. Rats must have had a lovely time in those days. I felt sorry for prisoners chained to these dungeon floors. They, at least, would have been allowed candlelight. And surely all the rats would have been driven out by now.

Darkness—the complete absence of light—can have a strangely stifling effect. Not only because my physical eyes could no longer see anything—but because my inner vision had gone sightless from fear. I hadn't even a blind man's stick with which to find my way. Nevertheless I couldn't wait hours to be rescued. I must find the stairs that would lead me to the floor above. Streetlights would show me the way to the reception desk and a telephone. Someone would come for me when I called. Though I wasn't sure whom I would call. But that was a problem that lay ahead—*when* I found my way up.

I'd closed my eyes, since it was better not to stare into blank nothingness. When I opened them to make my first steps toward escape, I realized that the darkness was not absolute—as it had seemed at first. My eyes had begun to adjust, and in the direction of what must be the front of the building a faint sliver of light came through. I remembered that I had seen arched windows under the high steps when we had come in. And there'd been a door between them.

Moving with my hands outstretched against collision, I found my way past pillars that rose into arches, and over rough brick toward the goal of lesser darkness. Once I bumped into a cabinet with a glass top that rattled and set echoes crashing around me. An exhibit of some kind, I supposed.

A few more steps brought me to the cold outside wall, where windows and a central door had been set into the brick. Useless, of course. The door was locked and the shuttered windows

185

wouldn't open. Now I was farther than ever from the stairs, but at least I knew they must rise against the wall opposite from this one—clear across the building.

Thanks to the tiny flittering of light and the adjustment of my vision, I could at least see the deeper blackness of brick columns, so I didn't run into them. Nevertheless I moved with my hands reaching straight out, still more or less blind.

When bricks turned to wood under my feet, and the floor sloped upward, I swept my hands to the side and found the rails of the "bridge" above the old seawall. I didn't want to go deeper into the dungeon, and I struck out in another direction.

Step by groping step, I moved toward what I hoped was the location of the stairs. They couldn't be that far away now. Hands outstretched, I could step ahead a little more confidently. Until, without warning, my fingers touched something that made me cry out in alarm. I had placed my right hand fully on warm human flesh. My recoil was one of terror. To come upon someone hiding in this place, knowing I was here, sensing me in the darkness! I screamed, as I'd done in the theater, and the echoes went crashing horridly around the groined ceiling, smashing silence with sounds that surely weren't coming from me.

Almost at once, I recognized that these were sounds I wasn't making. Someone—that face I'd touched—was laughing, and I knew the laughter was Valerie Mountfort's. I stood back against a column of brick, shaking and angry, unable to speak.

She flashed her torch on my face. "I'm sorry, Molly. I didn't dream you'd frighten that badly. I really wouldn't have left you here for five hours. I just wanted you to have time to realize how unwelcome you are in Charleston. We don't like pretenders here. So this was just a hint of the unpleasantness to come—more serious unpleasantness that could happen if you don't go away.

But I'll get you out of here now. First, though, tell me what you would have done if I'd left you here."

Somehow I forced myself to speak quietly, and regain some shred of lost dignity and control. "I'd have found the stairs and gone up to the telephone on the reception desk. Then I'd have called someone to come and get me. When they did, I'd have told them all about your trickery."

"Which wouldn't matter," she said lightly. "They're all used to my impulsive ways. In the past I suppose the family would have locked me in the attic and kept me a secret. Now I have the devotion of my sweet daughter, silly though she can sometimes be. And no one talks about madness. We use words like 'neuroses' and 'psychoses'—all treatable, of course. Only I refuse to be treated, and I am looked after and my wishes considered. Of course, I don't do anything too outlandish—most of the time."

She spoke with an amusement that didn't sound in the least mad—which made it all the more frightening. Probably the psychotic rationalized their own madness.

"I think you know exactly what you are doing," I told her. "It's *why* you are doing it that I don't understand. I appear to be Amelia's twin—but how can you really be sure? I don't know or care anything about an inheritance, though you may not believe that."

"Who would you have called?" she asked. "After four in the morning?"

I'd been thinking about that as I groped for the stairs. Not Amelia—she would be too stricken by our mother's actions. Not Honoria, who would rouse Porter. Not Charles. Never Charles—for some reason I couldn't explain. I might have called Garrett, but I needed a woman with me now—a woman's kindness and sympathy. So it was Daphne I'd decided upon. All along she had

187

struck me as the most sensible of the clan, and I knew she would come for me at any hour without any fussing.

"I would have called Daphne Phelps," I said.

"A good choice. Give me your hand, Molly, and I'll take you to the stairs."

Again her fingers seemed hot as I touched them, and I didn't trust her. She used her flashlight until we reached the bottom step of the stairs. Then she turned it off, leaving me in blackness again. I knew what she meant to do, and grasped her hand tightly. Her strength surprised me as she twisted away and ran up the stairs. I leaned on the banister as darkness returned to smother me.

She called to me from the floor above. "That's a good idea, Molly—to phone Daphne. So do it!" She ran away across the stone floor, and I heard the opening and slam of the outer door as it closed after her.

I was angry all over again, and just as futilely. At least she had led me to the stairs. I went up easily enough, guided by the rail, and into the welcome radiance from streetlights beyond the windows. The phone waited for me, reassuring me of help. I called information and asked for Daphne's number.

Eleven

Daphne sounded drugged with sleep when she answered my ring. However, she woke up quickly enough when I gave her the bare bones of what had happened. I told her I was stranded at the Old Exchange and didn't know the streets well enough to find my way back to the Mountfort house. She asked no questions, but must have caught a hint of my mental state, for she took over at once.

"Stay right there. I'll throw on some clothes and come for you as soon as I can."

I'd had enough of this gloomy, history-ridden place, and when I put down the phone, I let myself out the front door to the landing where the steps divided. From here I could look straight down Broad Street—a line that had once divided Charleston socially—to where St. Michael's lighted white steeple rose above the roofs and the few cupolas of the town. But it wasn't St. Michael's I saw.

The night air was gentle, and the iron railing felt cool under my fingers. The touch of it steadied me. The steeple I remembered was St. Philip's, and I found it comforting to recall that moment in the alley that ran beside the theater, when Garrett had presented his "surprise." Suddenly I wanted to tell Garrett what had happened to me tonight. He might not be sympathetic, he might even be critical of my actions, but he would listen.

"I like St. Philip's best," I assured the shining white steeple that overlooked Broad Street. St. Michael's, serene in its own beauty, didn't seem to mind.

Early-morning Charleston echoed with the sounds of a party breaking up at dawn, so that laughter and voices reached me through quiet streets. Lights came on where there were early risers, and from a distance I heard what might be Daphne's car. I went quickly down the steps to wait on the sidewalk. The huge bulk of the Old Exchange loomed massively behind me, and I was eager to escape its overwhelming shadow.

Dawn touched the sky over the water and I welcomed the full light of morning. A heaviness of realization about Valerie Mountfort pressed its own darkness upon my spirit. Perhaps she was only to be pitied, but she had frightened me—badly—and had seemed too close to a dangerous edge. I could never think of her as my mother now.

The car was indeed Daphne's, and when it stopped at the curb and she got out, looking calm and capable, I felt an enormous relief. She opened the passenger door and waited for me to get in, asking no questions.

"I'm not taking you back to the Mountfort house at this hour and under these conditions," she told me. "We'll fix breakfast at my place, and wait until Amelia is up before I return you to South Battery. In the meantime we can talk—if you'd like to tell me what has happened."

Daphne had rented a top apartment in a house that had been renovated. We climbed stairs that circled in a tight oval. At the top a door painted a soft blue welcomed us.

"I love this color," Daphne said as she took her key. "Of course, it's the blue they use in the Middle East to guard against the evil eye."

I didn't think Daphne would place much belief in evil eyes, but she enjoyed being unconventional. The moment I stepped through her blue door I felt comfortable—and safe. Rooms opened from one to another, though not in straight "railroad" fashion. She led me through a pleasant living room, where books spilled over onto chairs and tables, and waved a careless hand. "I'm always reading three or four at once."

The small dining area opened on a galley kitchen, and she told me to look around while she whipped up an omelet and crisp slices of bacon.

French doors opened upon a piazza that overlooked the brick-walled garden and neighboring houses. Now I could see St. Philip's steeple again, shining a few blocks away. Stepping-stones below cut a path through grass, and a graceful, very old pecan tree spread its branches in one corner.

"I need something cheerful and quieting right now," I said. "I've had too much excitement for one night."

191

We sat down to breakfast on the open piazza, and I told her what had happened. She listened intently, buttering toast and spreading marmalade, wasting no time on comments until I was through. When I described the moment when I'd touched Valerie's face in the blackness of the Old Exchange dungeon, she shivered.

"You're giving me goose bumps! I know that place pretty well, and I wouldn't want to be alone down there at night. Look —I'll talk to Valerie and to Amelia too. Though I'm afraid it won't do much good. My father will be livid when he hears about this—if we even tell him. Valerie's like a sister, and he worries about her."

"Is there an—imbalance—in Valerie?" I chose my words carefully. "Or was she putting on an act?"

"Perhaps some of both. Though she never carries anything so far that we worry about her seriously. She is known for her outrageous pranks, Molly."

I wondered how far was "far."

Daphne went on. "It's a good thing you didn't call the police. Perhaps she's never grown up. Everyone has always loved and protected Valerie. Your father treated her as though she were still the young girl he first knew. Southern women are hardly fragile, though that can be an act—an act that belongs more to the past than now. When tragedy hit, Valerie didn't change all that much on the surface. But a good deal of suppressed emotion got bottled up inside her—and some of it was anger. She's angry the way a child would be. Adulthood is something she's postponed."

They had all made excuses for Valerie Mountfort. Excuses that continued to keep her from growing up, though I couldn't help wondering why they insisted on doing this.

"In any case," Daphne added, "I don't think you should return to that house just now. Let's get you out of the city for a while. Evaline will put you up at the plantation, and I'll call a family conference to see what to do about Valerie. Of course, my father will probably blame you for anything that's happened. And maybe he'll be partly right, Molly. Whatever possessed you to go with her in the middle of the night?"

"I suppose she seemed excited in a rather appealing way, and I thought I might get to know her a little better if I humored her about whatever she wanted to do. Perhaps we might have come closer to an understanding—if she hadn't had something else in mind."

"It could be that getting to know her isn't such a good idea," Daphne said. "Anyway, you look out on your feet, so if you've finished eating, lie down and take a nap. It's still early. Then we'll go over to the house to pick up your things, and you can stay at Mountfort Hall for a few days. I'll call Evaline from the house and let her know you're coming."

"How will I get there?"

"I'll call Charles too. He can usually leave the office when he pleases, and I'm sure he'll drive you out."

I agreed to everything, enormously weary. It was a relief to lie down on Daphne's bed and go to sleep.

I must have slept for more than an hour, and I awoke re-freshed, and with more questions in my mind. Daphne was ready to leave, and I asked one of them as we went downstairs.

"I talked to Garrett at the Omni after you left. He walked me back to Amelia's car and showed me the earring you gave him. I supposed it had belonged to Valerie and that the other one had been lost. But tonight Valerie was wearing two earrings just like it, except that her lotuses were set in gold. Can you tell me about the earring?"

We were on the way downstairs and she spoke over her shoulder. "A child found it out at the plantation tangled up in fishing line and gave it to me. I was a little girl and I kept it as a treasure. Recently, I remembered it and took it to Garrett."

"Why?"

She looked uncomfortable. "Can we let that go for now? It's a complicated story. I'll tell you some other time."

She drove me the few blocks to South Battery while Charleston was still waking up, and let us in with her own key.

"I'll use the downstairs phone, Molly. You go up and pack your things. Don't wake Amelia if you can help it."

As I started up the stairs, I met Miss Kitty coming down. Usually she greeted everyone with a small mew, and talked very little. Now, however, she sat on her haunches on the bottom step, tipped back her head, and yowled piteously.

"Okay, okay," Daphne told her. "I hear you. She wants to go back to the plantation, Molly. She can take only a little of this house. She'd like to stay with Honoria, but my father doesn't care for cats. I'll get out her carrier and you can take her with you. I'll leave Amelia a note, so she won't go searching for you and Miss Kitty."

I bent to stroke soft gray-and-white fur, and at once she flung herself on her back to invite a stomach rub. I obliged for a moment, and then raced silently up to the third floor to my room.

Everything seemed quiet. Not even the rocking horse was creaking. I hoped I wouldn't need to see either Valerie or Amelia before I escaped. Miss Kitty followed me, watching with bright interest.

Before I was through packing, however, Amelia came to my door in her pajamas. "What's happening, Molly? Where are you going?"

"Daphne thinks it's best if I go out to the plantation to stay for a little while."

"Why? How do you come to be listening to Daphne?"

194

There was no escaping an explanation. "Sit down for a moment, Amelia. Perhaps you'd better know about this."

Once more I told the story of what had happened at the Old Exchange Building. Amelia grew white and teary-eyed as she listened. Before I finished she covered her face with her hands, crying softly.

I went to sit beside her. "Can you tell me the truth about your mother?"

She looked at me, her cheeks wet. "*Our* mother. When you were taken, she collapsed and was very ill."

"Mentally ill?"

"I'm not sure. Daddy never believed that about her. He felt that her physical state was affecting her emotionally. When she grew stronger, everything seemed to improve. Except that—" Amelia broke off. "Oh, I don't want to talk about it. Just let it go, Molly."

"We have to talk. Say what you were going to say."

She went on hesitantly. "Mama learned to manipulate the people around her by falling back on her very shaky emotional state. She learned she could perform in certain ways and get whatever she wanted. It's mostly acting, I think. She isn't crazy, Molly. She wanted to frighten you tonight, and she did. It's as simple as that, and you danced to her tune, just the way everyone does."

"But why? She said she doesn't believe that I'm her daughter. But the punishment she chose for me seems a little extreme, doesn't it? She talked about what she called my deception."

"Oh dear. Molly, this is all so complicated. It's true that you don't match the imaginary twin she's created in her mind and you're already asking too many questions about our father's death. I have a feeling that's what she's really afraid of."

"Why? Because of his letter?"

"Maybe we're all afraid of revelations out of the past. The murky pond was quiet until you came, but now it's being stirred up."

"I wonder if Garrett Burke has come across something that has set him on the trail, Amelia? If I go out to the plantation, perhaps I can find out. Daphne's calling Charles now to drive me out there. Why don't you come with us?"

"I wish I could. I'm working at the Historical Society today. But I'll put on some clothes and come down to see Charles before you leave."

She went off and I closed the suitcase and zipped my tote bag. When I went downstairs, Miss Kitty came with me and began to sniff around the carrying case.

"Did anyone hear you?"

"Amelia did. Valerie's nowhere to be seen. I had to tell my sister what happened."

"How did she take it?"

"With tears."

Daphne made an unkind sound. "That's Amelia. Maybe everybody's right to be afraid of what you may dig up from the bottom of our murky pond."

That was the same figure of speech Valerie had used, and I didn't care for it.

"Did you make your phone calls?" I asked.

"Yes. Evaline will have a room ready for you. And Charles will be here soon. Molly, that's a very determined expression you're wearing."

"It's not determination. I'm just looking grim."

"I'm still betting on you." She seemed ready to say more, but only added, "Anyway, watch your step, whatever you do. If Valerie meant to frighten you into leaving Charleston, she could be on the right track."

"I'm staying," I said. "For now anyway."

"So you do know what to do."

The door chimes sounded and she went to let Charles in. Amelia came running down the stairs, straight into his arms. He held her gently while Daphne put the cat into the carrier and handed it to me.

"If I can, I'll come out later," Amelia promised Charles.

He shook his head. "I don't expect to stay. I'll be in touch when I get back."

Once we were on our way, driving north through busy morning streets, I told my story for the third time, beginning to feel tired of repeating it, though Charles had to know.

When I'd finished, he reached over to touch my hand. "Poor Molly. I seem to have brought you into all sorts of unpleasantness. First the theater, and now this. Something must be done about Valerie."

His words were kind, disarming, and for a moment I wanted to lean on him. But the thought of leaning on Charles alarmed me. He was strictly off-limits. I moved my hand away from his.

"Daphne had the right idea," he went on. "It's best for you to get out of Charleston for a while."

"One way to get out would be to go home."

"You are home, Molly. Haven't you begun to feel that?"

"What I feel right now is that several people very much want me to leave, including Valerie Mountfort."

"I don't think you'll run because of that. Since I met you in New York, I've thought a lot about the differences between you and Amelia. You may look alike, but you're a very different kind of woman. You'll stay."

"I'm not sure yet."

"I think you are. You're not seriously afraid of Valerie, are you?"

197

"I was seriously afraid of her last night." I looked straight through the windshield, though I saw little of the route we were taking.

"Okay, that's understandable, but what about in the broad daylight?"

"Let's just say I'm looking forward to staying at Mountfort Hall."

Our talk had once more made me aware of the quality of his voice with its musical cadences that were very different from Garrett's harsher northern accent. I recognized again that Charles's speech had a special Charleston flavor and that there was no such thing as one southern accent.

"We're not going straight out to the plantation. There's a place I want you to see first. It's a favorite spot of mine. In fact, the whole family used to love coming here."

I knew he was being kind, but my aim was to reach Mountfort Hall and be alone. I needed thinking time. There was no way, however, to turn Charles from his course. As we drove, he told me a little about the place he wanted me to see.

"The whole area used to be planted with rice. But when new types of long-grain came on the market, our water-grown South Carolina rice was no longer wanted. So all the rice was taken out, and water pumped in from the nearby Cooper River. Cypress trees were planted and now there are acres of beautiful cypress swamp, with walks and azalea gardens all around. Next spring I'll bring you here when the azaleas are in bloom."

Next spring? I could hardly think ahead to next week.

We turned off the main highway onto a side road that ran east for a few miles. Signs leading to Cypress Gardens appeared, and we turned in through a gateway and found the parking area.

"Charleston's Department of Parks now owns and operates the Gardens," he told me. "At this hour we'll have the place mostly to ourselves. Its isolation and loneliness are part of the charm."

There was nothing to do but go along with Charles's wishes and pretend a pleasure I didn't feel.

We left the car windows open so Miss Kitty could be comfortable, and walked toward the water. A sloping bank led down to rowboats moored along the shore, and I looked out across the water in wonder. A smooth green film of duckweed spread as far as I could see, covering the surface so completely that no reflections showed.

A guide was available to navigate the swamp, but Charles preferred to take our boat out himself. When he had helped me to settle onto a wooden crossbench, he took his place behind me and picked up a paddle.

We moved smoothly away from the bank, cutting through the green skin of duckweed, so that pools of dark water appeared around the boat. As the red-painted prow pushed its way ahead, I began to relax. I had never experienced more peaceful surroundings. That sense of peace and the very loneliness that Charles had spoken of were exactly what I needed to rest my own spirit.

Charles used his paddle so expertly that only the soft sound of its dipping broke the intense silence. Now I could let everything that worried me go for a little while. Just as Garrett had made me that lovely gift of St. Philip's last night, so Charles was giving me this enchanted place. I would use this in some novel sometime, but for now I let the impressions of all I saw and felt become a part of me.

Thick green water lapped so close that if I wished I could trail my fingers along its surface over the boat's side. Silver-gray boles of cypress rose on every hand in thick, fluted ridges, and at times the boat slipped so close to a clump of trees that Charles would push us away with his paddle. The shore where we'd boarded was distant now, and even the occasional trilling of a bird seemed part of the magical silence. On ahead a long-legged blue heron stood poised on a log, watching for fish. When we drew near, he spread his enormous wings and flew off, long legs dangling. The sight took my breath away.

"Thank you, Charles," I said over my shoulder, whispering so as not to disturb the stillness around us.

Charles's paddle cut the water with hardly a sound as we slipped along toward the opposite shore. Growing out of mud on the far bank were protrusions of wood—hundreds of little stumps only a few inches high.

He saw the direction of my interest. "Those are what they call cypress knees, Molly. Suckers from the trees run under the water and come up where it's shallow and grow on the bank. All of those have been chopped off because the wood is prized for making lamps and clocks to sell to tourists."

Our boat glided into an even lonelier part of the swamp, and now some of the trees we passed bore small signs—arrows with numbers—to guide boats into the deeper channels.

"There's been a drought," Charles explained, "and some of the swamp is too shallow to navigate. Boats can get stuck."

In spite of all the beauty around me, I wouldn't care to be stranded out here until someone came to find us, or just happened by.

"Look out there, Molly." Charles pointed. "That floating log is the back and snout of an alligator. One doesn't go swimming here."

The quiet through which we floated—sometimes with hardly a thrust from Charles's paddle—gave me a sense of distance from any world I knew. A quiet greenish gloom pervaded all that lay around us. Though when I looked up to follow the pointing fingers of some tall cypress trees, I could see patches of blue sky beyond leafy clusters of green far away at the top.

Charles rested his paddle and let the boat drift. All of my inner turmoil was gone, and I simply rested—physically and emotionally. For a little while I was safe—with all my alarms stilled.

"Molly," Charles said, "dear Molly." He touched a finger to the back of my neck, lifting a strand of hair.

I sat very still beneath his touch, not trusting either him or myself. He leaned forward and kissed my neck lightly. "Darling Molly. Do you know how I feel about you?"

My sense of peace evaporated instantly. I bent forward, away from his touch. "No, Charles, you are not available, no!"

"I know this is wrong, Molly, but I have to tell you how I feel. I think it began when I first saw you in New York, and couldn't help staring. You were conscious of me too, weren't you? To me, you were Amelia, whom I love, but you were also someone more exciting—someone unknown and tantalizing. I had to find out about this paradox. I *had* to bring you to Charleston to meet your real family. Not only for them and for you, but for me."

I had to stop him. Never mind that something in me had liked the touch of his finger, his lips.

"Amelia is my sister." I sounded stiff, but that didn't matter. "I care about her, and it's clear how much she's in love with you."

"I know." He spoke sadly, dejectedly. "I never meant for this to happen. I even resisted it at first. I love Amelia, as I have since we were children. You're a woman and she is only a young girl. I'm not sure she will ever change. You're not Amelia, but if you hadn't looked so much like her that it was confusing to be with you—"

"You're right," I broke in. "I'm *not* Amelia!"

"I won't be able to stop what I'm feeling, Molly."

"That's your problem. As far as I'm concerned, nothing is happening! Let's go back to your car. You can drive me to Mountfort Hall and leave me there. Then you'll go back to Amelia, and this will never have happened."

"This *is* happening, Molly. I don't want to hurt Amelia, God knows. But it's too late to stop the way I feel. We're adults and things change."

He sounded sadly sure, and my resistance grew.

"I like you, Charles, and I'm glad you brought me to Charleston. I *think* I'm glad. But I'm not sure who I am yet. I need you as a friend, and I don't want to lose that."

He put both hands on my shoulders. "You're trembling, Molly."

"I'm upset! And you aren't listening to me!"

"I understand your loyalty to your sister and I admire it. Even though you hardly know her, there's a tie."

"Our birth ties me to Amelia, and there's nothing that ties me to you."

"Don't be too sure." He picked up the paddle and dipped it into green water so that the boat glided ahead, causing hardly a ripple. Only when wind stirred the surface did the duckweed drift aside. Then cypress boles grew inverted downward in strange reflections that showed blue sky in dark waters.

Charles went on. "You need time, Molly, and so do I. Too much has happened too quickly. I had to let you know how I feel. So I needed to find a place where I could tell you these things and you couldn't run away. Here you at least had to listen to me."

Run away? I began to smolder. This was the old male concept of flight and pursuit. I was *supposed* to run, and of course he needn't put any stock in that. It was what a woman did when confronted by a strong man who knew better than she what was best for them both. Only those ideas belonged to the age of the dodo. Some men just didn't realize this yet.

I knew I must stay here for a time. There were matters to be dealt with concerning my sister, my mother, and the entire mystery of why I was stolen as a baby. But a rowboat was no place for confrontation. I needed a place where I could *walk* away.

Ahead on the water a small bridge curved in an arc, offering the way to our landing area. We slipped soundlessly through the mirage of a moon tunnel made by the bridge and its reflection, having come full circle from the bank where we had boarded.

Another boat carrying visitors had thrust its prow out into the swamp. I caught the flash of a man's red shirt amid gray boles of cypress trees. Voices reached us as the boat turned out of sight, and the green film lay undisturbed again. For me, however, this was no longer a place of serenity, and I wanted only to be where I could run, if I chose to, even though I didn't care for that picture.

Neither of us spoke, as Charles helped me out onto the bank, his hands careful of me—his manner tender. We walked in silence to the car, and I glanced at him only once. The glint of amusement in his eyes didn't reassure me. I suspected that Charles Landry was a man who would wait, sure that in the end he would achieve whatever he wanted. I was beginning to feel very sorry for my sister. I could be rid of him, but what about her?

When we got into the car, Miss Kitty woke up and mewed plaintively. I took her out of the carrier and held her in my lap as we drove back to the main highway. She purred and looked up at me with that wide, deceptively innocent gaze. Only her long tail, striking across my knees, spoke a language of its own. I found comfort in holding her small warm body, and wished I could be as content as she.

We crossed the peninsula toward the Ashley River, and Charles continued to drive in silence. When we were once more on the wide avenue of live oaks, with the house looming at the end, he spoke to me gently, reasonably.

"Everything will be as it was, Molly. On the surface. Only you and I will know what happened this morning. I recognize that there are difficult decisions ahead. Don't worry about anything. Events have a way of working themselves out. Of course, I will need to talk to my mother."

I busied myself with putting Miss Kitty back in her carrier and didn't answer. Perhaps his mother would be more sensible than her son.

Orva Jackson must have seen the car from a window, for she had come out through the high Palladian doorway to greet us. I began to rearrange my thoughts. Perhaps Orva was the one I might talk to—if ever I could find a way past her careful reserve.

Twelve

"Please come up," Orva invited. "Miss Evaline is fixing your room, Miss Molly. Let me carry those bags for you."

"Thanks, Orva," Charles said. "I'll take them up. I want to see where my mother has put you, Molly."

I handed Miss Kitty to Orva, who looked disapproving. "When Miss Honoria's not here, this one digs her claws into furniture, knocks things over, and leaps up where she shouldn't be. She's like a little kid when teacher's out of the room. Come on now, Miss Kitty. Behave yourself."

The little gray-and-white cat sprang out of her carrier eagerly, ran to hook her claws into the nearest tapestry chair, and stretched herself full-length. Orva slapped at her futilely, and Miss Kitty withdrew to wash her fur disdainfully, indifferent, as always, to correction.

The guest bedrooms were on the top floor—a floor, Orva said, that I would have all to myself.

We climbed two long flights of stairs, and I looked down the hallway to the open door at the far end.

"Fine!" Charles approved. "This is the best room in the house, when it comes to a view, Molly."

He looked so pleased that I liked less and less the idea of being up here alone. Garrett Burke would be in the house only during the day, and there'd be no one around at night, except Evaline and, perhaps, Charles. I'd call Honoria and ask if she could come out for a visit while I was here.

"It's a beautiful room," I said, hoping that Charles would go away.

Instead he went to a front window and opened it. The muddy odor of the river, with its overtones of blossom scents from the land, came into the room.

"There!" he said. "That's our Low Country smell. You may not believe this, Molly, but you'll miss it when you're away."

Evaline Landry greeted me pleasantly, though I wondered how she would react if she knew about her son's interest in me.

"I like the room and the view," I told her, "but I'm not used to such an enormous house. Do you suppose I could be given a room downstairs?"

His mother shook her head. "I'm sorry, Miss Hunt, but there's no other room I could give you. There are only family bedrooms downstairs, except for the room Mr. Burke uses. We need to keep those bedrooms for the Mountforts and the Phelpses whenever they come out."

Orva Jackson had remained in the doorway, and now she spoke softly.

"If it'd make you feel better, Miss Molly, I can move into the room next to this one and stay at night for as long as you're here."

"A good solution." Evaline Landry agreed, but without enthusiasm. Clearly she felt scornful about my attitude, not given to flights of fancy herself.

"Thank you, Orva," I said. "I'd like that—if it doesn't inconvenience you too much."

"No, ma'am. My rooms're right down in the basement, so it's no big fuss to move a few things up here."

"Then that's settled," Charles said. "Though I wouldn't have expected you to be the nervous type, Molly. I'll get back to Charleston now—unless there's something you want me to do, Mother?"

She shook her head, and he looked at me. "See you soon, Molly."

"Perhaps Orva can help you unpack," Mrs. Landry said when he'd gone.

I didn't need anyone to help with the few things I'd brought, but I wanted to talk with Orva, so I said that would be fine. Mrs. Landry looked around the room one last time, wished me a pleasant stay, and went off.

For the first time, I relaxed a little. "Do sit down, Orva. There's nothing much to unpack, but I've wanted a chance to talk with you."

She sat down uneasily, and I tried to explain. "There's hardly anyone I'm sure of. So many strange things have happened. But I've had the feeling that I might be able to talk to you."

She said nothing, sitting on the edge of a chair, waiting. I wondered how far I dared go in speaking to her about Charles.

"Something has happened, Orva, that I don't know how to deal with. May I tell you about it?"

She bowed her head gravely, and I caught the glint of her half-moon combs. "I guess maybe it's Mr. Charles. I could see it coming."

That took me by surprise, but it was a relief to have her ahead of me. "He took me to Cypress Gardens on the way out here, Orva. It's a beautiful place, and I loved the boat trip through the swamp. But then—" I hesitated.

"It's hard for him, Miss Molly. You and your sister being like two peas in a pod—yet both so different. Maybe he's got himself all mixed up."

I hung my clothes in the armoire and tried to find the right words. "He cares about Amelia. I do believe that he loves her. But now he thinks he wants me, and—"

"And whatever Mr. Charles wants, he's used to getting. So maybe you can give him a real shock, Miss Molly. Wake him up to losing for once in his life."

"I don't even want to hear what he's saying."

Orva considered for a moment, looking out a window toward the river. "Maybe what you need to do is talk to Miss Evaline. He listens to her, and she'll know how to handle this."

I couldn't imagine talking about this to Charles's mother, and Orva saw rejection in my face.

"Never mind, Miss Molly. Miss Evaline will be watching him anyway. I'll think about this some and we'll talk more."

At least I'd shared my concern with Orva, whom I trusted and felt closer to than I did my frightening mother.

We left the door open as we went downstairs together, and I told her I was stopping off to talk with Garrett. She gave me a warm, serene smile that was somehow healing and went downstairs. Garrett's door was open, his typewriter clattering. I tapped on the panel and he looked around. Miss Kitty was already there —not dancing with sunbeams, but curled up asleep on a deep windowsill.

"Hello, Garrett," I said. "Is this a bad time to talk?"

"No, it's fine. You're not interrupting anything important. I seem to be blocked at the moment—not a useful idea in my head."

"I know the feeling. I haven't been able to think about my next book for ages."

"At least you're not bound by dull and stubborn facts when you're writing fiction. The so-called facts around Nathanial Amory's death are pretty interesting, but cloudy, and nobody in the family opens up. Even Honoria sidesteps some of my questions, as though she's afraid of stirring things up."

I had nothing to offer, so I watched the sleeping cat. Now that I was in the same room with Garrett, I didn't know what to say. I couldn't tell him about Charles.

He ran his fingers through his thick dark hair and pushed his chair back from his desk. "What are you doing out here, Molly?"

"I'm staying here now. For a few days anyway. It seemed a good idea to get away from Charleston for a while." I sat beside Miss Kitty on the wide windowseat, pushing her over a little. She opened her eyes, blinked at me, and went back to sleep. The tip of her pink tongue protruded a tiny speck, and I lost my heart all over again.

"What's happened?" Garrett said.

"It's a long story, and I'm tired of telling it. Let's just say that things aren't going well with my mother. Daphne thought I'd

209

better come out here, and I've been given a room upstairs. Orva is moving into the one next to me, so I won't be alone."

"A good idea. You should be fine here at the Hall." But I thought he sounded doubtful.

"I should be fine anywhere. What do you mean by 'here'?"

He got up and stretched widely. "You seem to have a talent for getting into trouble."

"Because there are those who want me to leave?"

Garrett pulled a sheet of paper from the roller, crumpled it, and threw it into a wastebasket that was already half full. "I can't move ahead on this until I pick up more facts. Porter wants me to let the whole matter—he calls it an 'episode'—of Nathanial's death go. Just skip it. But that's not what I want to do."

I couldn't focus on Nathanial now. "Can we talk about earrings?"

"What about earrings?"

"That one Daphne gave you yesterday—with the coral lotus. Valerie Mountfort has a pair almost like it."

"I know."

"Stop being enigmatic! Tell me what that one earring is all about!"

"Nathanial wrote a poem about earrings. I showed it to you."

"That doesn't tell me anything. Please explain."

Oddly enough, even when he was aggravating me, I felt more comfortable with Garrett than I ever did with Charles. At least he paid attention to what I said.

"Those earrings go back in history, Molly. But I'm not sure where they lead. The one Daphne showed me was found out here at Mountfort Hall. Something made her remember it recently, so she brought it to me and told me how she happened to have it. Maybe we'd better let it go at that—since I don't know any answers."

210

I wasn't ready to let anything go at this point. I *wanted* answers. "Daphne told me that a little girl—a friend—brought the earring to her years ago when she was a child."

"You're not part of this, Molly, and it's better to stay uninvolved."

"But I'm not uninvolved. I have a twin sister I'm worried about, a disturbed mother I've never known, and a father who died under mysterious circumstances. How can I ever be the same woman I was when I came here?"

He swiveled away from his desk. "All right—you have a point. I'll tell you what little I know. After I left you yesterday, I took that earring to the jeweler's shop in Charleston where it was made. The old man who created those little works of art is still alive, and he remembered the earrings very well. He was able to tell me who had ordered them."

Garrett paused again, and I prodded him. "I know that Simon Mountfort gave Valerie the pair she wears. Lotus earrings set in gold. The one you showed me was set in silver."

"Simon ordered the second pair too—those with the silver setting. I haven't an inkling of what this means or who they were intended for. It may not really matter. The world is full of lost and mismatched earrings."

"But you're pretty interested, aren't you? I suppose my father had a mistress, and he gave her the less expensive pair. So what?"

He stared at me thoughtfully. "Somehow, I don't think that's the case. Everything I've heard makes me believe that your father never looked at another woman, after Valerie."

I wanted that to be true, but I didn't know if it could be. "Daphne said the earring she gave you was brought to her caught in some fishing line. Do you think it was from Nathanial's boat? Why wasn't the boat ever found?"

"I can think of two possibilities. It could have been swept out

211

into the Atlantic by river currents. Or someone could have made sure it would never be found."

I sensed Garrett's sadness. His research had perhaps begun to involve *him* with a ghost.

"Why does Nathanial Amory's death matter after all these years?"

"Maybe everything's connected—past and present. Maybe it's all inevitably linked. I'd like to learn the truth for this book I'm working on. In spite of Porter, I'd like to make it an honest book."

"Will Porter allow that?"

"I'm not sure he'll allow anything I may write about Nathanial to be published. He claims he has nothing to do with Mountfort history. I'm not so sure, and I have to go ahead, whatever happens."

His concern with Nathanial seemed almost an obsession. Miss Kitty woke up suddenly and leapt from the windowseat, once more on her hind legs boxing with dust motes in a beam of sunlight.

"Honoria thinks she sees Nathanial," I said. "Perhaps he can't rest until the truth is known."

"Now you sound like Honoria, but who knows—maybe she's right."

"What has caught your sympathy so deeply about Nathanial?"

When he answered his voice was so low that I leaned forward to listen. "Nathanial Amory was my father. That's why I'm here. That's why I must follow through to whatever ending I find."

Everything fell suddenly into place about Garrett, leaving me not so much surprised as anxious. Ramifications opened in every direction, but I could find nothing sensible to say.

He went on quietly, watching Miss Kitty's antics. "My name

isn't Burke, of course. That's my mother's maiden name. Mine is Amory. Before my father died, my mother received a letter from him that she didn't show me until she knew her own life was almost over. My father had left her some years before he wrote that letter. He was working at Mountfort Hall as a tutor. I was only a few years old, but in spite of her hurt, my mother talked about him often. Perhaps she created more between them than there'd ever been. He came down to South Carolina because he wanted to track down some distant family connection. Perhaps on the left-hand side of the escutcheon. His own bloodline led to the Mountforts. While he was working here, he came upon some damning information—to one Mountfort, at least. In his letter he hinted to my mother that he might be stepping into dangerous territory, but by that time it was a matter of principle with him. Some wrongdoing needed to be exposed."

"And so he died," I said into Garrett's silence.

"Yes. When word came to my mother about his drowning accident, she didn't believe that it was accidental at all. But there was nothing she could do against the powerful Mountforts, and she lacked the means and the courage to try. I didn't know about this until two years ago, when she showed me my father's letter. Afterward I seemed to have no choice. I owed it to him to find out whatever I could."

"Your mother must have still cared about him."

"She did, though I never blamed him for leaving her. She was a difficult woman and they must have been very different. My mother was a realist. Nathanial's poetry meant nothing to her. They'd married too young, and had quickly grown away from each other. Though I think I mattered to him. He wrote me letters that I still have. Letters one might write to a small child. Before he had the time or means to come back to see me, he was gone."

"Honoria must have been enchanting when she was young."

Garrett smiled. "I'm glad they found each other."

"Does Honoria know who you are?"

"Perhaps she's aware with that extra sense she seems to have. I've never told her, but perhaps my father has—if he really comes through. She has mixed loyalties because of Porter. Only Daphne knows. And now you. I'd reached an impasse, Molly—until you came."

"How could I make a difference?"

"Everyone is reacting to you in different ways. I have the feeling that you've stirred up forces you may not be able to handle. So be careful, Molly. Stay on guard."

"But why should this be? There's nothing I know that would make me a threat to anyone."

"There's something. I'm not sure what. Has anything unpleasant happened since I last saw you?"

I hardly knew where to begin. I didn't want to tell him about Charles and the cypress swamp, so I described what had happened to me backstage at the theater when I'd stumbled and managed to knock myself out. And how I'd come to with that evil-looking halberd set deliberately beside me. I told him as well about the weird adventure with my mother in the dungeon of the Old Exchange Building.

Garrett listened grimly until I was through. "I don't know what the connection is, but we may be in this together."

"But not against all the Mountforts," I said quickly. "I've become very fond of my sister. I'm sorry for my mother, but I don't think I can help her. I haven't any idea which way to turn."

"I'd like to trust Honoria. Even though she doesn't know who I am, I suspect that she's tapped into some deeper feeling that makes her my friend. I know she believes that rowboat was scuttled by someone who knew Nathanial and knew he couldn't swim. Someone who lost an earring that became tangled in his fishing gear."

"Lost by the woman who scuttled the boat?"

"That's the obvious suspicion, but we don't know. A man owned those earrings first. There may be complicated possibilities."

"Simon Mountfort?"

"I didn't say that. The trail's too old to follow by this time, I'm afraid. The matching earring is probably hidden by whoever damaged the boat so that it would gradually sink once it was out on the river."

"Do you know who was here at Mountfort Hall at the time that Nathanial died?"

"Everyone was here for a party. Valerie and Simon came out. Daphne was a child, and she came with her father. Honoria was working at the plantation as a docent and came to the party. Evaline and Charles lived here, of course, as well as Orva and her little girl, Katy. She was the one who found the lotus earring and brought it to Daphne."

"Katy? I wonder why Daphne didn't mention that?"

"I didn't mention it either, until now. Does it matter who found it?"

"It might matter if Katy remembers something she hasn't told anyone. What about Daphne's mother?"

"Porter's first wife was an invalid and seldom went anywhere. I don't think she'd have come to a party."

A still greater dejection had settled upon Garrett, and my silent sympathy went out to him. He must have seen this in my face, for his look held mine, and for an instant a sense of something intangible—perhaps recognition—sprang between us. It was almost as if we had touched very briefly.

"Thank you, Molly," he said gently.

I moved toward the door, feeling uncertain—not sure what had happened. Or if anything had happened.

He let me go, and when I was out in the hall, I went toward the stairs. One room in the house drew me, and it was where I wanted to be. I saw no one on my way to the music room. The piano waited for me and I sat down before its closed lid.

This was where my father had played Debussy in the last moments of his life. How I wished I could have known him. Wished that I could talk to him now. Perhaps even about that moment between Garrett and me—and whatever it might lead to. But first, I felt compelled to find answers to old secrets.

Certainly I must talk again with Orva. And with Honoria. There must be a great deal both knew and had never told anyone over the years. I must coax these memories out into the open.

I put my arms on the shiny black wooden lid over the keys and rested my head upon it. Silently I spoke to my father: You loved me as a baby. Perhaps you love me now. If there is some essence of you in this house, in this room, help me to understand what I must do.

The strength of my longing was very great, but unhappily, no sense of his presence came through to answer me. I was ready to turn away from the piano when a sound told me that someone had entered from the hallway. Someone who stood silently behind me.

I stayed where I was, hoping that whoever had come in would go away. But the person behind me waited too, until I gave up and turned around on the bench.

Honoria Phelps stood in the doorway, watching me gravely. As always, she filled her small space dramatically. Her long batik garment hung to her feet in a pattern of startling royal blue and dark green. Copper earrings hung nearly to her shoulders and she looked exotic, and not at all like Porter's Dresden shepherdesses. Miss Kitty slept on her shoulder, as though part of her costume.

I could only stare at this sudden apparition.

"Don't look so surprised, dear," Honoria said. "You needed me, so I came. I brought Amelia along and she's visiting with Evaline. I've been feeling all morning that you wanted me to come, so when the feeling became acute, I drove out to find you."

"I was going to phone you," I said lamely.

"There was no need. I called Daphne's bookshop and she told me where you'd gone, and that Charles had driven you out here. She also told me what happened with your mother last night, and why she thought you needed to get away from Charleston. I'm not sure Mountfort Hall was the right choice of a place for you to come."

"I really have needed to talk with you," I admitted, feeling a surprising comfort in her presence.

"Then let's have a picnic outdoors. Evaline needn't bother serving us lunch. I looked in the refrigerator, and there's cold chicken, potato salad, and leftover corn bread—so we can have a feast."

She put the cat down, and I followed her into the big modernized kitchen, off the second-floor dining room.

When we'd packed a hamper, Honoria led the way down to the riverbank, where an ancient live oak spread its enormous limbs over the water and a small table and metal chairs sat in its shade.

We put out paper plates, but ate with the real silverware Honoria had brought, and drank lemonade from tall crystal glasses. The food tasted wonderful, and I was happy to be away from the house with all of its conflicting currents. For a little while I felt as if I could stop asking questions and let everything go.

Honoria did nothing to disturb my mood. "This tree is at least two hundred years old," she told me. "It has weathered wars and hurricanes, and I hope it will last through future storms. That's always the terrible aftermath of a hurricane—the loss of magnificent trees."

I'd begun to feel very relaxed in Honoria's company, and after we'd eaten, I was ready to talk.

"Charles drove me to Cypress Gardens this morning," I began.

"Of course he thinks he's in love with you," Honoria said calmly. "You're the other half of your sister—perhaps the half he's most attracted to right now."

Others seemed to be seeing what I hadn't noticed at all. Or hadn't wanted to? I set my glass down with a thump.

"Please! Amelia and I are two very different women, and he can't be in love with us both."

"You don't want him, do you?"

"Of course I don't!"

"That's not a given, as they say. He's a pretty attractive man."

I could hardly deny that, since I'd felt his charm more than once. If only I could talk to her about Garrett, who interested me much more. But I put the thought away quickly. Honoria was too good at sensing my thoughts. And as Garrett had pointed out, Porter was always there in the background when it came to Honoria.

"I'm going to stay out here for a few days," she went on. "At least for as long as you're here. When things have quieted down with your mother, we'll go back to Charleston. I'll have to commute for rehearsals, since the play will be opening soon. Though I'm not sure we'll ever be ready. But it will run for a week, and then I'll be free."

The last thing I cared about at the moment was the play, and I put one of my questions into words.

"When you spoke with me in Nathanial's old room, Honoria, you said that I might be the one to tell you why Simon Mountfort died. What did you mean?"

"I've done all I can. I've tried, believe me. But perhaps you will be the one to find out more about his death."

"Everyone says it was a heart attack—and then backs away."

"You might talk to Orva sometime. You're not exactly one of us, yet you have an old tie with her. Sometimes there's still a self-protecting attitude among older black people that started way back in slavery days, when it was a pretty good rule to follow. 'Don't get mixed up with white folks' troubles.' Perhaps Orva still holds onto a bit of that."

"Do you think she knows something the rest of you don't?"

"This is only a sense I have, Molly. She's never opened up with me. I don't think she trusts my spirits!"

"She's been very kind to me. She's even moving upstairs into the room next to where Mrs. Landry has put me. Perhaps I'll have a chance to draw her out while I'm here. Honoria, what am I supposed to be afraid of? Why are some of you trying to protect me?"

She raised her hands helplessly. "I've always seen a dark light around you—though I've never understood what it means. Tonight I mean to try a more direct way of finding out."

"How? What are you talking about?"

"Sometimes Nathanial speaks through me without any warning. But I can't count on that, and there's been no way for me to ask questions. So now I want to force him to come to me. And I want everyone to be there. I think you're the reason this will work."

I didn't like the sound of that. "I don't care for séance spookiness, and I don't believe in it."

"You have the wrong conception, Molly. I'm not going to hold an old-fashioned séance or call in spirits. I'll just set the scene in a special way, so that he will channel through me if he can. If he comes, then anyone there can ask questions—including you."

I still didn't like the sound of this, but I doubted that Honoria would let me off. "Will you invite Garrett?"

"Of course—if he cares to come."

Honoria began packing our lunch things back into the hamper. "You needn't come back with me, Molly. Explore a little. Do you see that path over there? It leads to a place that might interest you. Follow it. Perhaps something will come to you there."

She sounded as though she wanted to be rid of me, but it didn't matter. What else did I have to do? The path she indicated led toward a stand of woods, and I walked toward it slowly, lost in my own clouded thoughts. A quiet time for thinking might be just what I needed.

As it happened, I wasn't to have that quiet time, after all. Though I had no sense of anticipation as I began my walk through the woods.

Thirteen

The well-worn path led away from the river through trees left from what must have once been forested land. I walked slowly with a sense of moving toward some destination I wasn't sure of. Soon, I promised myself, I would turn back to the house and look for Orva Jackson. Somehow I must coax her into helping me.

As the path climbed, it took a final turn and emerged in a cleared area up a rise of ground. Suddenly I understood its reason for being. Crowning the rise was a low brick wall, beyond which

I could see granite headstones. This must be the Mountforts' private cemetery.

As I moved toward a gate in the wall, something close by shrieked raucously. The cry was one of terrible pain, and I turned, startled, to find its source.

A peacock picked his way across a field near the wall, trailing a heavy feather train, its iridescent colors flashing in the sun. The bird seemed unconcerned by my presence, and when he raised his slender, beaked head, his crown of delicate filaments trembled. Again he uttered his frightening cry.

I had never been so close to a peacock before, and I watched, entranced. Dozens of eyes in the bird's long train seemed to watch as I approached the closed gate of the cemetery.

A voice spoke to me from beyond the wall, and I knew immediately that I wouldn't need to wait to talk with Orva. "He's gorgeous, isn't he, Miss Molly? Miss Amelia calls him King Midas. You should see that bird when he's strutting for one of the peahens and puts up the fan of his tail."

Orva came to open the gate for me, and as I entered she waved a hand at a marble marker behind her. "That's Mr. Simon's grave right there. I bring him flowers every week."

I wondered if she was the only one who remembered.

The entire closed space had been neatly tended, so someone came often. A few of the stones were very old, their markings worn dim over the years. The most impressive stone belonged to Edward Mountfort, who had built the Hall and first lived here. A small monument topped with an angel marked his grave.

"Come, Miss Molly. There's a seat over here where you can rest."

Orva indicated a double seat of iron scrollwork, painted white. It was placed near Simon's grave, and I sat down in the shade of a magnolia tree, its white blooms still lingering overhead and scenting the air. Orva chose a mound of grass for her seat and pulled her knees up to her chin under her flowered skirt.

This was the chance I'd waited for.

"Thank you for moving upstairs for a few days," I told her. "I'll feel better having you there. I'm just not used to that big house."

"It's no trouble, Miss Molly." She nodded toward the grave nearby. "You were your daddy's special baby for that little while before you got taken away. And you were special to me too. I took care of you and loved you like you were my own—you and your sister both."

"You said you knew my father when he was young. Can you tell me about him?"

"Your grandma Laura—she's over there, not far away—used to teach Mr. Simon and me lessons together before we went to school. She taught me to read and to speak proper, though Katy says it never took too well with me."

"When my father died you were the one who found him, weren't you?"

She bowed her head silently.

"Will you tell me what happened?"

She spoke without looking up. "It was a terrible thing, Miss Molly. He'd been playing that beautiful music your mama loved —and then he stopped with a sort of crash. I was working at the other end of the hall, and I had a bad feeling right away. I ran down to the music room—and there he was slumped over the piano bench, with his head turned sideways on the keys."

Just where I had rested my head a little while ago.

Orva continued as though the words were wrenched from her. "I won't never forget the way he looked."

"How do you mean?"

223

"Scared, Miss Molly. Like something had come into that room and frightened him so bad that he died right there."

"Did you see anyone?"

She shook her head, still not looking at me. "If anybody'd come out of that room, I'd have seen who it was. But nobody did."

"Then there couldn't have been anyone there, Orva."

"There's a place I didn't think to look before I ran off to get help. Just off one end of the music room there's a small office Mr. Simon used. A long time ago it was where the mistress of the house sat to write her letters and keep her accounts. Somebody hid there until I went for help."

"Did you tell anyone about this, Orva?"

"Once I tried to talk to Mr. Porter, but he said that a heart attack could pretty much scare anybody into looking the way Mr. Simon did when I found him. Only it wasn't like that. Miss Molly, I think he saw something outside his own self—or heard something. And it scared him so bad his poor heart couldn't take the shock."

"Who might have frightened him like that, Orva?"

She was quiet for a moment, and then she raised her head and looked straight at me with wide eyes. "Miss Molly, it don't matter anymore. It's too late. Sometimes I get the feeling that all the ground around us is as quivery as a swamp. Mr. Porter told me not to let my imagination run wild, but one misstep and I don't know what could happen. It's better if you don't talk about this when we go back to the house."

This analogy to a swamp had been haunting me ever since I came. "Did you ever discuss what happened with Katy?"

"She was a young girl when your daddy died, and we haven't talked about it much since she grew up. Better not to. Better leave all that swamp water be."

224

"I've been trying to find my father ever since I came here— just to get to know him a little. I feel that how he died stands in the way. It's as though I'll never know him until I find out what really happened."

"He was a good man, Miss Molly. You can believe that."

"But he believed that he was responsible for something terrible."

"Never mind, Miss Molly. Never mind! Look over yonder in the far corner of this place. That's Mr. Nathanial's grave—sort of all by itself, wouldn't you say? It seems maybe his family was connected to the Mountforts, but nobody wanted to bury him too close."

I called her back to the subject that interested me. "Orva, do you remember who was in the house when my father died?"

"Sure, I remember. All the time there was parties going on, and the house was full! All of your folks and their friends came out from the city."

Just as had been the case when Nathanial died. But before I could push her further for answers, she stood up, moving with agility. "I better get to work now, Miss Molly. Miss Honoria's going to stay upstairs too, instead of in the main bedroom on the second floor, so I need to get a room ready for her. Now you'll have double company, and I reckon that's a good idea. I'm going along back, but you stay here, Miss Molly, and talk to your daddy for a while. Could be, *he* can tell you what you want to know. Miss Honoria thinks that can happen, and maybe I do too."

I could think of nothing to say to Simon Mountfort right now, but I wanted another chance with Orva. She had started along the wooded path, and I called after her.

"Wait for me a minute, Orva. Please! Then we can walk back together."

She couldn't very well refuse me, and she waited. I went into

225

the corner where Nathanial Amory's small headstone stood a little apart. No flowers had been left here, but I suspected that Garrett visited this place regularly. In my mind I formed words with an intensity that surprised me: *Help me to find the way. Help me to help your son—to help all of us.*

Nothing came to me as a sign. Or if I was given a sign, I lacked the sensitivity to interpret it. Beyond the wall, the peacock shrieked again, and I hurried to join Orva.

We walked through the woods in silence until the house came into view. My thoughts scurried, seeking some way to get her to talk to me—to tell me whatever she knew, or suspected. Nothing emerged, and I asked another question as we neared the house.

"Has Mrs. Phelps told you about her plans for this evening?"

Orva began to walk more quickly, perhaps eager to be away from me and my uncomfortable questions. "Miss Honoria mentioned something about that to me, but there's no way I want to be part of what she's got it in mind to do. Calling in spirits can stir up more dead things than she thinks. Let them rest quiet, I say. Don't you mess with any of this neither, Miss Molly."

"I can't stay out of it," I said. "I don't *want* to mess with it, but I have to."

She stopped abruptly on the path. "Then I'll come too. Maybe I have a little good magic, Miss Molly."

"Do you mean that Honoria's magic isn't good?"

"No, oh no! It's okay, but she don't know what the power is that she calls in. So I'll be there, Miss Molly."

Orva led the way around to the river side of the house. I noticed a door I hadn't seen before and I asked her about it.

"Maybe you'd like to see what's down there in the basement, Miss Molly. It's a real big surprise to most people."

Even though it had been the main approach in the days of river travel, the façade that faced the river was less impressive than the Palladian portico on the land side. Steps rose to a simpler entrance leading up from the water, and a carriage road circled around to meet the grander land approach. The steps to the doorway on the river side were built of decorative gray stone. Underneath, a door had been set into the stone at ground level, with two arched windows on either side. The arrangement reminded me uncomfortably of the entrance to the Old Exchange Building.

Orva opened the lower door for me and I stepped into a cool, shadowy, high-ceilinged space that seemed, astonishingly, to be the entrance to a Greek temple.

Orva chuckled softly. "It sure comes as a surprise, don't it, Miss Molly? That old Mr. Edward must've had fun with all this."

On each side of the entry stood a marble column, rising in Doric simplicity to the high ceiling. Or, at least, each was a portion of a column. Only one was topped by a finished capital of the sort that would have supported a roof. There were other columns standing about—broken, incomplete, yet impressive in their graceful ruin. Ahead, deeper into the gloom, rose several broken marble steps, topped by what looked like the remains of a hilltop temple straight out of Greece—two partial columns with a lintel piece resting overhead between them.

Since none of this was rooted in the earth, but seemed precariously balanced, the whole had a surrealistic look, as though painted by Dalí. These gleaming white pieces of marble must, indeed, have come from Greece at a time when that country's ruins had been plundered.

"Do you know why Edward Mountfort built this?" I asked Orva.

"Nobody knows for sure. Mr. Porter hopes Mr. Garrett will find old diaries or account books somewhere to give him an answer. Lots of bits and pieces were left over from marble used on the house—so maybe Mr. Edward just wanted to build his own little temple. It's all kind of spooky down here, and not too safe, they say, so nobody comes here much. Of course, Mr. Edward liked it, he even had himself painted in front of Greek columns in that picture upstairs. I thought you'd be interested to see what's here."

Even by daylight that came in through two windows, the place was certainly creepy, and I could imagine how eerie the illusion would be when moonlight found its way into this "temple" of ancient marble.

Orva led the way around steps that led nowhere, to a wide space of basement beyond, where the floor was paved in large gray stones—more ship's ballast, probably.

Sunlight reached through windows at the far end of a wide central hall, and Orva showed me where the servants' quarters were located. Before the Civil War, of course, there had been slaves housed in cottages—cabins—away from the main house. Afterward, when the years of poverty were past, servants lived down here.

There had been a huge open fireplace where cooking had been done, but now a modern kitchen had been put in for the staff, with a long table where meals could be eaten. Orva showed me her comfortable sitting room and bedroom, and her own small bath.

"I always stayed out here at the plantation when I grew up, Miss Molly. This is where I was born. I don't like the city much, though Katy's always after me to move in with her. Maybe even the ghosts keep me company out here—the ones I feel comfortable with."

"Which ones are they?"

She only smiled. "If you'll wait a minute, Miss Molly, I'll pack some things so I can move upstairs next door to you. Then I'll fix Miss Honoria's room. Someday we'll have an elevator in this big old place. Mr. Charles says it's one of the first things he'll put in after he gets married to Miss Amelia. Of course, the main kitchen is upstairs, so it's not like when meals had to be carried up in the old days."

"Were Charles and my sister planning to live at Mountfort Hall after they married?"

"Oh yes, ma'am. Mr. Charles loves it out here."

We left the basement and started to climb to the top. At the first-floor level, Daphne Phelps called to me from down the hall.

"Hi, Molly. I've been looking for you. We need to talk."

Everyone wanted to talk!

I thanked Orva and she went on upstairs as Daphne led the way into the formal drawing room and turned on a ceiling fan— a modern anachronism spaced between the great chandeliers. She seemed distraught, unlike her usual calm and collected self. We sat together on a green damask sofa, and I grew increasingly aware of her edginess.

"No bookstore today?" I asked.

"I have a good assistant. There were things I needed to do out here. I've talked with your mother and she's pretty remorseful about her behavior last night. I brought her out here this afternoon, and I think she wants to apologize to you—and explain. She even cried a little when we talked, so I hope you'll give her a chance."

The last thing I wanted was another session with Valerie Mountfort, and I suspected that what was worrying Daphne had nothing to do with my mother.

"I don't think I have anything to discuss with her," I said. "And I don't trust her tears and repentance."

"You're probably right to be cautious, but you'd better give in for now. You'll all be together for this performance Honoria is putting on tonight and I suspect it could be pretty enlightening.

Valerie and Amelia are at Evaline's now, talking wedding plans, and I know your mama hopes to see you."

"What is really upsetting you, Daphne?"

She jumped up and moved to a window, turning her back.

"I have the funniest feeling about tonight, Molly. In some ways Honoria is an innocent. I don't think she dreams of what she could release—something that might damage us all."

Orva had hinted at the same thing.

"I thought you didn't believe in Honoria's powers."

"It's not her powers I'm afraid of. It's other things, like the human element that may get frightened enough to become dangerous at a time like this."

"What human element? What are you talking about?"

"That's the trouble—I'm not sure. But I've told Dad what Honoria plans—she didn't tell him! And I hope he'll come out here and stop the whole thing. It's no parlor game she's proposing. I don't plan to attend, and I don't think you should either, Molly. Dad has never understood that he married a woman who was in love with a ghost. My father can be pretty arrogant when he chooses, and he has a whole set of beliefs of his own. To accept Honoria as she really is would be impossible for Porter Phelps. So he prefers to be amused and humor her. In his eyes she's a little doll who can do no wrong. He fools himself first of all. I just wanted to warn you, Molly, and keep you out of this. Games are games, but this could be destructive."

"Tell me what you mean."

"Never mind." Daphne turned from the window. "The less you know, the better. I need to find Garrett and tell him about Honoria's plans."

"He already knows."

"Not all of it—he doesn't."

"What more is there?"

She regarded me in sober speculation. "I can't talk about this yet. Maybe I'll never be ready to. There are too many lives that could be affected. Sometimes I think it's better to let everything alone."

"So that a murderer will never be exposed? Isn't that what Honoria is after?"

Daphne looked genuinely surprised. "I wasn't thinking about murder. I'm thinking about whatever it was that Nathanial Amory discovered before his death. Molly, you know who Garrett is, don't you?"

"Yes. He told me a little while ago. But if Honoria manages to evoke Nathanial's spirit, as she thinks she can, he will only tell us the truth. So what are you afraid of?"

"Don't be too sure about second-guessing a source we can't possibly understand. I expect spirits have their own agendas—just like human beings. Honoria is meddling and maybe she'll let the genie out of the bottle. I don't know what I think about all that. What really scares me are the lives that could be carelessly ruined."

"I don't think Honoria can be stopped at this point."

"Dad can stop her. If he chooses to. I'm going to look for Garrett now. So why not go over to Evaline's cottage and make your peace with your mother? There's a tour coming through here in a little while, so we might as well find someplace else to be. I'll see you later."

She hurried away down the long room and disappeared around a corner.

I decided that I might as well do what she'd suggested, and I turned off the fan and went outside.

Visitors were already coming from the parking area across the grounds, and scattering in different directions. One group wandered toward a little gift shop across wide lawns where sheep grazed. Others separated to visit the long low building where indigo dye was being prepared in the old way, and weavers worked at their looms. Charles had pointed out these places to me, and I had been fascinated. As I went past, I looked through a window to see a young potter at his wheel. The voice of a guide drifted out to me. At another time I would stay and listen, but Daphne's fears were contagious and I wanted to find my sister. Perhaps Amelia was my anchor to reality. Her happiness mattered to me, and when I thought about my twin, I could even dredge up the courage to face Valerie Mountfort.

Fourteen

The Landry cottage—once a slave cabin—carried few reminders of its past. Its bricks had faded to a softly focused pink, and rosebushes grew beneath the front windows. Shallow steps led to a narrow door, left over from the original cabin.

When I knocked, voices inside hushed, and Evaline Landry came to greet me.

"Good afternoon, Miss Hunt." She opened the screen to invite me in, and though her greeting was formal, she didn't seem unwelcoming. I stepped into what had once been the single main room. Charles's father had expanded it by building several rooms at the back.

Rustic furnishings made it quietly inviting. Mountfort Hall's elegance would be out of place here. Plaid chair cushions were secured with perky ties, and most of the furniture had been hand-crafted of local woods. For me, however, Evaline Landry seemed more in character as the chatelaine of the big house.

From a kneehole desk a framed photograph of her son looked out at the room. I knew that expression of cheerful confidence— not far from the arrogance I had first suspected—and I turned quickly away.

In the center of the room Amelia was being fitted for her wedding dress, and an elderly seamstress knelt to pin up the hemline. My sister smiled at me warmly, her head rising like a blossom from tiny ruffles. For all that she was my twin, *I* would never look as tenderly beautiful. Inner happiness had given Amelia a glow that I could never achieve. I hadn't looked like that even when Doug was alive, contented though I'd believed myself to be.

"Will I do, Molly?" she called to me, knowing very well that there was only one answer.

Thinking of Charles made it difficult to respond as warmly as I wanted to, but I managed to tell her how perfect she looked. Had I ever been as young as my sister? Her lovely innocence became her, even though that could be a treacherous quality as a woman moved beyond the age of innocence.

Movement in a shadowy corner of the room caught my eye, and I saw Valerie Mountfort rising to come toward me. She spoke quickly, without any greeting.

"Please come outside with me, Molly. I have to talk with you. It's very important to me."

234

Evaline Landry, hovering about Amelia and the seamstress, glanced at me briefly. Almost imperceptibly she nodded at me, and I knew I had no choice but to follow my mother out of the cottage.

"I'll be back soon," I told Amelia as my mother and I walked out into the warm afternoon.

Valerie led the way again, just as she had last night—but this time she kept up a stream of polite conversation, often looking over her shoulder to see if I were keeping up. I wanted to dig in my heels and refuse to go anywhere with her after last night. Where was she taking me this time and why was I going? I slowed my pace, forcing her to wait. As we neared the main house, she stopped and faced me.

"Don't be afraid," she said. "I don't blame you for feeling nervous. I behaved outrageously last night. Sometimes I can't help myself and your return has upset me so."

Apparently she thought this excuse seemed quite plausible and reasonable, in spite of her carelessly spoken "outrageously."

"I'm not sure there's any way to explain or excuse what you put me through," I told her.

She smiled without warmth. "I wish I could like you better. Perhaps that will come in time. It's not your fault. I always built you up in my mind in quite a different way. You could never match what I expected my Cecelia to be like. You must understand that I have suffered even more than you have."

We'd begun to walk again, and I picked up this strange conversation. "I haven't suffered at all. My adoptive parents loved me, and I grew up in a happy home. So I've never missed the life I might have had in Charleston."

We'd reached the steps on the land side, and she ran up them to the doorway. I followed as she went into the wide central hall. She moved directly to the music room, though she never glanced at the piano as she hurried past. A door opened off the far corner into a small room. This must be the office Orva had mentioned. A room my father had used.

One wall was lined with books and there were several pieces of good furniture, solid and large enough for masculine use. Valerie stood looking around for a moment. "I haven't set foot in this room for years, but it has been kept just as it used to be when Simon was alive. This was where he took care of plantation affairs. Of course, even then, Porter managed the more important money matters. Cousin Porter cared about Mountfort Hall more than Simon ever did. I think my husband spent a lot of his time in this room reading—to escape from things he couldn't cope with. Perhaps couldn't face. Do sit down, Molly."

I chose the straight desk chair. My sympathies were with my father. I'd begun to gather an impression of the man he must have been, and I liked him far more than I would ever like my mother or her cousin Porter.

"I want to tell you something," she said, curling up in one corner of the couch. "In this room no one can hear us and we can speak freely."

"About what?" My continuing resistance sounded in my voice.

Valerie seemed not to notice, intent on her own single purpose. "About your sister. You are the only one who can help Amelia avoid making a terrible mistake."

"What kind of mistake?" I asked.

"Oh, she doesn't know she's making one, and she would deny every word I say. Perhaps it's your fault that I've neglected her—because for so many years I could only think of the baby I'd lost."

This was so unfair that I didn't attempt an answer.

She uncurled herself and went to Simon's desk, where she picked up something from its surface before she sat down again.

Her small, strong fingers held a long paper knife in the form of a silver saber.

"I gave your father this years ago, before you and Amelia were born. He was very fond of it. Though once he cut himself with it."

She drew the slender weapon from its six-inch scabbard, and held it out to me. "You can see how sharp it is."

I didn't touch the paper knife. "Why did you bring me here?"

Carefully she replaced the saber in its sheath. "I know I'm delaying—because it's all so hard to say. Molly, your sister must not marry Charles Landry."

There was nothing I could say. My surprise was too great. Even though I might agree, I also felt certain Amelia would do as she pleased when it came to Charles.

"He's not in love with her," Valerie went on, "and that lack of love, once she recognizes it, will destroy her. Amelia's too much like her father—she's not as strong as I am. Of course Charles grew up with her, and he has a brother's affection for her. I think he even fooled himself for a while, convincing himself that he loved her. It's Porter who wants this, and Porter's influence with Charles is greater than anyone else's, even though Evaline is a strong woman who can usually manage her son. Porter will never listen to me. I'm just his feckless young cousin, and he thinks me unbalanced anyway."

I could certainly understand why Porter would think she was unbalanced, but I had no idea where this was going, or where I came in, and I waited.

"Amelia has stars in her eyes," Valerie went on, "and she has never loved anyone but Charles. Even when he was running after other girls, she waited for him. So it's hopeless to talk to her."

"If the marriage was stopped now, it would break her heart," I said.

237

"Broken hearts mend. It's a lot harder to mend broken lives."

Everything she was saying sounded perfectly rational and sensible. I had the same feeling about Amelia marrying Charles, but I had no idea how to stop her.

"How can you possibly change her mind?" I asked.

"I can't, Molly. But you can."

"That's foolish. She would never listen to me." If Amelia knew what had happened at Cypress Gardens this morning, she might blame me instead of Charles.

"It's not a matter of listening, Molly. I have a faultless plan. *You* are going to marry Charles. That will take care of the whole matter irrevocably."

Once more she had shocked me into silence, and she smiled at me, slyly triumphant. "You see how simple it is? You're attracted to him—women always are. And, obviously, he is already attracted to you. No, don't protest, I've seen the way he looks at you. So you'll be doing something that will be good for both you and Charles—and you'll save your sister at the same time."

She *was* a little mad, I thought—building her own fantasy world that no one could argue her out of.

"It's impossible, of course," I said.

That was the wrong word to use with Valerie Mountfort, and she merely shrugged it aside.

"You won't be able to help yourself, Molly. You will do this because you love your sister, and because the sooner it is done, the safer she will be."

"What do you mean—safe?"

This time she waved her own word aside. "Charles is being pushed into a marriage he doesn't want. You are the solution. And it's far better if Amelia hates you than if she does something that may very well push her over the edge and ruin her emotional stability for the rest of her life. You and Charles can run off together without any delay, and then neither Porter nor anyone else can do a thing about it. Your own inheritance from Simon will make Charles independent of Porter—*and* he'll have Mountfort Hall, which will make him very happy."

I stood up and started toward the door. "Perhaps there is someone else who would oppose this idea."

"Evaline? She and I are old friends. Once she gets over her first shock and realizes what Charles wants, it won't matter to her which twin he marries. Frankly, I think all she cares about is seeing the Hall come to Charles, so you see this is a perfect plan. And you will still be entitled to half of the inheritance you and Amelia were meant to share all along."

I didn't know Evaline Landry well enough to know how she would react about anything. I doubted, however, that she could be manipulated as easily as Valerie thought and I knew I couldn't be.

"Never mind, dear." Valerie changed her course, suddenly as sweet as magnolia blossoms—a change I distrusted entirely. "Let's not discuss this any more right now. You need to think about what I've said. I've brought you something—a little gift to make up for last night."

She took a small box from her purse and held it out to me.

I stiffened. Whatever it was, I didn't want it.

"I know you'll accept this because it's from Simon—your father. You can't refuse a gift from him." She picked up my limp hand and forced the box into my fingers. "Open it, Molly."

The jeweler's box was of blue velvet, embossed in gold, and I knew what the contents would be before I raised the hinged lid to see a pair of lotus earrings, made of coral set in gold.

"Put them on, Molly," Valerie urged.

It was easier to do as she wished and get away from her as quickly as I could. I realized again that she was incapable of listening to anything I might say. I clipped the earrings to my earlobes and hurried away from her through the music room, and toward the stairs. Behind me, I heard her laughing—that same eerie sound I'd heard last night in the darkness of that appalling dungeon.

I had promised Amelia to come back to the cottage, but I couldn't face her now. I ran upstairs to the second floor and found Miss Kitty watching from the top step. She began to stalk back and forth, mewing plaintively, obstructing my way.

"Look out, kitty," I said. "I don't want to step on you."

She promptly twined herself around one ankle and began to yowl. I was relieved when Honoria came out of Garrett's office and down the hall to see what was happening.

"I don't know what she wants," I said, "but I wish you'd make her stop."

Honoria, looking quizzically at Miss Kitty, came to unwind her from around my feet, and gathered her up soothingly. The cat would have none of this. She dug in her claws and sprang away. Back at the head of the stairs she sat down to resume her yowling.

"I don't understand your behavior, Miss Kitty," Honoria told her. "Molly, what do you think she's trying to tell me? I'm trying to get everything ready for tonight and I don't have time for this. The afternoon is practically gone, and I must see that the atmosphere will be proper for what we need to accomplish. Will you help me?"

At the moment I wanted neither Honoria's nor the cat's company.

"I'm sorry. I can't imagine what's wrong with Miss Kitty and I'm going up to my room for a while to rest. Can't you get Garrett or Orva to help you?"

"They've evaporated, since they don't approve of what I want to do. This isn't a séance, Molly. What we do these days is very different. We call it a sitting, and there's no ectoplasm, or table rapping, or ghostly voices. None of that phony stuff. Whatever happens is channeled through me. But go up and get your rest. I'll manage somehow."

Miss Kitty, now silent, watched me reproachfully as I climbed the upper flight to my room. Later I would wonder how matters might have gone if we had paid attention to the warning Miss Kitty was trying to give.

The door to my room stood closed, and I opened it to an unpleasant surprise. The rocking horse from the South Battery house stood in the center of the room. Whoever had put it there meant to upset me.

I heard Orva in the next room, and when I called to her, she came out at once and clucked over the presence of the horse.

"Did you see anyone bring it up here?" I asked.

Orva shook her head. "I didn't see anything, Miss Molly. But I reckon it was Miss Valerie's notion."

"But why put it in my room?"

"Something she's trying to tell you?" Orva suggested. "Just a reminder, maybe? Of course that rocking horse belongs out here at the Hall."

"At least it's not rocking the way it did in Charleston."

"Miss Honoria says it takes Miss Valerie being around to make it rock."

"What do you mean?"

Orva frowned. "I can't remember the word she used. Something that begins with 'kin'—some kind of energy."

"Kinetic? Kinetic energy might be a possibility, though isn't that supposed to be connected with poltergeist activity? I believe it comes from an emotional intensity so great that it can move objects. Usually only the very young possess it." Or the mad. A chill went through me.

In any case, I didn't want the wooden horse in my room. A fact that Orva had already recognized. She picked it up with little effort and carried it out in the hall, leaving me to rest.

I shut the door and lay down on the bed. For now, I wanted only to be still and not think about anything. I mustn't let what Charles had done, or what Valerie Mountfort had said, devastate me. Neither one could make me do anything I didn't want to.

So why did I have this sense of a net settling over me, entangling me in its folds? If I could sleep for a little while, perhaps I could get up with a clearer head and then look for Garrett. He was as far from Charles and Valerie as I could get, and something had seemed to begin between us. Perhaps he would offer me support and reassurance now. I seemed to be thinking about him a lot.

I was still tired from my loss of sleep the night before, and the few minutes I intended to rest grew into a couple of hours. I awoke suddenly, with the sense of a distant crash ringing in my ears, and a feeling that my bed had reverberated as though in an earthquake. I sat up and listened, my heart thudding, but there was no further sound and my bed seemed perfectly still. I must have had a vivid dream—otherwise I'd hear the sound of voices, of people running to investigate. There was nothing.

Someone had left a tray beside my bed. Since I had nearly two hours left to eat and dress, I took my time. Sandwiches had been wrapped in wax paper, and a covered slice of apple pie tempted me. Even a small percolator could be plugged in to give me hot coffee. All Orva's doing, I felt sure, but I was wrong.

A note lay on the tray. It was the first time I'd seen Honoria's distinctive handwriting—almost like calligraphy with its decorative flourishes. She wanted me to rest as long as I could. Then I was to eat and come downstairs—at least by seven-thirty. Her words concluded: "This may be the most important night

Mountfort Hall will ever see. All the answers are to be made clear. I feel sure of this. Honoria."

A tall order, considering the turbulent years these walls had known, yet a new sense of anticipation grew in me. I felt refreshed and even hungry. After I plugged in the percolator, I showered, then I came back out and sat down to eat.

Afterward I put on an azalea-pink silk shirt that I could wear with white pants. No bandeau, though I clipped on the lotus earrings, feeling a little defiant. Though I wasn't sure of whom or what.

By seven-thirty I'd put on my lipstick and a touch of blush, since my skin was too pale. The reflection I saw in the mirror was Molly Hunt, and not Amelia, and that was the way it should be. I wanted to hold tight to my own identity tonight, whatever might happen.

When I reached the room that had been Nathanial's, I looked first of all for Garrett. He stood away from the others, leaning against a desk that must have been used by his father. He met my look without smiling, and I knew he saw the earrings. For a moment his eyes held mine and I sensed the strength he offered me. Strength and something more. I smiled at him warmly, accepting. Something *had* begun, and I felt almost happy.

Honoria had dressed for her role—of seeress? She wore a white silk robe with flowing Japanese sleeves and a wide sash tied with a flat bow at the back. In this kimono-like garment, she looked not so much young as ageless. A tiny enchantress.

Beside Garrett and myself, only Amelia, Charles, and Orva were present. I suspected that Orva was here only because Honoria had insisted. Aware of her fear of Honoria's "meddling," I went to sit beside her.

"Porter should be here soon," Honoria told us. "He may be late leaving the city, but he will come. Of course, he's argued

243

against what I want to do, but higher voices have advised me, and nothing can stop us now. Evaline is coming, and of course Daphne, though I don't know about Valerie."

"Daphne told me this afternoon that she wouldn't be here," I said to Honoria. "She was pretty convincing about not wanting to come."

"And Evaline doesn't feel that Mama should join us," Amelia said. "Though I don't know how she can be kept away if she decides this is what she wants to do."

Evaline *had* managed to convince her not to come, as she explained when she arrived a few minutes later.

"I don't think Valerie should be here, Honoria. She was already in an excitable state, so I gave her a tranquilizer and she's sound asleep."

Charles's mother looked no more relaxed than the rest of us. She wore a violet frock of soft chiffon that gave her a look less severe than usual. Nevertheless I had the strong feeling, as she sat down next to her son, that she greatly disapproved of whatever Honoria intended here tonight.

We all watched as Honoria performed a ritual of lighting tall white candles around the room.

"We need white for protection," she informed us. "Though these will burn with a yellow flame that is spiritual, and that is also protective."

Charles's eyes followed me as I went to sit beside Orva, and I could only hope that Valerie hadn't told him of her foolish plan. Amelia still looked innocently happy, her hand confidingly in his. Watching my sister, my spirits sank. I could see no happy future for her if she married Charles. My mother was right. Amelia was emotionally fragile. Could Amelia end up like Valerie? Is *that* what my mother feared?

At the last minute, just before Honoria was ready to start,

Porter appeared in the doorway, bristling with indignation. Before he could burst into words, however, Honoria spoke to him sweetly, her tone somehow compelling.

"Please join us, dear. We're about to begin."

Whatever his intended objections, his wife's voice seemed to quiet him almost hypnotically. He sat near the door, containing himself, but exuding disapproval of whatever was about to take place. Daphne had been wrong—Porter would stop nothing.

I noticed Miss Kitty stood at the threshold of the room, but did not enter. Did she know something we didn't?

Call it séance or sitting or whatever, this entire scene had trappings I didn't care for. A round teakwood table had been placed in the center of the room, and at a gesture from Honoria, Garrett sat in a chair placed opposite her at the table. His own tension was clearly high, and Honoria reached to place a hand on his arm.

"Let everything go. Let your anxious feelings float away from you. Free your mind of doubt. We need to be empty—free of disbelief before the spirit we seek can come in."

Again her voice, her words, seemed to have an hypnotic effect. Garrett relaxed visibly, and perhaps the rest of us were affected to some extent, so we could let anxiety float away.

A slight breeze from open windows caused the candle flames to dip, and shadows moved around us with a seeming life of their own. Reflections stirred in an inverted crystal bowl that had been placed in the center of the table. A bowl for flowers in another life? Cut-glass facets broke flickering light into rainbows that were never quiet.

I tried to hold on to some last bit of reality. I didn't want to lose myself so deeply in Honoria's spells that I could no longer judge objectively.

Across the table Garrett and Honoria faced each other, and

both stared into the shimmering rainbows of light. I stole a look around the room at the others. Porter poker-faced, Evaline Landry remote and probably wishing herself somewhere else, Amelia holding Charles's hand tightly, and Charles with a look on his face that I recognized—amused and superior to all this nonsense. Only Orva, beside me, kept her fingers tensely interlaced in her lap. I wished that Katy had been invited. Instinctively, I knew her presence in this room would make me feel more comfortable.

"We must be very quiet now," Honoria said. "It takes a great energy for an entity to come through—energy that can weaken quickly in the face of adverse emanations. Whatever happens, we mustn't interrupt. Only Garrett will ask the questions."

She seemed calm and accepting—ready for whatever might occur. "Before we begin, we must ask for help," she added.

Her few, almost inaudible words were of prayer. Then she placed her hands palms down on the table and stared intently into the pulsating lights in the crystal bowl. It seemed a magical living sphere now, its humble origin forgotten. Softly she began to speak, and white light seemed to radiate from her silk robe.

"Will you speak to us, Nathanial? Your son is here and he has questions to ask of you. Please come in."

Someone gasped at the word "son." Probably Porter. Orva reached her hand for mine, steadying, as though she knew and reassured me. Suddenly a voice that was not Honoria's normal tone spoke in the room. A voice I had heard before in this house, when it had come through uninvited.

What are the questions?

The channel had been taken over. Honoria was only a vessel now, and it was up to Garrett to carry on. He spoke simply and directly.

"Are you Nathanial Amory?"

246

There was no answer. Probably no energy would be wasted on what might be considered obvious. Garrett spoke again.

"We want to know how you died."

Drowned. Only one word.

"Was it an accident?"

No.

"Who caused your death?"

A long silence followed, and Garrett repeated the question. The voice spoke again, strong enough to be heard, but sounding as though the effort to use human vocal cords was something long forgotten.

Notebook. Find. Notebook.

"Find where?"

Again the long hesitation, the obvious effort. *Hidden. Marble.*

"Please tell us what you mean."

Stolen. Money stolen. The voice was fading, as though its power to speak was lessening.

"Did the person who caused your boat to sink steal something?"

I had the feeling that the voice was struggling to answer, but suddenly Honoria gasped as though her breath had been snatched away. She moved convulsively and her face contorted. Something —something other than Nathanial—was trying to force its way into the channel.

Honoria sighed deeply, as though she surrendered, and a new voice shrilled through her—strong and terrified. Terrifying!

No no no! Help me, help me!

Garrett recovered first. "Who are you? How can we help you?"

Too late! The temple has fallen.

An empty silence followed. The channel was clear, and no further words came through from any source.

247

Honoria stirred and spoke in her own trembling voice. While she had taken no active part, she knew all that had happened. "We must go at once! Help me blow out the candles, Orva. The only temple I know of is the marble one old Edward Mountfort built in the basement. We must go down there right away."

Porter tried to stop her. "Don't, Honoria! You're carrying this too far." He was white and sweat rolled down his face.

She brushed past him blindly on her way to the door, and he let her go. Amelia had begun to shiver, and looked as though she might faint. Evaline Landry was very pale, but she put an arm about her as she spoke to her son.

"Go with them, Charles. I'll take Amelia back to the cottage."

For a moment I thought Charles would object, but Amelia beseeched him with her eyes, and he let her go off with his mother.

Garrett caught my hand and held it tightly, pulling me into the hallway after Honoria. It was as though he had a right to draw me with him, and I held on to him gratefully. Orva followed us, as Porter stumbled almost blindly toward the stairs.

Miss Kitty waited for us at the top of the stairs, and again I had the eerie feeling that she'd known something all along and had even tried to warn us of what might happen. Now, when she saw that Honoria meant to go downstairs, she neither howled nor mewed, but flew ahead, pausing now and then to look back and make sure we followed her.

At the basement level, the stairs ended in the section farthest from Edward Mountfort's whimsical "temple." Miss Kitty didn't hesitate. She bounded ahead along the central hallway, still leading the way. Someone turned on lights, so that white columns of marble sprang to life ahead of us. But now the configuration had changed from what I had seen with Orva that afternoon.

One column at the top of the wide marble steps had fallen, dropping the gray lintel stone it had helped to support. Miss Kitty sprang onto the fallen lintel, and every hair on her body bristled. Someone lay beneath the heavy stone and I saw that blood had stained the marble. An arm flung to one side displayed a woman's hand, wearing a distinctive jade ring. I recognized the ring—it belonged to Daphne Phelps.

For a moment we all stood motionless, stunned with horror. Then Garrett knelt beside the marble beam, and his hand shook as he touched Daphne's wrist. "I think she's been dead for a long while," he said grimly. "Hours, perhaps. The crash down here of marble falling must have rocked the house. Didn't anyone hear?"

Apparently no one had. Then I remembered being shaken awake by what I'd thought was a dream. Later I was able to pinpoint the time for the police, and it was an hour when everyone else, except Daphne and me, seemed to have been out of the house.

Porter's voice shook as he spoke. "Send for an ambulance, someone!" He seemed incapable of moving, riveted to the spot by disbelief and a numbing grief.

Orva ran off to telephone. Garrett appeared to have himself sternly in hand, while Charles looked sick and close to collapse. Full realization would strike us all later, but perhaps Honoria was closer to this state because of her channeling, and she began to cry softly.

"That doesn't help," her husband told her—the first time I'd ever heard him sound impatient toward Honoria.

I sat down shakily on a marble step, unable to accept the fact of death. How could Daphne be so suddenly gone? Had she leaned against that column—jarred it into falling? I felt wet tears on my cheeks.

The remaining column towered above me like a threat, and I

249

got up to move away from that menacing weight. An appalling thought had come to me. What if someone had deliberately pushed the column over when Daphne had stood beneath the lintel?

Honoria stopped crying and spoke the words I'd been thinking. "Someone shoved that column over! That's what Daphne was trying to tell me!"

"What do you mean?" Porter asked sharply.

"The channel was open because of Nathanial, and Daphne took it. She spoke through me, calling for help, although it was already too late and she knew it."

Porter sat down on another stone, well away from the lintel, as if his legs would no longer hold him. He stared at his wife as though everything about her suddenly sickened him.

Under her white silk garment Honoria wore jeans and a shirt. She removed the gown and spread it sorrowfully over Daphne's body. At once a streak of scarlet stained the white cloth. But when she turned to her husband, Porter drew away as if he couldn't bear her touch.

"What you've done tonight is unforgivable," he said, seeming to blame his wife for what had happened to his daughter.

Honoria answered him quietly. "I am not responsible for Daphne's death, my dear. It was necessary to contact Nathanial, if I hadn't, Daphne might not have been discovered for days. She was a newer, stronger, more frightened spirit, so she could take the power from Nathanial and reach us. I suspect that she's here now, watching us."

Porter covered his face with his hands, but when Honoria touched his arm, he flinched and drew away.

Unexpectedly, it was Charles who took a practical approach. "The police will ask questions. Maybe it's just as well if we don't confuse them with side roads. They'd never understand that Daphne led us down here."

Porter agreed at once. "Nobody should talk about that rigmarole upstairs. It has nothing to do with Daphne's accident. Does anyone know why she was down here?"

I surprised myself by answering, since I'd intended to keep still. "Nathanial said something was hidden in a marble place."

No one picked up my words, and when we heard sirens, Garrett went outside to bring in the police officers. The ambulance rescue squad arrived soon after, though "rescue" was no longer a word that applied.

I stood back and watched, a growing sense of sorrow for Daphne filling me. She'd been kind and sensible last night, when I'd needed her. Irrelevantly, I remembered that I'd promised to sign books for her—and never had. Little things. . . .

Honoria's agile mind was already concocting a story. She explained to the police that we had no idea why Daphne had been down here. It was only by chance that she'd been found, when Honoria had come in from an errand, through this river side. I offered my memory of a jarring dream some hours earlier, when everyone else was apparently away from the house. The others were silent.

The sirens and lights brought Evaline, who arrived shortly after the police, with Valerie on her heels, having refused to be left behind. My mother's state was one of high excitement. At least I was glad that Amelia hadn't come with them.

Evaline registered the scene quietly, with no reaction that I could read. However she might feel, she would be wise enough to offer no opinions to the police.

There was, however, no way of stopping Valerie. "Daphne's been asking for trouble!" she cried to anyone who would listen.

251

"She's been inviting something awful to happen to her!" Valerie clutched at her gown and began to moan.

Both police officers looked interested, but Valerie was obviously in no condition to be questioned at the moment. Porter put an arm around her in an effort to soothe her. As we all watched, one officer knelt to take a small object from Daphne's fingers. He held up a single lotus earring set in silver.

Valerie stared at the object in his hand for a frozen instant. Then she began to scream hysterically. The sound crashed from stone floor to marble columns deafeningly, until Porter took her by the shoulders and shook her into silence. Wild hysteria subsided, and her words came in a whisper.

"Simon! I know it was Simon. He hated us all so much. And now he's come back to do this."

Porter pushed Valerie into a chair that Orva had brought, and I was close enough to hear what he said to her.

"Poor Simon is dead. Do you really want him brought into this? The past has nothing to do with what's happened here, so pull yourself together."

Valerie quieted, her hands clasped tensely in her lap. Evaline Landry bent over her, murmuring something.

"Amelia needs us now," Evaline said so we all could hear. "Let's go back to the cottage."

Valerie rose obediently and went out the door with Evaline. Not even the police tried to stop them. Questioning would come later.

Fifteen

Everyone had gone off except Honoria, Garrett, and me. The medical examiners had come, and Daphne's body had been removed sometime before. Porter had gone to Evaline's to pick up Valerie and Amelia and return to Charleston—something Honoria herself had suggested. During this time of confusion, Orva managed to disappear and no one inquired after her.

Before they left, the police told us that the county sheriff would return in the morning and would want to see everyone who had been here the previous evening.

Honoria stayed on at the Hall, as she had originally planned. Porter would need time to himself, she told us calmly. That was the way he would work through his grief. Now she sat on a chunk of marble that left her feet dangling, and stared into space. Miss Kitty sprang onto her lap, beseeching, until Honoria began to stroke her absently. Honoria looked deeply exhausted, yet remote and unapproachable.

Garrett touched my arm. "Let's get out of here, Molly."

His voice carried an edge of pain. He had been closer to Daphne in recent years than almost anyone else—they'd been good friends. As I stood up to go with him, he spoke to Honoria gently.

"What happened wasn't your fault. Don't take on all the blame."

Her eyes opened widely, as though she saw him for the first time. "Fault doesn't enter into it. Unfinished business does. None of us is safe until we *know*. Daphne knew too much."

"Then perhaps you'd better not stay here alone," Garrett told her.

"I'm not alone. I'm waiting for Daphne. Perhaps she can guide me through this maze."

I hated to leave her there the way she sounded, but Garrett drew me out the door.

"I don't think anyone will hurt her, Molly. The damage has been done. But perhaps she'll find some answer in her own way."

We walked around to sit on a bench to watch the moon paint silver shafts across the water. The air felt warm and, as always at night, flower scents drifted on every slight breeze. It was late, but Garrett didn't seem ready to return to Charleston, and I hated to go back into the house.

"What do you think happened upstairs?" I asked him. "Do you think Nathanial really came through?"

"If he did, he left us with a lot to consider. He certainly didn't reveal how his boat was scuttled or who was responsible."

"But he wouldn't have known that, would he? He'd have died not knowing who sabotaged his boat, who stole his life."

"I suppose you're right."

"Do you believe in Honoria's channeling?"

"Believe? Disbelieve? Either word implies finality. I can only say I don't know. I've read a bit about the subject since I came here. There are various theories. At least on the part of those who don't dismiss channeling completely. Honoria believes that some entity from outside her body speaks through her vocal cords. There are others who think this voice comes from some 'higher self' within the person who channels. Perhaps from some part of the brain that we haven't learned to harness. Or there might even be access to some larger, more universal fund of knowledge. Jung believed that."

I didn't want abstract speculation. Something had touched Honoria that appeared to be outside human experience.

"Let it go, Molly," Garrett said. "For now let it all go and just *be.*"

This was what he had done for me when he'd shown me a lighted spire against the night sky—something so serene and quieting that for a little while I'd let all anxiety flow away. But now I sensed his sadness, his own grieving for Daphne.

"I'm sorry, Garrett. I know how much she meant to you."

His fingers tightened about mine. "She's been a good friend ever since I came here. I could talk to her about anything. I loved her and I'll miss her. But I wasn't in love with her, Molly."

There was nothing I could say, and after a moment he stood

up. "I'll walk you up to your room and then I have to get back to Charleston."

He hadn't moved away from me, and I felt comforted. We went into the house after pausing briefly at the basement door to check on Honoria. She had gone and the lights were off, so that piles of marble shone dimly in the shadows.

When we reached the upper hallway, Garrett stopped beside the rocking horse. "What's this?"

"A long story. I'll tell you another time."

He accepted that. Gently he touched my cheek with a finger, lifted a strand of hair. Then he went off down the hall with that springy step that was natural to him, even in times of stress.

I entered my dark bedroom, turned on a light and gasped with fright. Evaline Landry sat in a chair near a window, and she stood up as I came in.

"I hope you won't mind my waiting for you, Miss Hunt. I didn't mean to alarm you," she said gravely. "I had to return to see you."

"Please call me Molly," I said automatically, my body still trembling from her unexpected presence. "And of course I don't mind."

But I did. Every bone in my body seemed to ache, and only the solitude of my bed appealed to me. I wanted no discussion about anything.

She sat down when I did. "Porter has taken Valerie and Amelia home. So I came here. I wanted to reassure you about your mother."

It wasn't Valerie who concerned me now, and I waited.

"She has told me about her plan to have you marry Charles. Of course I've talked to her sensibly, but she persists in thinking it is an excellent idea."

256

I had always sensed an underlying strength in this woman, but I still wasn't sure of her motives.

"I'm glad you've talked to her. Of course this is a foolish idea, and nothing I have wanted. She is not well. Do you know why she started to scream when that police officer found the earring in Daphne's fingers?"

Mrs. Landry hesitated. "Perhaps it reminded her of something she finds it hard to live with. I'm afraid your mother's illness is growing worse. She has had no professional help, of course, since she refuses to air her problems with a stranger. But the family has protected her for too long."

I had no thoughts about any of this, and she saw my weariness. "I won't keep you. I didn't know whether I would see you alone in the morning and I did want a word with you. Good night, Molly."

She went off and I wondered briefly why she had come at all. At least I'd indicated that I had no interest in Charles, and perhaps that was what she wanted to hear.

I undressed as quickly as I could and was asleep the moment my head touched the pillow.

In the days that followed, no one revealed anything to the police about Honoria's "sitting." They were told that Daphne hadn't been seen for hours before Honoria found her.

The investigation revealed that the weight of the column that had fallen had begun to crack the stone floor at its base. A tilting that had resulted must have been increased by Daphne herself. She had always been fascinated by this "temple," and she must have stood directly under the lintel stone. Her weight on the cracked floor could have made the difference, so that the column had fallen, dropping the stone to pin her beneath it. The second column remained firmly on level stone, where no cracking had taken place. The family, influenced by Honoria, thought differently, but with no evidence to go on, nothing was said. The press made enough of what they were given, and though I was sure the police were not totally satisfied, they had no reason to delve any more deeply into our lives.

There were other developments during this period that had nothing to do with the police. Porter, infuriated to learn that he had employed a man whom he now termed a "spy," discounted all the good work Garrett had done on the history of the Mountforts and fired him for not revealing his relationship with Nathanial. The book would be published, but it would go no further than Nathanial Amory's death.

Garrett phoned me and told me of his decision to remain in Charleston for the duration of the play, and then return north. In spite of the falling out with Porter, Honoria had begged him to stay. Amelia had decided to dedicate the play to Daphne. The opening night was to serve as a sort of memorial service to her, with a few close friends invited to come up on the stage after the play to pay tribute to her. At first I had thought it odd for the play to go on, but I had come to realize that it meant a great deal to Daphne's friends and relatives to feel they were doing something for her.

I saw nothing of Garrett during this time, though he called me on two other occasions and sounded concerned. Concerned, but a little distant. He even advised me to go home to Bellport— something I wouldn't do. Not yet. Not until I could figure out what was going to happen with Charles and Amelia.

It was a sad, rather lonely time for me. Garrett no longer came out to the Hall. The plans for the memorial service, the play, and the wedding were keeping Amelia away from me and I knew I wasn't wanted in Charleston. I felt sure Porter had a part in this. More than anyone else, *he* had seemed to want me gone. Apparently Porter had decided he needed Honoria and she too had gone back to the city. She told me confidently that I would be quite safe, although she didn't tell me why she thought this.

At least Orva was close by, and in my mind I allowed the date for the play to be my deadline for making a decision about staying or leaving. I wanted to see them all together one more time—but I wasn't sure I could bear to stay for the wedding. I locked my door at night and felt anything but comfortable, though something in me insisted that I stay at Mountfort Hall. There was still a last act to be played, a last chapter to be written before I could be free. Garrett was waiting for something—I could sense that—and until whatever it was happened, everything between us was in suspension. I didn't dare to think ahead, but I was keenly aware of how much I missed him.

Evaline Landry kept a concerned eye on me. She insisted that a proper dinner be served every night in the small dining room on the second floor. She often joined me and tried, in her rather stiff way, to make me comfortable. At least I was thankful that Charles didn't attempt to see me at this time. I felt sure he had chosen what was the only wise course for him to take. Poor Amelia.

I went with Evaline to Daphne's funeral service, where there was a large attendance of relatives I'd never met. Porter had persuaded Valerie not to attend, feeling that her state was still too excitable and uncertain. Amelia sat beside me and we held hands. For that little while I felt that we comforted each other. She was profusely apologetic about not seeing more of me lately, but told me we'd have lots of time after the play closed. I didn't mention that I might be gone then.

Charles sat on Amelia's other side, and there was one unpleasant moment when he held my hand, kissed my cheek, and

259

called me "cousin" in a faintly mocking tone. I could tell he hadn't changed his feelings toward me, but he would do nothing that might attract Porter's criticism.

Afterward the cortege drove out to the plantation, where a new grave waited.

By the time the opening was only a week away, I began to find my own suspended role more than I could endure. Perhaps the most disturbing event was a visit from Honoria. She came out to the Hall to see me, since, as she assured me, I needed to know what was on her mind. She told me she had done the wrong thing in trying to call Nathanial back. She sat perched in a chair in the family parlor and told me this without blinking an eye.

"Of course," she assured me, "Daphne's voice didn't speak through me that night. I am sensitive, and perhaps I felt something—oh, I don't know."

"Is Porter brainwashing you?" I asked bluntly.

For an instant the old Honoria looked at me, and then she turned away.

"I know you want to stay for your sister's play, Molly. But after that perhaps you should go home."

"Because Porter doesn't want me here?"

"There's no real place for you here, is there, Molly? It hasn't worked out for you. I'm sorry."

Miss Kitty, who had attached herself to Orva these last days, had followed Honoria into the room. But now she sat aside, staring at Honoria as if she sensed a stranger. When Honoria invited her onto her lap, Miss Kitty began to lick her fur indifferently. She felt the change too.

Night was the worst time to get through because I couldn't roam around the plantation after dark, and all the wrong memories returned to haunt me. I even remembered that frightening moment at the theater when someone had left the threat of the halberd beside me. And of course I lived over those moments with my mother in the dungeon. In a different way, but just as disturbing, was the time spent with Charles at Cypress Gardens. Finally, and worst of all, I kept remembering the vivid picture of Daphne crushed beneath the heavy marble.

I asked myself at least a hundred times why I didn't go back to the inn in Charleston, but I could find no real answer. For reasons I couldn't fathom, I wanted to stay here. Perhaps it was Mountfort Hall's connection to my father, or the very unreal idea that a piece of paper with his handwriting made this place belong to me.

If only I could substitute thoughts of Garrett. I wanted to talk with him more than I wanted anything else. I'd felt the strong attraction that existed between us, but I still had no idea what Garrett wanted in his life beside the answer to his father's death. I could understand how that had become an obsession. Now that Porter had dismissed him from his work on the Mountforts' history, I didn't even know whether he would continue his search.

Somehow, when I wasn't looking, I'd begun to care too much about Garrett. This was the last thing I wanted—he was too uncertain a quantity. But when did love ever ask permission? This seemed all the more reason to get away and start rebuilding my own life—put a distance between me and this unwelcome yearning toward a man I hardly knew.

Much of each night I lay awake and listened to the house, to the lapping sounds of the river and the cries of the night birds. More than once I watched moonlight fade at my windows.

During this idle time I should have been working on my book. On the day before *The Shadow Soldier* was to open at the Stage Center Players Workshop, I made one more effort. I carried a notebook and sharpened pencils down to the bench near the river and began to make notes.

For once I managed to concentrate, and as bits of story came to mind, I jotted down whatever occurred to me, playing a little with the conflict of possible characters. Long before I could begin to write, all this planning and exploration must be done. Some writers could plunge in with only a scrap of an idea to set them off. I needed to know a great deal about my people before they would come to life for me. I must know about their struggles, their secrets, and about those conflicts that would arise among them to build my story.

My hero began to evolve nicely—or so I thought, until I read what I'd set down about him and began to laugh to myself. Garrett's words returned to needle me. Would I really want to spend my life with a Rochester or a Heathcliff? Or even with Daphne du Maurier's Max de Winter? I would never be able to stand one of those glowering, inconsiderate, domineering men. Not for five minutes! My new heroine would have none of them this time either. I knew her well enough by now to be sure of that. Bits and pieces of me got into every woman I wrote about, but only close friends could tell what was real and what was fictional. Sometimes I didn't know myself.

Garrett had suggested that I think about Harry Lime from *The Third Man*. Just to use him as a springboard to a new sort of hero for me. Harry had charmed those who cared for him, but he'd also tricked and deceived them, and he'd done some pretty evil things. The secret of his charm might be useful—but I didn't know what it was. Perhaps it had been Orson Welles's own personality that charmed. Anyway, I didn't want *him* for a hero either.

I tore up my notes on this unnamed character and started all over again. My new version might seem an enigmatic man at times, but he would be basically wise and sensitive. Even gentle, with a basic kindness in him that those overpowering characters never had. He would never push my heroine around, or bring her to tears. This wishful thinking brought me to a halt very quickly. It just wasn't real in my experience. Besides, if no conflict developed between my two main characters, I'd have no story. Conflict was basic to any man–woman relationship in fiction, as in life. Though perhaps in an ideal situation each could help the other to grow, if enough breathing space was provided.

Hah! I thought. *What* ideal situation? I read over the sketch I'd been writing and realized that it was a fantasy version of Garrett Amory. A real man would be far more complex than what I'd set down on paper, and I tore this up too.

At the moment I couldn't work on the man in my novel, and I found myself bored with a heroine who could do everything so well. In real life *I* had been left helpless to take any decisive action—something that never happened to the women in my books. But what action could I take—except to go home? Valerie and I would never be close, and that no longer mattered. I'd had a loving mother whom I'd grown up with, and whose place I never wanted to fill. Amelia was getting ready to make a terrible mistake and I was not doing anything about it. And Garrett had removed himself from me completely.

So why stay for the wedding? Why even stay for the opening of Amelia's play? I would go inside right now to a telephone and find out whether I could reserve a plane seat for New York tomorrow. At least, this plan gave me something to do, and it was better than staying around for reasons that weren't very good. So why did I feel more miserable than ever?

I picked up my notebook and pencils, and started back toward the house. Or, at least, that was the direction I'd meant to take. My feet chose another way.

Once more I walked through the woods in the direction of the Mountfort cemetery, and I knew why. There was one person I wanted to say good-bye to, perhaps even apologize to, because I had failed him. My father.

Today the shrieking peacock had gone elsewhere, and old gray stones drowsed in hot sunlight—as they had done, some of them, for more than a hundred years. Only Simon's, Nathanial's, and Daphne's graves were recent, and I was startled to see Garrett standing in the far corner near his father's grave. I saw him before he saw me, and I was all too aware of my own reaction and the way my heartbeat went suddenly fast. At once I felt impatient with myself. Why should this happen? Honoria would probably say Garrett and I had known each other in previous lives. But I only wanted to know him in this one. He lacked Charles Landry's good looks, but that wasn't important. Everything about Garrett was right. I wanted to touch his hair where it grew above his ears. I wanted him to put his arms around me—and I knew exactly how they would feel.

He heard me and looked around, cool, unsurprised, probably indifferent. My heart thudded back to its normal rate.

"Hello, Molly," he said.

"I just came to tell my father good-bye," I told him hurriedly. "If I can catch a plane, I'll leave tomorrow. That will be best for me, and for everyone else."

He came toward me and stopped beside Simon's stone. "You're not staying for your sister's play?"

"There's no point in staying. I feel deserted by everyone. I'm surprised to see you at the plantation, Garrett."

"I'm breaking a few rules. Only Orva knows I'm here. I've been staying in her downstairs rooms, while she's upstairs next to you. I've been trying not to run into you or Evaline and give myself away."

"Why?" I was stunned. I couldn't believe he had been here this whole time.

"Unfinished business. A search I've been trying to make."

"Couldn't I have helped?"

"I didn't want to involve you, but I have been keeping an eye on you. I'm glad you're leaving, Molly. Whatever happens, you ought to be safely away."

"Please explain." I was no longer sure I wanted to be away—now that Garrett was nearby.

"I'd rather show you. Maybe *you* can help me, if you want to."

I wanted to, and we started back through the woods together. He seemed carefully impersonal, and that wasn't what I needed.

"You remember those voices of Honoria's?" he asked as we neared the house. "The voice that was supposed to be Nathanial's spoke of a *notebook*, and used the word *marble*. This could only mean Edward's temple? Somehow Daphne must have believed something was down there too. I've spent hours searching through those piles of marble—with no luck. Yet I'm sure the answer is there. Maybe we can search together and cover more ground. Maybe you'll even bring me luck."

He flashed me a look that was not impersonal, but then turned away quickly. I wanted to say, "Stop protecting me. Let me in!" But I couldn't be sure how he felt.

We went around to the river side and stepped into that cool quiet place I had never wanted to see again. The fallen column had not been moved, nor had the lintel stone—except when it had been lifted from Daphne's body.

Garrett waved a hand. "I've been through nearly every chink on that side and found nothing. But unless someone else found it first, I still feel that my father's notes are hidden here some-where."

I looked around in dismay. There were hundreds of cracks and crannies where a thin notebook could be concealed.

"If Nathanial hid something here," I said, "perhaps Honoria should try to reach him again. All this looks hopeless."

"I don't think there's a hot line to another world. So let's get busy."

A voice spoke from beyond the remaining upright column. As though my words had summoned her, Honoria stepped out of the shadows.

"Nathanial never knew exactly where I hid his notebook, and neither did Daphne. Only that it was here somewhere. Daphne got her inspiration from one of Nathanial's poems that she showed me. About something hidden in a temple. I took the notebook before he died and wrapped it up carefully and put it away. Of course I didn't tell Daphne that I knew where it was or that I was the one who put it here all those years ago."

Leave it to Honoria to choose an unlikely hiding place! But this was neither the spirited Honoria I'd first met, nor the meeker one who allowed her husband to lead her around. She wore no "costume" today, and indulged in no dramatic performance. Her jeans looked worn, and her cambric shirt was a simple unpatterned white.

Shocked into silence, Garrett and I watched as she moved among piles of discarded marble, kneeling finally to reach a crevice we might never have found. When she drew out her hand, she held something wrapped in waterproof cloth that might have been cut from an old rain slicker. She balanced it for a moment in both hands, her eyes closed as though she experienced some feeling that carried her back in time to the day when she had placed the packet here.

When she looked at us again, she smiled faintly, almost herself. "I've startled you both, haven't I? This is a diary your father kept for a little while, Garrett. A record, really. I knew I must retrieve it now before the wrong person discovered it. There was only a remote chance of that happening, before the night we spoke with your father."

She gestured toward scattered blocks of marble.

"Let's sit down and I'll tell you quickly what Nathanial wrote and why I took it and hid it. I don't mind your being the ones to know. It's been a heavy burden for me to carry. Even though I haven't seen these lines for years, I remember every word, and all he told me besides."

Garrett remained standing stiffly, as if on guard against some emotional blow, but I sat down on a chunk of marble, feeling its chill through my summer slacks. And I braced myself against whatever was about to be revealed.

Honoria went on as calmly as though she related events that had happened to someone else long ago. Porter Phelps, she told us, had once been a compulsive gambler; that was his secret vice, though only a few members of the family knew. He had taken— "borrowed"—large sums of money from the bank of which he was president. And he had lost all of it at the gaming tables. The time came when exposure and disgrace were certain if the money wasn't replaced. In those days he hadn't achieved the iron control that was now a part of his personality and made him the ruling member of the Mountfort clan.

"He loved me—and I was in love with Nathanial Amory." Honoria spoke quietly, as though all shattering emotion lay in the past. "Porter's wife had died and he urged me to marry him. Nathanial wasn't free, and perhaps never would be. He had found the family thread he'd come here looking for, and was staying only because of me. But he had nothing to offer me, not even marriage, and Porter had everything. In those days I thought wealth and position mattered. I hadn't learned then to listen to my guides. I found that out too late, after Nathanial was gone. It seemed best for me to give up Nathanial and marry Porter. When Porter felt sure of me, he threw himself on my mercy and told me that he had done something illegal. Discovery would have meant prison for him, and disgrace for the family. As much as he loved me, he could never marry me until he was free of this enormous debt. I still loved Nathanial, and in my shocked state I went to him and told him everything. That was my mistake. He wrote down every detail I gave him about Porter in these pages—so that he could hold something over Porter's head if that became necessary. He didn't want me to marry Porter, of course."

Honoria paused, lost in the past, and Garrett spoke tensely. "Do go on, please."

About that time, she told us, something had happened that she could never account for, and that she'd been afraid to think about. Money had been put into Porter's hands—though he would never say where it came from. Not enough to pay back all he owed, but a considerable sum. Still being a gambler, he did what gamblers do. He went to New Orleans and played every cent of it at roulette. What happened was not what usually happens to the desperate. Honoria had gone with him, and she saw to it that he came home with his winnings, so that he was able to return all he had stolen before the loss was discovered.

After that, he never gambled again. Honoria changed him. Perhaps some awakening power came to her assistance, and for a time Porter forgot that she was a lovely little toy he had collected and wanted to possess. Though as the years passed and he became more secure in his own material power, he returned to being amused and tolerant in a superior way toward his wife's "hobby."

"At the time all this was happening," Honoria went on, "Nathanial knew everything—through me. He was angry because I was turning to Porter, but at first he didn't know what to do."

She broke off, staring at me, and I found that I'd begun to tremble.

"This is the terrible part," she went on, "though I still don't know the truth and neither did Nathanial. One of the twins had been kidnapped, and Nathanial began to suspect that the child had been sold to raise the amount that saved Porter and the family. This was a dangerous position to hold. I love Porter, but he's the wrong man to falsely accuse of such a terrible crime. Nathanial knew too much, yet not enough, and I grew afraid for him. I also knew that Porter had nothing to do with Cecelia's kidnapping. He may have been a gambler, but he would *never* do anything like that. I hid Nathanial's notebook in this pile of marble, so that it wasn't a threat to Porter. Then, before I had time to worry about what action Nathanial might take to prevent me from marrying Porter, he was dead. While I could bring myself to protect Nathanial from himself, I could not destroy his journal."

A flood of emotion caught Honoria and she stopped being the cool narrator and turned to Nathanial's son—as if for forgiveness she knew was impossible.

"I still must know what happened to my father," Garrett said quietly.

"And that's what I need to know too—or I did," Honoria said.

I hardly listened now, however, because I had focused on one appalling event—my own kidnapping. If I had been taken in order to save Porter, who had been responsible? Had Honoria told us all the truth—about herself, and about Porter?

269

Honoria saw my expression and shook her head at me. "Don't try to follow old trails, Molly. They don't matter anymore. When you first came here, I wanted to know the truth about your kidnapping and Nathanial's death, but I was foolish. After Nathanial mentioned the notebook, I couldn't let you find it by chance and misread everything. The notebook is yours now, Garrett—for whatever good it will do you."

"But how can we let this go?" I asked. "Daphne was searching for this when someone killed her. And that is *now.*"

Garrett supported me. "My father died because he knew too much and might have used it. So all this is alive and dangerous in the present, Honoria. We can't let any of it go."

At least I could experience one moment of relief. "Simon Mountfort had nothing to do with what happened. I can be thankful for that, at least."

"He knew about Porter's money problems," Honoria warned. "He knew what Porter had done and he found it difficult to live with himself, but for Valerie's sake, he couldn't speak out. Porter was like an older brother to Valerie. Perhaps in his heart he felt that one crime leads to another. I don't know."

So that was the guilt my father had carried for so long.

"Death doesn't exonerate, Molly," Honoria said. "So just let it all alone. What do you intend to do, Garrett?"

He was silent for a few moments, and then spoke to her directly. "Whatever I do I'll keep to myself. Molly is leaving tomorrow, so she'll be safely out of whatever happens."

"You sound as though you're sure something is going to happen," Honoria said.

"Right. You, of all people, should be able to sense that. When pressure builds, there has to be an explosion. And there's no doubt in my mind that it's building. I'm going back to Charleston now, since there's something I can do there. Look after Molly, Honoria, until she's on that plane."

I didn't want to be left in anyone's charge, but Garrett went off in a rush, before either Honoria or I could say a word.

Honoria watched me and she saw more than I wanted to reveal. "So it's like that—the way you feel about Garrett? At least that will settle Charles's nonsense. Though I feel a bit sorry for him—being in love with twins. It's a good thing you're leaving, Molly."

By now I'd begun to wonder if I really was. How could I possibly go away when so much hung in the balance, including Garrett's own safety?

"I'll leave," I said. "But not until after the play tomorrow."

"That's not wise. Why should you stay, Molly?"

I couldn't answer because I wasn't sure myself. "Let's get out of this place, Honoria. It gives me the creeps."

"You go upstairs," she told me. "I still have some thinking to do. And I know I must do it here—where I'm in touch. Then I'll go back to Charleston."

I left her, but I didn't return to my room immediately. I wanted to find Orva, who would be somewhere around, busy with her household duties. Perhaps I could have lunch with her and we could really talk. She was still holding something back about my father, and it was time for her to tell me what it was.

As I climbed the stairs, I thought about Honoria. Not about the terrible implications of what she'd told us, but about *her.* When she evoked Nathanial's "spirit" on the night when we'd found Daphne, she had spoken only what was already in her mind. All along she'd known about Nathanial's notes and where they were hidden. No "message" had needed to come through to

271

her from the outside. Could she also have known that Daphne was dead?

I couldn't seriously suspect Honoria of any crime, but I wished I knew whether she fooled herself first of all, or whether the whole "sitting" had been staged.

Sixteen

My search for Orva didn't succeed. I looked through several rooms, ending in the upstairs kitchen. There Evaline Landry was talking to the cook. When I asked for Orva, she looked displeased.

"I'd like to know where she is myself. She left a note saying that she was taking some time off—and simply vanished. I've tried to reach Katy at the library, but she has the day off too. So they're undoubtedly together. Now I must find extra help somewhere, and it couldn't be more inconvenient. So much needs attention in order to get ready for the wedding."

"I'm sorry," I said. "I won't bother you, but as long as we're together, you should know that I will probably leave Charleston right after the play."

She came out of her domestic abstraction and focused on me. "I'm not sure that's wise, Molly. What about Mountfort Hall? What are you going to do with it?"

"I don't know. I need some time to think. You'll hear from me soon. I promise."

I thanked her for her hospitality and said good-bye, in case I didn't see her again.

She looked very upset, but there was nothing I could say to reassure her. I really *didn't* know.

I walked toward the stairs, feeling uneasy about anyone else "vanishing." But at least Orva had left a note, and she probably was with her daughter.

As I climbed the stairs, I heard a sound from the upper floor that made me stop with my hand on the banister. That creaking rhythm could only be the rocking horse. I ran up the remaining steps and looked down the long hallway toward my room.

The horse was indeed rocking, but this time it had a rider. Katy Jackson sat sidesaddle, holding on to Applejack's head, her feet crossed at the ankles, and a pensive look on her face as she kept the wooden horse moving. When she saw me, she slipped down from its back, laughing.

"Hello, Molly. I hoped you'd come up to your room. Applejack is a friend from my childhood, so I was renewing an old acquaintance."

"Do you know where your mother is?" I asked a bit too abruptly.

"She's moved in with me for now. She's more upset than I've

ever seen her, though she won't tell me what's worrying her. She needs a change and a rest, and I'm happy to have her with me. Molly, can we talk?"

"Of course. I'm glad to see you before I leave Charleston."

She followed me into my room and we sat down. "When will that be?"

The air conditioner hummed while I considered her question. "I'm not exactly sure. I'd like to stay for the play, at least. I don't want to disappoint Amelia by taking off too suddenly. Anyway, if Orva isn't here, I don't want to remain in this empty house."

"That's why I've come. My mother thinks you shouldn't be here right now. Valerie is out here staying with Mrs. Landry, and Amelia is alone in the South Battery house. That's where we think you should go—so you can keep each other company. If you'll pack up your things, I'll drive you back to the city. I've taken the day off to be with my mother, since she's so upset."

I hated to think of Orva as anything but calm and reassuring.

Katy went on. "She's been tied up with the Mountforts all her life, so she thinks of them as though they were *her* family. But they're not, and I want her away. Daphne's death has hit her pretty hard, as it has me too. She was a good friend."

"There's something I wanted to talk to Orva about, Katy. Has she said anything about an earring Daphne was holding when she died? When the policeman held it up, Valerie screamed, and I wonder if your mother knows why."

Katy seemed startled. "She hasn't said anything about that. But then, she hasn't talked much about what happened. Was it a lotus earring?"

"With a silver setting—yes. I understand you found it when you were little girls and brought it to her."

"That's right. It was a pretty thing, and Daphne was my

friend, so I gave it to her. And I didn't think anything more about it until all these years later."

"You found it tangled in some fishing line that washed up on the riverbank?"

She nodded absently. "When Daphne brought it out again recently, she asked if I remembered anything more about finding it. But I didn't know anything else, so I couldn't help her."

"Have you any idea who the earring might have belonged to?"

"Perhaps Honoria?"

"I don't think so. Whoever dropped that earring might have had a hand in Nathanial Amory's death. And Honoria was in love with him."

"I don't know anything about that," Katy said, and I sensed her withdrawal. She didn't want to know.

"I'd better start packing," I said, and brought out my bags.

She watched me perform the quick task, though I felt she was hardly in the room—all her concern focused on her mother.

When I was ready we went downstairs to let Mrs. Landry know that I was returning to Charleston. Katy explained that her mother was feeling tired and had come to her for a short visit. She would be in touch.

Evaline Landry was still upset and anxious, but I think she was glad to have me leave, and she didn't suggest that I see Valerie again. She told us that she would stay out here with Mrs. Mountfort on the night of the play—tomorrow night. It would be best that Valerie not attend in her present emotional state. Apparently Mrs. Landry was willing to pass up the opportunity to see her son perform on the first night of *The Shadow Soldier.*

Before we left, I tried to phone Amelia, but no one answered.

No one was in sight at the former slave cabin as we went past and I was glad to escape without seeing my mother again.

During the drive we stopped for lunch at a roadside place, and Katy and I talked in a desultory way. We were both preoccupied with our own problems. Under different circumstances, we might have become friends, I thought regretfully.

When we reached the Mountfort house, I sat for a moment longer in the car with Katy. "After I've seen Amelia, would you mind if I came to your apartment to talk with Orva?"

She looked doubtful. "Let me ask my mother first. Then I'll phone you."

We left it at that, and she watched me go up the steps. Amelia had come home, and when she let me in, Katy waved and drove away.

Any doubts I might have had about whether Amelia would want me with her vanished as she threw her arms about me and whirled me into the hall.

"I *so* wanted you to come in early for the play!" she cried. "I saw Garrett for a few minutes and he said you were leaving Charleston as soon as you could catch a plane. Of course we can't have that! You can't possibly leave before my wedding, let alone before the play."

She sounded excited and breathless as she drew me up the stairs, and my apprehension returned.

"I'll come back for the wedding," I promised. "We're not going to part forever."

"But you'll stay now, won't you?" she entreated. "For my play and for our tribute to Daphne. You've never seen the whole play. Now I have a surprise for you. Come and see."

Once upstairs, she pulled me into her room and waved a dramatic hand. A crinoline costume lay across the bed—tiers of frothy lace, tinted a lovely shade of lilac and decorated by Miss Kitty, asleep among its folds. Amelia clapped her hands at the cat, who flew off the bed and sat down for her usual bath. Amelia brushed a few white hairs away and held the dress up for me to admire.

"Won't I look gorgeous, Molly? The color is exactly right, and since I'll be wearing this for the last act, I can keep it on for the gathering afterward."

She ran on, still excited. "Daphne made this dress for me, so I must keep it on. It's ironic that lilac is a mourning color.

"But this isn't all," she continued. "You haven't seen my surprise yet. A special present for you. Come along, darling Molly."

She was like a young girl—the girl I'd never known in our growing-up years. I went with her across the hall to the room I had occupied. But when she pushed me through the door, I stopped in dismay. There, across the spread, lay another lilac dress —an exact duplicate of the one Amelia would wear.

"Daphne made a copy for you, Molly. She was a wonderful seamstress and we cooked up this little bit of fun together. You can wear whatever you like earlier, but then you'll slip into the dressing room and change for the tribute. And when we stand side by side on the stage, no one will know which one of us is which. This will be such fun, Molly! And Daphne would love knowing we wore them."

A sense of foreboding filled me. Perhaps only because I'd always disliked the idea of either of us trying to pass for the other. That was a charade I wanted nothing to do with. But Amelia looked so happy and was waiting for my reaction so eagerly that I gave in. After all, what did it matter? Our duplicate appearance wouldn't fool anyone for long, and I could do this one last thing to please my sister.

She took it for granted that I would agree. "You've arrived just in time. I need to go to the Historical Society for my stint this afternoon. But you're at home here now, and I'll see you for dinner. Do you want to be the cook?"

Cooking wasn't my favorite pastime, but I would manage. When she'd gone, I went into the kitchen to check simple possibilities. Miss Kitty came with me, more hopeful than she should have been. An extension phone rang while I was investigating the refrigerator.

It was Katy, calling from her apartment. "Mother says she'd like to see you, so you can come over anytime, Molly. Just don't upset her, if you can help it. I won't be here because I've offered to work a later shift at the library. How is Amelia?"

"Everything seems fine. She's pretty keyed up about the play tomorrow night. Is your mother coming?"

"I don't know yet."

"Will Porter be there, do you think?"

There was a brief silence. "You'd have to ask Honoria, Molly."

When I next saw Honoria, we might have other things to talk about, and it didn't matter anyway—whether Porter came or not.

When we hung up, I decided that I could manage spaghetti and meatballs, with the help of a canned sauce. Then I sat down with a map to locate Katy's building. It was not too far from the Gadsden Inn, and I could walk there easily. Driving was often difficult because of all the one-way streets in the Historic District.

There was a feeling now of summer heat coming, and the city lived in a hum of air-conditioning, with drips of water along the sidewalks.

Katy lived in a ground-floor apartment off a long brick passageway. When Orva opened the door at my ring, I stepped into a large cool room decorated with articles brought home from Katy's travels. I glimpsed native pottery from Africa, tie-dyed panels of batik from Bali, masks from Peru—all fascinating, though I had no time to look now. An arched doorway opened into a courtyard filled with plants and flowers, and I caught a whiff of honeysuckle, common all over Charleston.

Orva invited me to sit down, and took a chair opposite me, upright and stiffer than I'd ever seen her. Her hands were clasped tensely in her lap, and this new Orva worried me.

"I'm sorry, Miss Molly," she apologized, "but Miss Honoria just phoned to say she had to see me. She's bringing someone with her, but I don't know who. She didn't mention. I told her Katy said you were coming over, and she told me to see you some other time. That's what she said. I'm real sorry. I tried to phone you, but you'd already left."

I made an effort to set her at ease. "It's all right, Orva. I'll come another time—then we can talk more quietly."

She could hardly wait to be rid of me, so I left at once, though the coming meeting with Honoria was clearly not something she looked forward to.

I returned through the dark passageway and walked along the sidewalk until I found a low wall, half hidden by rhododendrons. There I could sit and watch Katy's house. I didn't mean to return to South Battery until I knew who Honoria was bringing to see Orva.

I hadn't long to wait. Honoria's car pulled into a space at the curb across the way, and she and Garrett went inside. Garrett! At the sight of him—so close, so out of reach—my whole nervous system jumped a little. I'd have given anything to know what this meeting with Orva was about, but my presence obviously wasn't welcome and I walked back to be greeted by Miss Kitty in an otherwise empty house.

There I sat down in the big drawing room, with Simon Mountfort's portrait watching me, and thought about Honoria. My feelings about her seemed to change from moment to moment. Some of the time I liked her enormously and respected her own belief in her "talents." Yet she had been able to give up Nathanial Amory to marry Porter, and had lived with him for all these years. She had admitted that wealth and position meant a great deal to her, and I suspected that they still did.

Certainly she was capable of concern for others, but I wondered how deep her compassion went. She also enjoyed her own dramatic performances. I had never been able to pin her down into three dimensions, because a fourth always hovered just over her shoulder. When she told me her large tales, I never knew what was truth and what was fabrication.

The phone rang in the outer hall, and I hesitated to answer. It was unlikely that anyone would call me here, but perhaps I could take a message for Amelia.

When I lifted the receiver, Porter spoke to me. "Molly? Amelia told me you'd returned to Charleston. May I come over to talk with you for a few minutes?"

I didn't want to see him, but I had no choice, so I said he could come when he wished, and he assured me he would be right over.

It wasn't ten minutes before the doorbell rang and I let him in. We sat together in the drawing room, under Simon Mountfort's eye.

He began in his usual autocratic way, so that I stiffened immediately.

"I understand that you've decided to stay in Charleston in order to attend your sister's play tomorrow night. This is something you must *not* do. I have reserved a first-class seat for you on a plane to New York that leaves tomorrow morning. Of course, I will be glad to drive you to the airport."

I could hardly believe such high-handedness. "Thank you,

but I expect to leave day after tomorrow, and I'll take care of my own arrangements."

For a moment we stared at each other, and then the challenge of his manner seemed to dissolve. The harsh lines melted from his face, and his expression crumpled into something like despair. For the first time I glimpsed the man that Porter Phelps concealed behind his arrogant manner. Unlike the way I saw Honoria, I'd always viewed Porter in two dimensions. In one of my novels he would have been a simple, easily taken for granted character. All his surface behavior would fit under the heading of "domineering." Now he seemed a troubled, suffering man whom I didn't know at all. Honoria had given me brief glimpses now and then that I'd never really accepted.

"Why are you so anxious to have me leave at once, Mr. Phelps?" I asked.

"Both Charles and Amelia are very dear to me. I can't stand by and allow a foolish infatuation to destroy their lives."

"What have I to do with that? I'm not infatuated."

"Charles is infatuated with *you*. It will be better for everyone if you leave at once."

Annoyance with the whole Mountfort clan filled me all over again. I looked up at my father's portrait, but he had nothing to offer me. Nor did anyone else. I was entirely on my own.

"Better for whom?" I asked. "Charles can hardly marry me without my consent. I'm not in love with him, and I do care about someone else."

A bit of Porter's natural arrogance returned. "You don't know Charles! He's a fine young man. I'm proud to have been able to help him. His father died when he was young, and I suppose I've stepped into that role. His mother grew up with Valerie, almost like a sister, and Charles belongs with Amelia."

"So?" I said.

"It is right for him to marry Amelia."

"I'm not sure what is right for my sister, but I'm afraid nothing will change her. Charles will marry her—not me."

Though he didn't seem to accept the fact that I had no interest in Charles, I sensed that something lay behind an urgency that was out of proportion to his words. Some reason moved him that had nothing to do with Amelia and Charles. Suddenly, disturbingly, I realized that Porter was a frightened man. The underlying emotion that had brought him here was close to terror.

"Why are you afraid?" I asked bluntly.

A man I had never seen before looked at me out of Porter's eyes as he surrendered and spoke without equivocation. "I am afraid for you, Molly. I can no longer help my daughter, but perhaps I can influence you to save yourself in time."

Such palpable fear carried its own contagion, and an echo of what he was feeling stirred through me. This was an infection I couldn't accept.

"But I'm in no danger," I protested.

"Murder becomes easier with practice, Molly. You *are* a threat —to someone. I haven't any proof to give you, but I know you must leave Charleston as soon as you can."

I remembered my first meeting with Honoria, when the word *murder* had been spoken, supposedly in Nathanial's voice. Now it had returned, chillingly, through Porter.

"I've promised Amelia to stay for her play tomorrow night," I said weakly.

He sighed and settled back in his chair. His next words wandered far afield, surprising me.

"I'd like to tell you about your mother when she was a young girl. Valerie had so much spirit, so much beauty."

As he talked, I had the feeling that he'd almost forgotten my presence. This man, whom I'd thought cold and remote, was now allowing emotion to surface from long-suppressed depths.

"Of course, I was a number of years older, but I fell in love with Valerie when she was seventeen. We were second cousins, not first. She had the same wild dramatic streak that she has today. But in a young girl it was more attractive. She and Evaline, who hadn't married Jim Landry then, ran away together when something went wrong for Valerie and she wanted to fly in the face of her parents' wishes. The two girls took the spending money they'd been saving and a bit of jewelry they could sell, and ran off to New Orleans. They stayed in the French Quarter and lived high and recklessly. It was only luck that kept them out of serious harm. Your grandfather sent me after them. He didn't trust Simon, who was also in love with Valerie, to do the job. And of course I managed, even though it lost me Valerie forever."

He looked so stricken by these memories that I tried to bring him back to the present. "Honoria's a hundred times the woman Valerie is—and much more stable."

He smiled rather sadly. "I know that. But first love . . . perhaps that's the love no one ever gets over. Anyway I got rid of the unsavory friends the two girls had made and brought them both home. In thorough disgrace with the family, of course. Valerie's answer was to run off the following year and marry Simon—partly, I think, to punish me. And Evaline married Jim Landry, who had always wanted her. I managed to console myself in one way or another, and I had a good life with Daphne's mother."

These confidences made me wary. I still didn't understand the reasons behind them. I didn't understand his fear.

He'd looked away from me—off at Simon's portrait—the man who had married Valerie and was my father.

Now Porter seemed to rouse himself. "Women often bore me.

But Honoria has never once failed to hold my interest. You're quite right about her."

"Yet you don't approve of her behavior," I reminded him, "on the night of . . . Daphne's death, you left her."

"I felt as if Daphne's death was my fault. If I hadn't been caught up in Honoria's nonsense, I might have found her in time."

I doubted that would have been possible. Without knowing her reason, it would have seemed unlikely to him that Daphne would have been down in the temple at all. There was no way he could have saved her.

He went on, perhaps trying to reassure himself. "Amelia will make Charles a good wife. You're too much like your mother."

"I can't see myself as anything like Valerie Mountfort."

"You've only seen the sad, misguided woman she's become. The pranks of a seventeen-year-old wear a little thin at her age."

Pranks and madness were not the same thing, but again I said nothing.

He read my silence easily. "Valerie is emotionally fragile at times, but she's not ill. Most of us wear layers of conventional behavior, while she sheds all that and acts out her fantasies. She just needs to be kept occupied and happy."

I remained unconvinced, but I'd begun to feel a little sorry for Porter Phelps—something I'd never expected to be.

He chose still another direction. "Daphne and I didn't always get along as father and daughter, but I was proud of her. She was smarter than most of the family, and I admired her especially. She never let me run her life. I wish we could have known each other better. I cared about my daughter, but I never made her understand that. This is a guilt I'll carry all my life."

"I liked her very much," I said gently. "Even though I didn't know her for long."

"There's still a reckoning to be made for her death." The words were quiet, faintly ominous in their restraint.

Before I could say anything more, he stood up and bowed to me courteously. "Thank you for seeing me, Molly. I'm not sure what has been accomplished, but perhaps you'll think about what I've said."

I went with him to the door, wishing I could have been as free of convention as my mother. I still couldn't trust him altogether, yet I couldn't tell him that. Had Porter Phelps played a role in my kidnapping? Had he perhaps been getting even with Valerie for rejecting him, at the same time that he'd saved his own fortune?

When he'd gone, I found that the contagion of fear he'd left behind had taken root in me. It seemed all the more frightening not to know the direction of the danger that might threaten me. I only knew that I couldn't leave my sister while some unresolved threat hung over us. If I were in danger, she might be too. I was beginning to feel like a twin.

A strong sense of foreboding warned me not to relax my guard—that every shadow might be haunted. For the next twenty-four hours, I was as careful and watchful as I had ever been in my life.

Seventeen

Amelia was gone for part of the next day, so Miss Kitty and I kept each other lazy company.

I wished it could have been a more restful time. Amelia's excited edginess about the play made me nervous, and I would be glad to have the whole thing over. I'd made my plane reservation, so I could leave early the next day. Amelia had taken our lilac dresses to the theater and I was to put mine on there when the time came.

During these hours I saw nothing of Charles—which was a relief.

Garrett stopped in briefly to see how we were doing, but he seemed in an unsettled state, and I knew he couldn't talk in front of Amelia. Mainly he wanted to know when I was leaving, since he, too, thought I shouldn't stay for the play.

"Of course she must stay!" Amelia sounded mildly indignant. "In fact, I don't want her to go away at all, and I don't see why she thinks she must."

There was no point in arguing, and Garrett kissed us each lightly on the cheek and went off. I was sure he had learned something from Orva that might upset a few applecarts, but he wouldn't tell us now. Perhaps the outcome would have been different if he had opened up—but who could know about that?

I had time to think during that long day, and I wondered mainly about Cecelia Mountfort. Who was she to me—that baby self I had lost so long ago? Now that I'd spent time here, and grown closer to Amelia, I knew that Charleston would always pull me back, and I wasn't sure whether this made me happy or sad.

We had an early supper that evening and ate lightly. Just as we were leaving for the theater, the phone rang, and when Amelia answered, I heard alarm in her voice.

"Yes, of course, Evaline. We'll be on the lookout. Perhaps you'd better stay there, in case she comes back. Thanks for letting me know. Good-bye."

"That's all we need," she said as she hung up. "Mama's given Evaline the slip and gone off in a car. She's in a terribly agitated state and she's probably coming to the theater, so we'll set a watch for her. She may try to come in by the stage door, where she won't be noticed."

Amelia, already nervous as both actress and author, didn't

need this additional worry, and I tried to reassure her. "Perhaps Valerie will simply come home and not go to the theater at all."

"I don't think so," Amelia said darkly. "I wish I knew what she means to do."

There was no way to guess. We drove the few blocks to the theater, and Amelia was able to park her car easily, since we were early. As we went in through the front lobby, Amelia stopped the first man we met and asked him to watch the stage door for Mrs. Mountfort.

"Just call me or my sister if she appears," Amelia told him.

With an hour still to spend before curtain time, we went directly to the dressing room. Three or four women who played small parts were already there, and a little buzz of excitement had begun.

I set myself to helping Amelia dress in her first-act costume. She'd already done her hair at home, and had insisted on combing mine in a duplicate style that suited the period of the play—a central part, with smoothly drawn wings, and a chignon pinned on at the back. She'd even provided that for me, matching the dark color of our hair. I still disliked the idea of what she'd planned for the tribute afterward, but the deception couldn't possibly last for long, and then it wouldn't matter if we were dressed alike.

Now that Valerie Mountfort might be out there somewhere, I began to feel as tense as Amelia looked. Some wild plan must be motivating her, and it wasn't possible for me to settle down in my theater seat in the second row, so I stayed backstage. I saw Garrett and Charles in their uniforms of blue and gray, but only in passing. Amelia managed to warn them that an unpredictable Valerie might turn up at the theater. Katy, trim in her maid's costume, was told as well, and she sent a note out to Orva in the audience. So several of us were on the lookout for Valerie.

There was no more time to worry about anything but the play. Now and then someone went onstage to peek through the curtain, and returned to report that the house was a sellout. It seemed as if all Charleston was here!

When the curtain went up on the first scene, I stood in the wings, where I heard the first warm sound of applause and felt as pleased as though I'd been Amelia. However, as I nervously moved about backstage, I managed to get in Honoria's way more than once and she banished me to the dressing room.

At least I had seen the stage earlier. The exterior of a plantation mansion had been beautifully depicted on the backdrop, and the garden scene, where the duel would take place, provided a live oak with moss dripping from its limbs.

The first scenes ran on, and from the dressing room I could hear voices, though not the words. When the duel was fought, the clash of swords rang out, and the curtain came down on the dying Union soldier—to enthusiastic applause. Amelia had already come back to change into her lilac crinoline, and would be ready to kneel beside her dying lover when the curtain went up on the second act. She'd left the dressing room in a hurry because she got word that someone needed to see her. I put on my copycat dress, and listened to the chatter from the other actresses about how much Amelia and I looked alike.

With the intermission nearly over, Honoria came backstage to the dressing room. "Do hurry, Amelia! You need to take your place for the last act, so the curtain can go up."

"I'm not Amelia," I said. "And don't look so upset. This trickery isn't my idea."

Honoria rushed off to look for my sister, and by this time Charles, too, was searching for Amelia. Somebody thought they'd seen her out front, and they both took that direction.

Everyone had gone, and as I sat there, uneasy and uncertain, remembering Porter's words, a subtle awareness stole through me, as though I could sense another's fear, even greater than my own. With a strange intensity that I'd never experienced before, I knew it was Amelia's fear. My sister was in some terrible danger because someone thought she was me. Her terror reverberated through me, and I knew it would lead me to my twin.

For no other reason would I ever have ventured alone into that shadowy world behind the stage. I left the dressing room, moving almost like a sleepwalker.

No sooner did I reach the confusion of aisles than I was accosted by an excited young man. "I'm sorry, Amelia, but your mother wouldn't wait. She pushed through the stage door and ran off among all that junk back there."

I didn't tell him I wasn't Amelia. "Thanks for trying. Don't worry. I'll look for her. See if you can warn Honoria," I whispered to him.

When he'd gone off I struck out into the uncharted territory of criss-crossing aisles. It would be futile to search for Valerie back here—it was Amelia I must find. Hanging bulbs shed a pale diluted illumination that left shadows everywhere, deep and impenetrable. I tried to move softly in my billowing dress, listening intently for the least sound that would betray a living presence. The pull I had felt toward Amelia had lessened because of the new threat—Valerie.

The hum from the auditorium became quickly distant. I knew the curtain was still down, and couldn't go up without Amelia. I dared not call out for Valerie, since that might only send her into hiding. Yet I knew she must be here somewhere. Somehow I must hold on to that signal I'd received from my sister.

Unfortunately, I felt more lost than ever in this jungle of articles collected over the years. Shelves of assorted hats towered above me on a high shelf, and costumes whispered on racks as I passed, as though someone hid among them.

Valerie, if she were still here, was being utterly quiet. Once more I stood still, listening, and now I heard a voice speaking from the back of the huge old warehouse—only a mumbled sound, but evidence that someone was there.

I moved softly. There must be two people if one was speaking. Amelia and Valerie! A mother who thought she was speaking to the wrong daughter. But I had to be sure before they discovered my presence.

As I turned down another aisle, however, I found myself blocked. A woman in jeans and a man's shirt, her fair hair floating free down her back, stood before me. In one hand she held the halberd I remembered only too well. Valerie Mountfort looked wildly excited, and I knew where the danger lay.

With a swift movement she transferred the halberd from her right to her left hand, and reached out to grasp my arm with a grip that hurt. Not for a moment was she confused about my identity.

"Molly," she whispered, "come with me and be very quiet. We've got to stop what's happening. Don't make a sound."

I could have pulled away, escaped from her, but because of my sister, I went with her. My dress caught on some protruding object and I heard it tear. Valerie moved toward the distant voice, picking her way silently, pulling me with her.

Space opened out at the back, and here the floor had been covered with old ballast stones. Wide railingless steps led up to a second level, where scenery flats and lengths of lumber seemed to have been stored. I could glimpse their shadowy piles.

Valerie squeezed my arm. "Listen!"

Amelia wasn't answering the woman who was speaking. Chilled, I knew why. Amelia, by her silence, allowed the other person to believe she was me. In spite of that surge of fear that I'd come close to now—Amelia's fear—she said nothing.

The voice went on in cold assurance. "My son will never lose the plantation, Molly. I'll not have my plans interfered with. From the time the twins were born, I knew that Charles would grow up to marry Amelia. The entire inheritance from Simon must go to her, and through her to my son—Porter's son."

Amelia gasped softly, and a note of triumph came into Evaline's voice.

"No one has ever guessed. But now you know. After your mother and I ran off to New Orleans, and Porter came to bring us home, Valerie would have nothing to do with him. I had always loved him, but he had loved your mother. I thought he would love me if we had an affair, but his parents didn't want him marrying a girl with nothing. Not even Charles knows who his father is—but Porter has known all along. When I suddenly married Jim Landry, he knew why."

For the first time Amelia spoke, though only in a whisper. She still wanted Evaline to believe she was Molly–Cecelia. This was a brave and dangerous game my sister was playing, and I knew the risk. But when I tried to pull away from Valerie, she tightened her grasp, warning me to be still. We both listened.

"Porter gave you that second pair of earrings, didn't he?" Amelia whispered, doing a pretty good job of sounding like me. "And you lost one when you damaged Nathanial's boat."

Evaline laughed—a terrifying sound—and again Valerie's hand warned me to wait.

"Nathanial believed he was related to the Mountforts, and he had a foolish loyalty to them. He could have exposed Porter and ruined the family. God only knows what would have happened to us all then. Nathanial found out that I still had some pretty sleazy friends in New Orleans, and he suspected that I'd orchestrated

293

the kidnapping to raise the money to save my son's future. I could give that money to Porter and he would do the right thing for Charles. There was still one baby left, the one my son would marry."

Her utter callousness, her single-minded blind intent, was more paranoid than anything Valerie Mountfort could create. And the very fact that she was telling everything meant that she didn't intend for the woman who listened to live. Looking up, I could see that my sister's back was toward empty space. One shove would send her over.

Amelia moaned softly. I wanted to shout to her to tell Evaline who she was and save herself, but Valerie held me silent again.

"Wait, Cecelia," she whispered. "Let her set her own trap."

Step by careful step, Valerie began to climb toward the lighted platform, drawing me with her. The halberd pointed upward like a spear as that cold dreadful voice went on.

"I tried to warn you, Molly, that first day back here in the theater. You fell and knocked yourself out when you tried to run away. So I put that stage weapon beside you as a warning—to leave. I didn't know then that Simon had left the plantation to you or I might have gotten rid of you then. When Charles fell in love with you . . ."

"That's not true! Charles has always loved *me!*" Amelia cried, giving herself away.

There was an instant of silence as Evaline recognized her mistake. *"You're* not Molly! You tried to trick me, you stupid girl!"

Valerie let go of my arm, and this time I ran up the steps past her. "I'm the twin you're looking for! You can deal with me now —not Amelia!"

Amelia stepped away from the platform's edge as Evaline caught hold of me. Strong hands swung me around, thrusting me toward the spot where my sister had stood. Below lay ballast stone and for a moment I looked my own death in the eye.

But even as I struggled, an ax head struck at Evaline's arm, and a lance point was suddenly at her throat. I whirled her around while she was off guard, so that *her* back was toward open space and I could step to safety.

"I never took your sleeping pills," Valerie told her, thrusting with the lance point. "I knew what you were up to, but I went to the house first to check—so you reached the theater ahead of me."

Again she prodded with the halberd, and Amelia cried out. "No, Mama, no!"

Valerie ignored her. "You were going to kill Cecelia, just the way you did the others. Nathanial and Daphne. Now it's your turn."

But she held the lance point still, no longer touching Evaline. The woman took another step, terrified now, without caution, and went backward into space. She screamed as she fell, and we heard the sickening crack of her skull against stone.

Then everything was frighteningly still. I ran down to the stones below, but suddenly Honoria was there ahead of me, kneeling beside Evaline's body.

"Daphne told me to come!" she cried. "I heard her voice clearly." She looked up the steps, where Amelia and Valerie had started down. "I should have known! Why didn't Nathanial tell me?"

Valerie had dropped the halberd behind a flat from some old play, and I knew no one would find it for a long time.

"I couldn't let her hurt either of my daughters," she told Honoria.

Honoria hadn't seen the halberd, but she smiled at Valerie. "You did very well. Now I'd better go call the police."

"No!" Valerie cried. "No police until you know what to tell them."

"You're right. Evaline has taken her punishment and there's no point in feeding the press with everything that led to this. It might even mean prison for Porter. Old scandals won't help anyone."

Over the years the Mountforts had grown skilled at deceiving the police—and perhaps they'd get away with it one more time. They had the name and a great deal of local respect on their side.

My fiction writer's brain started to plot. "Can you figure out a reason why Evaline came back here and fell from the platform?" I asked.

Honoria smiled at me grimly. "I needed a prop and I told her where she could find it for me. There was no one else to send, and I never thought she'd be careless up where there was no railing."

"But how could Evaline have mistaken Amelia for me—when Amelia was dressed for the play!" I puzzled.

"Evaline knew there were two dresses because Daphne had worked on them out at the plantation. And she knew about Amelia's plan. So she'd expected Molly to be dressed like her sister, and she'd have thought Amelia would be onstage. Why *did* you come back here, Amelia?"

"Mama phoned me here at the theater—from our house. She was too late to catch me, but she warned me about Evaline and said she'd be right over. So I came back here to watch for her. Evaline was searching too, and she took me for Molly. So I thought I might draw her out. When she told me my mother had run up there to the platform, I believed her. So I climbed up, expecting to find you, Mama."

"My beautiful, brave daughter," Valerie said. "Now don't cry, or you'll spoil your makeup. They're holding the curtain, aren't they?"

Honoria said, "I'll go and announce that the play can't go on."

"No—wait!" Amelia hugged her mother and then turned to me. "I knew you'd come, Cecelia. I was calling for you to come."

"I know," I whispered. "I felt you calling." Now I understood about being a twin.

For an instant our cheeks touched, and then Amelia turned in the direction of the stage. "They're waiting for me. It's *my* play and Daphne's tribute. I won't let Evaline win!"

She ran toward the stage, drawing her billowing dress past objects that might have caught the skirt, moving far more gracefully than I ever could—my courageous, remarkable sister!

"Now I *will* call the police," Honoria said. "Can you two wait here until I get back? Then we'll talk to them together."

When she'd gone, Valerie gestured toward a white garden bench nearby, and we sat down, well away from the platform and Evaline's body. Before she'd gone, Honoria had found a length of bright brocade to throw over her. Inappropriate, but it served.

We sat quietly for a little while, each lost in her own thoughts. Garrett would be playing his spirit role onstage in Amelia's play. Nothing was settled between Garrett and me, but I knew how much I needed him. Wryly, I remembered that the heroes in my novels were always there to rescue the heroine. But tonight we hadn't needed a hero. We had done it all ourselves— Valerie and Amelia and I. Mountforts!

Yet so much still remained to be done, aside from talking to the police. Charles would have to be told that he was Porter's son, that his mother was dead, and what she had done. I had no idea what would happen now between Amelia and Charles, and I spoke this thought aloud.

Valerie answered quietly. "Charles will need Amelia now, and she will be there to support and love him. Perhaps they will both grow up. At least he will know he is Porter's son. I think it will be all right, Cecelia."

In an unexpected way, my mother had comforted me. But there was more I wanted to learn.

"How did you know it was Evaline?" I asked her.

Valerie didn't hesitate. "Daphne told me the day before she died. She'd been suspicious of Evaline for a long time. She guessed that Porter had given Evaline the silver lotus earrings similar to the ones Simon had had made for him, and that she'd lost one when she damaged Nathanial's boat. That's how it came to be tangled in the fishing gear. Daphne thought that if she could find the matching earring in Evaline's things she'd know the truth."

"But wouldn't Evaline have thrown the other one away where it could never be found?"

"Not if she didn't realize where she'd lost the first one. So that day, when Evaline was at the Hall, Daphne came back to the cottage to search. She went into Evaline's bedroom and looked into the jewel box on her dressing table. She didn't know I was in the cottage, and I walked in to find her holding the second earring. That's when she told me all she suspected about Nathanial's death. It was bad luck that Evaline came home unexpectedly and found her there. I stepped out of sight and she didn't see me. But Daphne was holding the earring—and Evaline *knew*. She tried to put on an act of indignation, but Daphne only laughed at her and went off, taking the earring with her."

I was beginning to understand. "Evaline got Daphne to meet her down in the temple area where they could talk?"

"I expect that's what happened. It's a pretty secluded place, and Daphne had been hunting for something down there. She

298

wouldn't have been afraid. Perhaps Evaline never knew she'd brought the earring with her. When she found an opportunity to push over that teetery marble column, she thought she'd made everything safe."

Of course. I remembered the moment when the police officer had held up the earring he'd taken from Daphne's fingers, and I understood why Valerie had screamed. She'd known exactly how Daphne had died.

The bench was small, so though Valerie and I sat near each other, we weren't touching. Yet I could feel that all the distrust between us was melting away.

"Why did you stay at the cottage with Evaline after Daphne died?" I asked.

"She wouldn't let me go. She kept telling me she was looking after me, helping me. She kept giving me pills. I wasn't myself— I was terribly afraid. She kept me from talking to Porter or anyone else. Until I got away from her tonight."

As Porter had said, murder became easier with practice, and Evaline, seeing only her single-minded goal, might have disposed of Valerie eventually too. She would have known that Porter, no matter what he suspected, would never give her away. I understood now why he had been afraid for me and hadn't wanted me to stay in Charleston even one more day.

"Poor Simon," Valerie said. "He must have known about Porter's debt to the bank. He felt guilty, but he kept still to spare the family. Orva knew something too. Evaline walked into the music room that day and told Simon the truth. That's why he had a heart attack. Orva saw her go in, but she never told anyone but me, and I didn't have a clue as to what happened."

So! I thought—that was why Garrett had gone to talk to Orva. This was what she had known all along.

Honoria, her phone call accomplished, returned to join us, her back to that length of brocade.

"Amelia is a hit," she told us proudly. "She's remembering her lines and carrying the whole thing off like a pro. Charles is playing up to her convincingly, and she'll never believe he doesn't love her."

"He does love her," I said. "I'm only a passing aberration."

"Of course, he must be told about his mother as soon as the curtain comes down."

I wanted to ask about Garrett—about how his role was going. My longing to see him had grown, and I still had a tendency to shake. I needed him just to hold me.

Porter had found us there. He hadn't wanted to watch the whole play and had come looking for his wife. Honoria explained everything quickly—even what the police must be told—and he took charge calmly. In spite of the awfulness, he must have felt an enormous relief. Though his long years of suppressing all emotion stood him well now.

Much later, when the police were gone and Evaline had been taken away, I sat alone again in the empty dressing room. Amelia and Charles were somewhere together—perhaps finding each other for the first time. I hadn't seen Garrett at all for a while, so I simply rested, trying to catch my breath, trying to regain some sort of equilibrium.

When Garrett found me, I was staring at my own reflection in the mirror, wondering in a confused way who I really was. He came quietly into the room and stood behind me, so that I looked up into his reflected face. He still wore his Union blue, and I my southern belle's costume. Confusion prevailed and I could see my twin in the mirror.

I spoke my thought aloud. "Who am I?"

He smiled, a new tenderness in his face. "You're Molly Hunt and you're Cecelia Mountfort. Not everyone can have two identities. What you'll never be is your sister Amelia."

That wasn't altogether true. There had been moments tonight when we'd communicated with each other in a way that only identical twins could.

As I watched Garrett in the glass, he touched a place between my brows. "There's a frown line there. Just a small one that comes when you're worried. Amelia's beautiful face wears very little of life—because she hides everything inside and pretends to be happy and carefree. You let yourself frown, and you let one corner of your mouth droop a little, because you don't pretend, the way she does."

His finger smoothed a corner of my mouth and my skin tingled beneath the slight pressure.

"But your eyes tell me something else. There's an eagerness for new experience. There's a clear-eyed reaching out. You want to *know*. You want all the things the women in your books experience, and you're not going to shut yourself off any longer. You'll deal with what's happened to you tonight, and for the last weeks. And you'll go on from there."

I watched the woman in the mirror shake her head. "You don't know any of this about me."

"Maybe not. But I think I'm guessing right. From the first day in Daphne's bookstore, I wanted to know more. You must have seen how I watched you. But I couldn't reach for you suddenly—you might have run. You had your own unhappiness to move away from, so I had to wait and give you time. It wasn't easy. How could I know that a feeling like this could hit me suddenly—without warning? I didn't ask for it. Even now I'm not sure about anything. Least of all about how you might feel."

301

"I'm sure," I said.

He leaned over my shoulder and kissed my cheek. "Come away from there. I can't hold a woman in a mirror."

I went into his arms so easily—as though I belonged there. All the heavy questions I'd carried around for so long dissolved and fell away.

"You've been cheated, of course," he said when he'd stopped kissing me, teasing me a little. "In your books the hero comes riding up on his white horse to rescue your heroine in the climax scene. But I wasn't even there."

"It wasn't *then* I needed you. It's now that I want to be rescued."

"Let's get out of here," he said.

The theater had become a haunted place, and I, too, wanted to be free of it.

We went out through the door to the alley, where we could look up at that magical spire standing against a sky that carried the reflection of Charleston lights.

From the street that ran past the theater we could hear voices, and we walked toward them. I fitted very well into the circle of Garrett's arm as we moved away from the past and into a future we would learn about together. I felt light enough to float. Not lighthearted—too many terrible things had happened—but as though there in the dark, we moved into a beam of Charleston moonlight that felt warm and strong and very real.

About the Author

PHYLLIS A. WHITNEY was born in Yokohama, Japan, of American parents, and also lived in the Philippines and China. After the death of her father in China, she and her mother returned to the United States, which she saw for the first time when she was fifteen. This early travel has exerted a strong influence on her work; many of her novels are set in areas she has visited in Europe, Africa, and the Orient, as well as in the places she has lived.

Phyllis A. Whitney is the author's maiden name. (The "A" stands for "Ayame," which is the Japanese word for "iris.") She is a widow, and lives near her daughter in Virginia. In 1975 she was elected President of the Mystery Writers of America, and in 1988 received the organization's Grand Master Award for lifetime achievement. She is also the recipient of the Agatha Award for lifetime achievement given by Malice Domestic.

Since 1941, when she attained her first hardcover publication, she has become an international success. Over thirty-five million copies of her novels are in print in paperback editions. Her novels for adults now number thirty-five, and her devoted following has made bestsellers of most of these titles, including *The Singing Stones, Rainbow in the Mist, Feather on the Moon, Silversword,* and *Dream of Orchids.*